PRAISE FOR *DEJA WHO*

"Brisk pacing; knife-edge danger; heart-pounding, chilling suspense; compelling, complicated characters; and a surprising romance all mix together into one electrifying story . . . Scary, explosive, and captivating, *Deja Who* will snare you into its tangled web and won't let you go!" —Romance Junkies

"[A] suspenseful and witty series launch." —*Publishers Weekly*

"You can always count on Davidson to take a premise and then yank it hilariously sideways, and she doesn't disappoint with her new reincarnation-themed Insighter series . . . This new tale has all the snappy dialogue and off-kilter humor that is a Davidson trademark, so settle in and enjoy!" —*RT Book Reviews*

"[A] cool urban fantasy series with a murder mystery at the heart of the plot . . . [A] great concept that ultimately delivered." —Smart Bitches Trashy Books

"*Deja Who* had all the silliness and wacky fun I'd expect out of a book by MaryJanice Davidson. Plus, it had a complicated, tangled storyline that kept me wondering who the bad guy was until almost the very end." —Harlequin Junkie

PRAISE FOR MARYJANICE DAVIDSON

"Delightful, wicked fun!"
—Christine Feehan, #1 *New York Times* bestselling author

continued . . .

"No one does humorous romantic fantasy better."
—The Best Reviews

"[Davidson's] adventures are laugh-out-loud entertainment."
—Fresh Fiction

"[Her] prose zings from wisecrack to wisecrack."
—*Detroit Free Press*

"Sexy, steamy, and laugh-out-loud funny." —*Booklist*

Anthologies

CRAVINGS
(with Laurell K. Hamilton, Rebecca York, Eileen Wilks)

BITE
(with Laurell K. Hamilton, Charlaine Harris,
Angela Knight, Vickie Taylor)

KICK ASS
(with Maggie Shayne, Angela Knight, Jacey Ford)

MEN AT WORK
(with Janelle Denison, Nina Bangs)

DEAD AND LOVING IT

SURF'S UP
(with Janelle Denison, Nina Bangs)

MYSTERIA
(with P. C. Cast, Gena Showalter, Susan Grant)

OVER THE MOON
(with Angela Knight, Virginia Kantra, Sunny)

DEMON'S DELIGHT
(with Emma Holly, Vickie Taylor, Catherine Spangler)

DEAD OVER HEELS

MYSTERIA LANE
(with P. C. Cast, Gena Showalter, Susan Grant)

MYSTERIA NIGHTS
(includes *Mysteria* and *Mysteria Lane*, with P. C. Cast, Susan Grant,
Gena Showalter)

UNDERWATER LOVE
(includes *Sleeping with the Fishes*, *Swimming Without a Net*,
and *Fish out of Water*)

DYING FOR YOU

UNDEAD AND UNDERWATER

DEJA
NEW

MARYJANICE
DAVIDSON

BERKLEY
NEW YORK

BERKLEY
An imprint of Penguin Random House LLC
375 Hudson Street, New York, New York 10014

Copyright © 2017 by MaryJanice Davidson
Penguin Random House supports copyright. Copyright fuels creativity,
encourages diverse voices, promotes free speech, and creates a vibrant culture.
Thank you for buying an authorized edition of this book and for complying with
copyright laws by not reproducing, scanning, or distributing any part of it in any
form without permission. You are supporting writers and allowing Penguin
Random House to continue to publish books for every reader.

BERKLEY is a registered trademark and the B colophon is a trademark of
Penguin Random House LLC.

Library of Congress Cataloging-in-Publication Data

Names: Davidson, MaryJanice, author.
Title: Deja new / MaryJanice Davidson.
Description: New York : Berkley, 2017. | Series: An insighter novel ; 2
Identifiers: LCCN 2017026990 (print) | LCCN 2017030071 (ebook) | ISBN
9780399585432 (eBook) | ISBN 9780425270417 (softcover)
Subjects: LCSH: Murder—Investigation—Fiction. | Private
investigators—Fiction. | Reincarnation—Fiction. | Paranormal romance
stories. | BISAC: FICTION / Romance / Paranormal. | FICTION / Fantasy /
Contemporary. | GSAFD: Mystery fiction. | Love stories.
Classification: LCC PS3604.A949 (ebook) | LCC PS3604.A949 D44 2017 (print) |
DDC 813/.6—dc23
LC record available at https://lccn.loc.gov/2017026990

First Edition: November 2017

Printed in the United States of America
1   3   5   7   9   10   8   6   4   2

Cover art by Blake Morrow
Cover design by Katie Anderson
Book design by Kelly Lipovich

DEC - 2017.

*For anyone who ever had that unshakable feeling of déjà vu
and secretly worried they were going insane.*

AUTHOR'S NOTE

Mozart loved poop jokes. It's true! He wrote entire songs about poop, which he shared with his friends (sang to? played for? I must find the answer!). This is how I know my love of profanity means I'm really a genius. Mom and Dad, you were wrong about me. *And* my genius.

The great state of Illinois has dozens of prisons. For the purposes of this story, I've made up the Illinois Correctional Campus, mostly because this is a world that accommodates Insighters and past lives, and the rules are a little different than the prisons in our world. Also, I wanted a prison with an acronym that would be pronounced "ick." Because who wouldn't?

Edward Gorey wrote some of the most wonderful and disturbing stories in the history of the written word. He wrote about lonesome socks, but he also wrote about sociopaths who killed children. Even now, I have no idea if his work was intended for children (like the first three Harry Potter books) or adults (like the last three Harry Potter books).

I also have no idea if he was some kind of literary/theater snob (he wrote and directed shows for which he made papier-mâché puppets, and he called this scripted weirdness *Le Theatricule Stoique*), or a giddy pop-culture fan (he liked *The X-Files* . . . and *Buffy the Vampire Slayer*!).

It's probably some combo of all of them, but no one's ever going to be sure. This is the same man whose work has earned major critical props over the years, which is cool, but he also described his work as "literary nonsense," which is cooler.

Basically Mr. Gorey is a mystery to me, which is why he's wonderful. Check out *The Gashlycrumb Tinies* or *The Beastly Baby*, if you get the chance, but be warned: His stories are like nachos. Strange, surreal nachos. You can't stop with one.

Joseph Vacher was a French serial killer nicknamed *l'éventreur du Sud-Est*. (I don't speak French, but I'm assuming that translates to something terrible.) Before he started killing people, he tried to kill himself, so it's doubly tragic that he was better at murder than suicide. He committed violent acts against unsuspecting shepherds and was finally, thankfully caught in 1897 and executed the winter of 1898. He pled insanity, and while I'm no psychiatrist, I think the guy who heard voices, ate most of his meals out of garbage bins, and killed shepherds in a frenzy was completely crazy. Detective Kline is right to dismiss the idea of being Vacher in another life, but for all the wrong reasons.

The frosting Angela drools over exists and it's specifically for frosting brownies. And not just regular brownies, still-hot-just-out-of-the-oven brownies. The secret ingredient is honey, which pulls it all together. It's friggin' exquisite.

Chief Leschi was chief of the Nisqually tribe in the 1800s, who were screwed out of land by the United States government.

And when Chief Leschi dared protest, he was unjustly hanged in 1858 on a charge most people—the hangman included—knew was false. He went bravely to his death and was vindicated by a Historical Court of Inquiry and Justice in 2004. For whatever that's worth.

The Donner Party. Wow. Where to even start? Their bravery? Their despair? The fact that virtually every decision they made was the wrong one? For those who don't know, the Donner Party was a group of families trying to make a fresh start in the mid-nineteenth century. Through a series of setbacks, which at the time didn't seem fatal but, like a Michael Crichton novel, were actually a domino effect of disaster, half the party died. The survivors lived through the disaster because they dined on oxen, horses, their own belts, and their dead travel companions.

The first of the dominos to flip: They got a late start. In the twenty-first century, a late start can mean missing a plane. Back in the day? It could cost you everything, up to and including your life. A late start meant they were trapped on the wrong side of the mountains when winter closed in.

The exciting new path guaranteed to be a shortcut? Not only was it a lie pitched by someone who had never taken that route, others tried to warn the Donner Party it was no good, but the warning letters—and there were several—either didn't make it in time, were lost entirely, or—worst of all—were deliberately withheld.

Every chance the Donner Party had to abandon the new, untried route and get back on track with the old one was vetoed because, ironically, they felt they were losing too much time. Going back and getting reorganized would, they thought, be riskier than keeping with the "shortcut." They told themselves the worst was over. Repeatedly.

For an excellent account of the entire horrifying/courageous story, give Ethan Rarick's *Desperate Passage: The Donner Party's Perilous Journey West* a try. Mr. Rarick doesn't sensationalize the lurid details, but he doesn't pull any punches, either, which is exactly the treatment such a terrible, ultimately triumphant story of survival demands. Be warned: If you're anything like me, you'll need frequent breaks from the book to go stand in front of your fridge and reassure yourself with the sight of food. And you'll probably want to wrap yourself in a blanket first.

BBC's *Sherlock* fanfic is the greatest thing in the history of things. Archive of Our Own has devoured so many hours of my life. (Worth it.)

Colonel Charles Rowan was a British Army officer and the first Commissioner of Metropolitan Police. He and his bestie, Richard Mayne, helped found what would later be known as Scotland Yard. In three months, they found, hired, and trained close to a thousand men. (They must have been champion delegators. Or micromanagers.) In that same period of time, they arranged for uniforms, equipment, and a place to work (and furniture and supplies!) for their recruits, and then they *really* went to work. Rowan retired at the tender age of sixty-eight, but only because cancer made him.

Jesse Tafero, convicted murderer, was executed on May 4, 1990, in Raiford, Florida. He was exonerated later that year by his former friend, Walter Rhodes, who confessed to the murders of Highway Patrol Officer Phillip Black and Constable Donald Irwin. And though he lied to put two people behind bars, one of whom was executed, Mr. Rhodes served no additional time after confessing. For the purpose of this book, I moved Mr. Tafero's execution back to May 1985.

All the past-life flashbacks are based on real historical events and people, but John Perry's case is an amalgam of several instances when people were convicted of murder, only for the "victim" to show up alive and well. Which is horrifying to contemplate.

The rules for visiting ICC were taken directly from the Illinois Department of Corrections website.

I've somehow made it into my forties without having to visit anyone in prison (which, given my distinguished family history of trailer-park-dwelling substance abusers, is odd), so I was amazed at all the hoops visitors have to jump through to see incarcerated loved ones. I came away from my research with respect for the pain these families must endure year after year after year. I'd heard the cliché that "nobody does time alone," and after researching this book, I think that's true.

Elizabeth "Betty" Parris was nine when she started accusing random townsfolk of witchcraft. This "I'm bored and the Internet hasn't been invented yet" mind-set led directly to seventy-two trials and twenty state-sanctioned murders. And though I gave her (and her father) a motive in my book, I don't know if that's how it all started.

I am not a historian and this is total, uneducated speculation, but I found it odd that many of those accused were rich, or owned multiple businesses, or had been in monetary disputes with their accusers' families, or had vast land holdings in the area, and after their trials and deaths, a lot of townspeople made out pretty well.

Curious. And maybe just a coincidence.

The graveyards of history are littered with merciful men.

—UNKNOWN

This is the happiest moment of my life.

—GEORGE ENGEL, NOVEMBER 11, 1887, MOMENTS BEFORE HIS EXECUTION

I write of melancholy by being busy to avoid melancholy.

—ROBERT BURTON, *THE ANATOMY OF MELANCHOLY*

Cold Case: "For the Illinois State Police, a case becomes 'cold' when an investigation for a murder, kidnapping, abduction or missing person 'is pending due to insufficient solvability factors.'"

—GERRY SMITH, *CHICAGO TRIBUNE,* "RECENT ARRESTS SHINE LIGHT ON CHICAGO-AREA COLD CASES"

You are a liar! I am no more a witch than you are a wizard, and if you take away my life God will give you blood to drink.

—SARAH GOOD, JULY 19, 1692

I felt then I was hanging an innocent man, and I believe it yet.

—CHIEF LESCHI'S HANGMAN, FEBRUARY 19, 1858

Problem-solving is hunting; it is savage pleasure and we are born to it.

—THOMAS HARRIS, *THE SILENCE OF THE LAMBS*

Grief is a selfish emotion.

—SOME GUY

Almighty God, thee only have I; thou steerest my fate, I must give myself up to thee! Give me a livelihood! Give me a bride! My blood wants love, as my heart does!

—FROM THE JOURNAL OF HANS CHRISTIAN ANDERSEN, C. 1825

The black dog I hope always to resist, and in time to drive, though I am deprived of almost all those that used to help me . . . when I rise my breakfast is solitary, the black dog waits to share it, from breakfast to dinner he continues barking . . . night comes at last, and some hours of restlessness and confusion bring me again to a day of solitude. What shall exclude the black dog from an habitation like this?

—SAMUEL JOHNSON, JUNE 17, 1783

Make no little plans, they have no magic to stir men's blood.

—DANIEL HUDSON BURNHAM

PROLOGUE

He walked in on a nightmare and realized at once why his brother had been murdered. The how was also immediately apparent: two in the face. Point-blank.

He's dead. And my life is over, too.

To put it mildly. Who was he without his brother? He had always been prepared to go first—at times, he would have welcomed it. But he couldn't spin this, couldn't fix it, and he couldn't run from it, either. He had his family to think about.

He tried to look down a tunnel of years without his brother and drew a total blank. It was unfathomable.

There was nothing for it but the truth. This one time, he would tell the exact truth: In an act of carelessness and envy he'd killed his brother, and he would accept whatever punishment was assigned. He wouldn't try to wriggle free of it. Ever.

And he wouldn't let anyone else get him free of it. Ever.

When he heard the sirens, he felt nothing but relief.

ONE

"Everybody, listen up! Our cousin and Leah Nazir will be here in twenty minutes. *Twenty minutes!* So everyone get your pants on!"

"Pants tyrant," came one response, and "We have a cousin?" was another, and "Angela, shrill is not a good look for you," and "If I didn't put my pants on for the mayor, I'm not doing it for Leah Nazir. Or our brother."

"He's not *your* brother," she said, pointing to Mitchell. "He's your cousin. He's *your* brother." Pointing to Jordan.

"No, he's mine!"

Other families, she thought, *are not like this. I'm pretty sure.* "You think I won't tell your girlfriends? The ones lucky enough to have them? They'll hear everything. They'll *see* everything." Angela Drake shook her phone in their direction. "I will take sooooooo many pictures of you guys without your pants. The girls will mock you and dump you in a flash." Unlikely. But she was desperate.

"How long have you been a hostile pornographer?"

"Nineteen minutes."

"That's how long we've got to re-robe," one explained, "not how long she's been a hostile porn peddler."

"Just . . . come on," she said, and she definitely didn't whine. Nope. Too much pride and class for that. Right? Right. "Guys? Come on? Pants? Okay?"

Grumbling, they complied. She was careful not to let the relief show on her face. Her plan, hatched at age ten, had a much better chance of working if everyone played nicely together.

So it was good to see amusements (cookbook, TV, phones, gambling sheets) were set aside as the lot of them changed out of one thing (swim trunks, hot pants, boxers, culottes, briefs) into another (khakis).

The lot of them. That was just right. Because she was a bad person, Angela found her brothers and cousins generally interchangeable. They were all young and lanky and had messy mops of thick dark hair, from lightest brown (with gold highlights— her brother Jack, the lucky creep) to near black (her cousin Jordan, another lucky creep—why were long eyelashes wasted on boys?) and everything in between. They all had blue or green eyes or, in her cousin Archer's case, one of each. Long noses, wide mouths, long limbs, big feet, deep voices (except Jack, who was sixteen and still occasionally squeaked, to his annoyance and everyone else's mirth). They were a pile of energy when they weren't a pile of sloth. Looked alike, talked alike, annoyed alike.

In fact, if some of the family gossip about her father and

uncle was true, some of her brothers were actually her cousins and vice versa. If it turned out to be true, not a single one of them—herself included—would have been surprised. Which reminded her . . .

"And we're not going to bring up family scandals." Even as she said it, she understood at once it was a lost cause. Because Jordan, Jack, Mitchell, and Paul all knew the reason Archer and Leah Nazir were coming to town was . . .

"Isn't that's why The Skull is coming to town? The family scandal?"

"Don't call her that!" The worst part: "The Skull" wasn't even the nastiest nickname the public used for one of the best Insighters on the planet. "And I meant the other family scandals. Don't talk about those. Any of them. Well, maybe that thing with the orange. That wasn't too bad. Nobody called the cops, and we eventually got the stains out of the carpet. No, scratch that, leave all the scandals out of it. Just to be safe. Okay?"

"Didn't Archer kill a guy last month? I mean literally murder the hell out of someone?"

"*Don't talk about that, either!* Honestly! It's like you guys aren't even reading the memos I send out!"

A low sigh from behind her. Another problem with a large family: You were always surrounded. "I've told you before, hon. Shrill isn't your best look."

"I remember, Mom." The Scandal No One Should Talk About had blighted Angela's childhood and stolen her mother. Mrs. Emma Drake had turned into a shadow the day her brother-in-law pled guilty to murdering her husband. Angela knew that threatening the lot of them with ". . . or I'll tell Mom!" would never have worked. Mrs. Drake was so unplugged from herself, strangers (and neighbors, and family members) often assumed she was sedated. "And I'm not being shrill. I'm being authoritative."

"Authoritative in a high, shrieky voice," one of the pack commented.

"Firm!" she definitely didn't yelp. "I'm being firm. Because I want to make a good impression on—on—"

"The Skull," everyone in the room said just as Angela finished with, "Archer."

A barrage of scornful hoots was their simultaneous rebuttal. "Since when—"

"When, Angela?"

"Since when do you—"

"Archer? You think we're buying that? You want to make a good impression on—"

"Oh, this is too *too* rich . . ."

"*Archer?* The one you treated like a house pet that never quite figured out house-training? That Archer?"

"I did not!" Well, maybe sometimes. During middle school, possibly. Maybe once or twice in high school. "All of you, back off. And back *up*." They'd all climbed off or from beneath various pieces of furniture and were closing in, which was as dreadful as it sounded. "We didn't get along when we were kids, but that was years ago."

"Years."

"Years, she says."

"Hey, guys, it's all in the past because, y'know, Angela here says it's been years and *years* and—"

"She thinks last Christmas is 'years'?"

"She thinks last month is 'years.'"

She groped for the flyswatter hanging on a nail between the living room and kitchen, then lunged forward like a fencer on the offense. "Back! All of you, get back!" The Horde collectively flinched as the swatter swung and hissed through the air.

"Oh, gross."

"Seriously with this, Angela?"

"Don't point that thing at me."

"We have a flyswatter?"

"Yeah, it's usually on one of those little hooks on the keyboard."

"All right!" Swish, lunge, parry. *If I didn't know better*, she thought, *I'd think I was a fencer in a former life.* But nope. Alas: She'd been nothing more exotic than a minor league baseball pitcher just after World War I.

Which was probably why she didn't consider softball a real game. "You're right."

"Hear that? I'm right!"

"Which one of us is right?"

"Shut up, you're all basically a hive mind, anyway." She'd stopped ducking and weaving (literally as well as figuratively) and held them all at flyswatter length. "I admit it: I was a shit to Archer through most of our childhood—"

"The sordid truth comes out!"

"It was awful, *I* was awful, and I've apologized to him." So many apologies. Even now, she flushed hot with embarrassment when she remembered the cutting things she'd said over the years. The fact that, as an adult, he tolerated her with absent good humor was more a testament to his easygoing personality than to her amends. Which she found perversely irritating. *The guy can't even hold a grudge right.*

But, again: The Plan.

"We need to put that behind us now because— Oh, my God they're here!" She almost dropped the flyswatter, hesitated—it had kept the throng at bay pretty well—then hung it back up. She would not meet Leah Nazir with a flyswatter in one hand. Most likely.

"This is the most excited I've ever seen you."

"Of course I'm excited! She's the Mangiarotti of Insighters." She could actually *feel* the puzzled silence, and tried again. "The Mozart of Insighters."

"She's a famously immature genius harpsichord player who loves jokes about shit?"

"Scatological humor," she corrected automatically, then cursed herself. "I mean, no!" She flinched as she heard car doors *thunk*ing shut in the driveway. They'd be heading up the walk to the front door. They'd be *entering* the front door! Her cousin/maybe brother/worst enemy and the James L. Brooks of Insighters! Here! In her house! Where she'd been stood up for prom! Twice!* "Please. I'm begging you guys. Be nice. Be . . . not weird. I mean—as best you can," she modified.

No use asking for miracles.

---

*In fairness to the Horde, on the following Mondays Mitchell and Paul beat the crap out of the boys who blew her off. Or maybe it was Jack and Jordan.

TWO

The James L. Brooks of Insighters stared at the cream-colored two-story house and tried not to vomit.

"Home," Archer announced (unnecessarily), already tugging their suitcases out of the trunk. "The place where they are morally and sometimes legally obligated to let you in."

"I don't think I can do this," the Mangiarotti of Insighters muttered.

"What's that, babe?"

"I said I don't feel well."

"Okay, let's get you inside and you can have a ginger ale and lay down."

Ah, Archer Drake. The love of her life. (Well. This life.) Straightforward and not a man to get lost inside his own head. Product of a close, large, loving family. Brave and sweet and gorgeous.

And clueless. Also, *lay/lie* was one of her peeves. "It's *lie.*

Unless you are physically laying me down, it's *lie*." Her peeves were legion.

"You'll lay yourself down," he said, with aggravating cheer. "I stand by what I said! And you know it's totally fine to be nervous, right? Hell, I've met all the players, and *I'm* nervous. Actually that's probably why," he added thoughtfully. "I know 'em. But they'll love you."

Leah found a smile. "I'm certain that's a lie."

"Well, they won't hate you."

"That's better."

"They can't hate you, they know you're here to solve a murder."

"Why are they so adamant the wrong man is in prison? Is it—" Her experience with such things was nearly non-existent, so she chose her next words carefully. "Is it a family thing? Or is it more objective than that?"

"A little from Column A and a little from Column B. Listen: There's no way my father killed his brother. They were always tight, to the point where my aunt hated it. My dad adored his brother. Still does, how's that for depressing?"

"I don't know."

"And anyone planning a murder would make sure they had a much better alibi than Dad did. It's stuff like that, all little things. You look at the facts, and you can't shake the idea that something's missing. Something huge."

Her normally good-natured sweetheart had gone pensive, so she held off from more questions. "This won't be an instant fix, you know. I'm not sure your cousin understands that."

Archer's brow furrowed. "What? I'm not following."

Before she could say anything else

(*not a fix—and also, get me out of here*)

(what was I thinking)
(I mean it, get me out of here!)

the front door popped open so hard, it rebounded in the face of the young woman standing just inside. "Archer!" she called as she wrestled with the screen door and bounded out in a burst of energy with which, by now, Leah was familiar. The woman—his cousin?—strongly resembled Archer, with the same long limbs and barely suppressed hyperactivity, the same bright eyes, and a mouth made for smiling. Her hair—a riot of shoulder-length reddish-blond waves—was the only visible difference. Well, the hair and the breasts, too. Obviously.

"Huh," Leah mused. "You're all like that."

"Only when we're freaked out. Or nervous. Or horny. Or in fear for our life . . . yeah," Archer finished, giving up. "We're all like that. All the time. Except my aunt. But you'll see for yourself."

Splendid.

Archer's cousin had finally fought free of the screen door. "Hi, it's so great to meet you oh, my God, I can't believe you're here how was your trip oh, my God!" This as she rushed over so quickly and shook Leah's hand so enthusiastically, she nearly knocked her back into the car.

THREE

They're insane. I should be terrified.

And perhaps she was. Deep down inside, where she crushed most of her fears. Mostly she was fascinated. It was like observing a pack of Archers in the wild, and she was the hapless nature lover trapped in the high hide, praying the predators were vegetarians. Or at least full, and thus would not eat her.

Angela had begun by introducing her brothers and cousins. Or her cousins and brothers; there were a lot of them, they all vaguely resembled each other, and they all spoke in unison.

"Guys, this is Archer's fian—"

"Hi."

"Do you know who James L. Brooks is? Will you tell us?"

"Arch captured you, right? Set some sort of bizarre trap and you fell right into it? Blink twice if you want an extraction team."

"Man, not cool. Archer doesn't like 'Arch.'"

"He also doesn't like when you insinuate he makes a habit of felony kidnapping."

"He didn't like Toe Cheese, he didn't like The Thing That Smells Like Gym Shorts, now he's yanking 'Arch' from circulation . . . Cripes, what *does* he like?"

"It's nice to meet you, Leah."

"Angela made me put on pants. You're welcome."

"It's nice to meet you," Leah managed. Probably. There were a half dozen of them, all gangly and dark-haired and energetic. The youngest—Jack? Jordan?—was still in his teens, the oldest—Mitchell? Paul?—was in his early twenties. Angela was the oldest of them all, at twenty-five. "All of you."

"What?"

"What'd you say?"

"Hon, you'd better speak up if you want to be heard over our actual voices *and* all the voices in our heads."

"She said—shut up—she said she—shut up, you guys, let me talk! *She said it was nice to meet you!*" Angela made a visible effort to calm herself. "Which is a lie, obviously, but she's being a good guest."

"I've been called many things," Leah said, and found a smile, "but never once 'a good guest.'" Possibly because she was rarely invited anywhere. Who'd want to be around someone who could see all your sins from all your lives? Answer: no one who didn't need something.

"Aw, Angela." Archer was grinning at his cousin, who looked capable of murder, or at least assault. Leah didn't blame her; she couldn't imagine growing up in such a din. "I missed how you shriek us into submission."

She let out a snort. "Sure you did."

"But listen, can I get a ginger ale or something for Leah? It was a long drive and she—"

"Long drive?" a cousin (or brother) asked. "From where? We all live in Chicago."

"Yeah, but they're suburban, we're city."

"Which suburb, though?"

"Unless the suburb is five hundred miles away, it's not a long drive."

"A suburb five hundred miles away isn't a suburb, you deeply pathetic idiot."

Then the ghost drifted by, and Leah—who hated clichés— nearly jumped out of her skin. At least, that's what it felt like. She did a double-take and realized that this woman—whoever she was—was just a shell. A living breathing shell, a walking talking ghost. "You need something to drink?" the ghost asked vaguely. "Nice flight?"

"They drove, Mom," Angela put in before Archer could say anything. Leah noted that he shot his cousin a sympathetic grimace. "They don't live very far away."

"Actually, they live in a suburb five hundred miles away."

"Shut *up*, Jack."

"Oh, well, you'll be visiting lots of times, then," the spirit predicted as she began to drift away. She followed that with a non sequitur: "I picked up the mail."

"Thanks, Mom. We know that's your thing." To Leah: "It's her thing. She's in charge of the mail, everyone else is in charge of everything else."

Curious, Leah broke her own rule

(don't touch people just to peek at their lives. it's only okay to in-

vade people's privacy when you're on the job, but holy God what is up
with this woman? is she here? are we?)

and extended a hand. "It was kind of you to invite us."

"Oh, well," came the vague reply. "I didn't, really. Angela did."

"I'm Leah Nazir. It's nice to meet you."

Mrs. Emma Drake gave Leah her limp pale paw and Leah saw

nothing

nobody

alone

always

alone

(but . . . on purpose?)

always

alonealonealone

(should have stuck to the rules)

FOUR

It could be worse, Angela reassured herself. *It could be a lot worse. The boys are behaving. Mom is being . . . Mom, but I never expected anything else. Archer seems fine, he's even teasing me a little. Ms. Nazir seems . . . er . . . hard to tell, actually . . .*

And that's when Leah Nazir's big brown eyes rolled back and she pitched toward the floor. She would have face-planted if Archer hadn't been so quick.

Her mother blinked, her way of showing extreme alarm. "Oh. Huh. I think she needs to rest. I'll go check the . . ." And she drifted away, probably to check the guest room, which Angela already knew was perfectly appointed.

Coward. The thought rose in her brain like a bad-tasting bubble and, for once, Angela didn't try to squash it. Her mother had been through a lot. Her sister-in-law succumbed to cancer a year before the murder, leaving her to raise all those kids on her own . . . (she'd taken the cousins, too, as they were virtual orphans). It had been tough, no question. But it hadn't exactly been a laugh-fest for the rest of them, either, and Angela became a de facto parent at age thirteen, the minute the hearse pulled into Graceland Cemetery.

Still a coward, though. And Dad would have hated what she turned into. He wouldn't appreciate her abandoning his brother, either.

Angela shoved all that away. "You got her? C'mon, let's stretch her out on the couch. Should we take her to the ER? I can call 911."

"I'll do it!" From Paul.

"Bullshit!" From Mitchell, predictably, since he lived to keep track of everyone's turn. "You got to call 911 when Jack fell out of the tree house. It's my turn."

"No, the last time we called 911 was when the neighbors called the cops on *us*—"

"Why are we always surrounded by tight-ass neighbors?"

"I'm already dialing, it's done, I'm doing it," Paul announced. "See? Niiiiiine . . ."

"Hang that up unless you want to be on the stretcher next to me," Leah managed from Archer's arms.

"Okay," Jordan said. "That's pretty cool. I'll hold Paul down for you, Leah, and you can work the body. I suggest starting with the lower ribs. Or his upper lip."

"I'm fine," she continued, waving away Jordan's offer to help her assault his brother. "Temporary setback. I'll be okay once I get off my feet."

"You *are* off your feet," Angela pointed out. She followed them, fretting the length of the hallway to the guest room. "Are you sure you don't need a doctor?"

"I'm fine."

"Do you often faint?"

"I did not *faint*. Silly ingénues in bad movies faint."

"Silly what now?"

"I temporarily blacked out. *Very* temporarily. For barely a second. Half a second. Thank you," she said as Archer deposited her on the bed with a flourish. "I was already a little under the weather, but I don't need 911 or a doctor or an exorcism or anything of the sort and also, stop fussing."

"Okaaaaaaay."

"I'm pregnant," Leah added, and grimaced.

"You're—really?" Angela felt a huge grin break over her face. *Why the grimace? Is she not happy? No, stop reading into it—she fainted in front of the in-laws. She's a little embarrassed—because she doesn't know how many people have swooned in our family room over the years.*

"Yes, really," Archer replied, smiling and puffing out his chest a bit, probably because he got to have sex.

"Well, that's great! You're gonna be a dad!" Angela was impressed, and not for the first time. Archer had been the first to

(flee)

leave home, hold down a number of odd jobs,

(Jordan kept a chart of them, and the thing was eye-popping)

fall in love, foil a murder, get engaged, and now to have a baby on the way. (In that exact order, too, she realized.) He, unlike the rest of them, had moved on. And not just on . . . *forward.* He was a grown-up, and not just chronologically. "That's really great."

"No, it's not," Leah said dully.

(??????????)

Angela managed to tactfully say nothing, or even raise an eyebrow, and when Archer didn't scowl, or burst into tears, she realized that whatever was upsetting Leah about being pregnant, he knew all about it. Which in its own way was kind of cool.

Leah broke the short silence. "I'll explain."

"You don't have to," Angela replied at once, not meaning a word of it. *Please, please explain! Explain until you're blue in the face! But not really!*

"I know I don't *have* to," Leah snapped. Her lips thinned and she added, "I'm sorry. I'm in a foul mood. It's like this: I had a terrible mom."

"Okay." Angela knew Leah's mom; everyone did. A B-list actress from the nineties, a gorgeous redhead in the style of fifties pinup queens, never as famous as her daughter, and went to her grave trying to change that.

"So I don't know how to do it. I'll be bad at it." She met Angela's gaze dead on. "I'm afraid. That's what this is. That's all this is: pure fear."

"I'm sure that's not true."

"It's absolutely true: I am scared shitless."

"No, no, I meant about your mom."

"It's definitely true," Archer cut in. "Leah's mom was the worst."

"Not that, either! I *meant* that Leah won't be a bad mom just because she had one. It doesn't . . ." Her gaze went from Archer to Leah and back to her cousin. "It doesn't always follow. There's not an Insighter in the world who won't tell you that. We see a lot," she said, turning to Archer. "But it's not all bad. That's one of the myths. We see plenty of the good in people's pasts."

A weak snort from the bed. "Stop generalizing. And 'bad mom' doesn't do it justice."

"Okay, but it's not like you cornered the market in crap parents." Although it sure sounded like Leah's B-lister mama *had* been a worse-than-usual momager . . . at least, according to the tell-all book by the actress who only *played* her daughter.* "I mean—jeez. You know about my dad. And what we've got to try to do for my uncle. It's the whole reason you came to town. And my mom freaked you out so hard you hit the floor."

Angela's Insighting ability was nothing compared to Leah's. If Angela's ability could be likened to being the best actor in drama club, Leah's made her Sir Anthony Hopkins (who, rumor had it, had been the Sun King in an earlier life); but it was strong enough that Angela didn't go out of her way to touch strangers. She'd been amazed when Leah had stuck out her hand, and even more amazed when her mother had shaken it. "You *hit* the *floor.*"

Leah was already shaking her head. "That was—that was more morning sickness than anything else."

"Sure it was." *I'll bet you don't go out of your way to touch strangers. Quite the opposite, I think. So why'd you want to touch my mom? I think I know.*

The color was coming back into Leah's face and for the first time, Angela knew how to talk to her. *She's really invested in the bad-mom thing. Okay. She feels better if she fights back a little. Okay.* "It can't have been that bad."

---

*"She took me out for drinks a few times but would only ever give me an empty glass. Said even air would make me look fat. But her hair was glorious." Excerpt from *My Year with Nazir* by Amy Ackman.

"Mine was the stage mom from Hades, and that was on her *good* days."

"Mine's a ghost," Angela said.

"Mine exploited me for money."

"Mine is so out of it people think she's on tranquilizers. PS: She's not on tranquilizers."

"Mine slept with the judge assigned to my emancipation trial, which is why I remained un-emancipated for so long."

"Mine slept through all my birthdays, both my graduations, and Archer's crime prevention award from the city of Minneapolis."

"Mine— But you've never lived in Minneapolis."

Archer shrugged. "Long story."

Leah stared at the father of her child, and Angela had the impression she was holding back giggles. "Okay, we're definitely discussing that later—"

"Oh, God." He groaned.

"But getting back to the more interesting and depressing conversation, my mother slipped Valium in my tea, then brought me to a plastic surgeon's office. The only reason I didn't get non-con breast implants at age thirteen was because I woke up too soon. And also, the surgeon wasn't a sociopath."

"Mine left all of us alone for two days because she forgot she had children. You know, the way some people forget their keys."

"I swore off tea forever. And I loved tea! In fact, I refused to eat or drink anything she touched until I was emancipated. I spent years terrified I'd be roofied by my own mother."

"Mine *forgot she had children*."

"Mine's dead."

"Mine might as well be."

"This," Archer announced, "is a terrible game. And I think I'm calling a halt to it. Yeah, I'm definitely calling a halt. If you two will let me. And how the hell do you even know who wins?"

Leah grinned and sat up. "We both did. Or we both lost. Either way: I have to say I'm feeling better."

"Good enough to go back out and face the throng?"

"Christ, no," Leah said, flopping back down.

FIVE

He's dead.
    (thud)
Murdered.
(thud-thud)
Your father's dead.
(thud-thud)
Your uncle murdered your—

                ∽

ANGELA OPENED HER eyes. The words that changed every-
thing, the words that decimated her childhood. But the—
   Wait.
   Where am I again?
   Then she remembered: This was no ordinary car-ride snooze.
She'd actually dozed off in Archer's car while he drove her and
Leah to a state prison to visit her incarcerated uncle and put

phase two of her long-game plan into action. In a downpour, no less, and his wipers needed changing. *Thud-thud.*

How the hell did I sleep?

"She's back!" Archer cried, catching her gaze in the rear-view as she sat up, rubbed her lower back, smacked her lips. Bleh, nap-breath. She'd throttle someone for a Tic Tac. "Let me guess: You stayed up all night freaking out about our visit, and when you finally calmed down, you conked."

"No," she denied automatically. The "Shut up!" that followed was also automatic. She could feel her face get warm as she flushed. *Jesus, how old are you?* "Sorry. Force of habit."

"Ah, that takes me back," Archer said, adjusting the mirror so he could keep torturing her with sporadic eye contact. "Back to hell, in fact, which in this case means Iowa."

"We only made the one trip to Iowa."

"Yes, because the state trooper who put out the fire politely asked us to never, ever return."

"He was really nice," she said, remembering. "He could have arrested some of us. Or all of us." It was one of the reasons she'd wanted to get her Insighting license—to work with the police.

One of the reasons.

"Angela has a soft spot for cops," Archer told Leah, which was embarrassing beyond belief.

"I do not! Well, good ones I do," she admitted. "They make things better. And easier."

"The good ones usually do," Leah agreed. "In our work, we— No?"

"I wasn't talking about work. This isn't— I mean, I didn't

just suddenly become interested in my father's murder case again. I've never stopped working it."

"Since the day after my dad took a plea bargain for killing your dad." He paused a beat, and then he and Angela added, "Allegedly!" in unison.

"Ha! Jinx," her cousin chortled.

"Ugh, you're endlessly annoying."

At that, Leah burst into giggles, and Angela was able to see her as a real person instead of the glorified Insighter ideal for the first time. It was as sobering

(heroes are just ordinary people having a series of bad days)

as it was exhilarating.

(oh, my God she's so cute when she laughs!)

"Do you still dream about it? The night you found out your dad was dead?"

"Actually I've been thinking about Mom's one-eighty on the whole accident-versus-surprise thing." Hopefully Archer wouldn't notice she hadn't answered the question.

"'Accident-versus-surprise'?" Leah asked.

"Yeah." Angela leaned forward so her head was between both of their head rests. "The first time I did the math, I saw I was older than my parents' marriage and asked about it. Turns out they *had* to get married; Mom got pregnant and Dad wanted to do the right thing. My dad always said I was a surprise. When I asked the difference, he said: With an accident, if you could do it differently, you'd go back in time and undo it. But with a surprise, you'd never go back and undo it."

"And what did your mother say?"

"Oh, the reverse." Angela laughed, but there wasn't a lot of humor in it. "One the reasons I was so surprised by the depth of her grief was because mostly I remember them fighting all the time. It wasn't some great love match. So when I found out they had had to get married, it made sense. And, Archer, you're not saying anything, so I'm betting you knew what was going on."

Archer didn't reply. Just kept driving. Leah's gaze met Angela's in the rearview mirror. "I'm afraid I don't understand."

"I wasn't an accident. Mom got pregnant on purpose. She'd wanted to get married for ages but Dad had, y'know, *zero* interest. Here's the irony—Dad wanted Dennis's life. And Dennis wanted Dad's."

"So you were . . ." Leah paused.

Archer filled in the blanks: "Bait in a trap. Personally, I liked Uncle Donald's version of the story."

"Well, yeah, I did, too. When I was six."

"And I think your mom was a real jerk for telling you the truth."

Angela shrugged. "I'm glad she was honest. And I give Dad props for sticking around." Was that why her mother had made grieving her full-time job? She had gone to such lengths to haul Douglas to the altar, losing him was too much? Something to think about. "Also, I'm not sure I was bait. I think I was more like the canary in the coal shaft."

"Angela, that's awful!" Leah cried, but then couldn't stop giggling. "You guys have the oddest way of looking at the world."

"Look who's talking," Archer said fondly.

Angela had to admit it: She hadn't thought they'd all be

laughing as they drove through the gates of Illinois Correctional Campus. What did that say about her? And them?

That things will be different this time. Because I'm different, and Archer's definitely different, and we have Leah Nazir, and a new detective, and we're finally going to get it done.

Please God.

SIX

Paucis notus, paucioribus ignotus, hic jacet Democritus
Junior, cui vitam dedit et mortem Melancholia.*

So it was coming for him again, the serious ailment, the settled humor. The timing was dark and sweet because with the beauty and simplicity of knowing when you are predicted to succumb, if one so chooses, you can make the astrologer a seer or a liar.

"So, a seer," he said aloud. Friends would have been surprised to hear how low and hoarse he sounded. When it was on him, he went days without speaking. Or bathing, he remem-

---

*"Little known, and even less forgiven, here lies Democritus Junior, who gave his life and death to Melancholy. Died 9th January, 1639." Epitaph from the monument to Robert Burton.

bered, glancing at his reflection in the mirror. Or shaving. Or eating. He couldn't even muster the will to gasp in horror at his reflection. What little energy he had he needed for breathing. There was room for nothing else.

Ah, but euphoria might be on the way! He knew that as a dying brain fought and clawed for oxygen, chemicals flooded the system with joy and jubilation in a burst of biochemistry. That would be delightful, but it wasn't a requirement. All he required was nothing. Forever.

He changed into a (reasonably) clean suit even as part of him knew it was idiotic: He'd shuffle off the mortal coil, but not before pissing and shitting himself. But the idea of ending it all in the same pajama pants he'd lived in for the last month was unpleasant.

He found the rope, ran it through his fingers for the tenth, sixtieth, hundredth time. Sturdy, strong. The knot would hold, and the beam, and the chair (until he had no use for the latter—or, he supposed, the ladder he needed to reach the noose).

No note, at least not in the traditional sense. Friends would say he had been writing his suicide note for the last three decades: *The Anatomy of Melancholy.** Five printings in seventeen years, and every page dedicated to recognizing, treating, and enduring that wretched and serious ailment.

His friends would also point out his inconsistency on suicide. He had expressed conflicting points of view about the last act, stating at times that taking one's own life was a natural

---

*Full title (and it's a mouthful!): *The Anatomy of Melancholy, What It Is with All the Kinds, Causes, Symptoms, Prognostics, and Several Cures of It, in Three Main Partitions with Their Several Sections, Members, and Subsections. Philosophically, Medicinally, Historically Opened and Cut Up.*

consequence of the fiend Melancholia, as a tumor was of cancer, and other times seeing it as a moral choice. Readers had chided him for the disparate views, as they did not understand a fundamental truth of his condition: Sometimes he wished to be dead. And sometimes he did not.

It would never be done. *The Anatomy of Melancholy* could never be done, which was the work's most dreadful and wonderful characteristic. And he was tired.

So then, what next? He positioned the chair, tossed the rope, tightened the knot, and wondered about what he would face as he left. Nothing? Or choirs of angels? Or another life?

What if I come back? What if Melancholia finds me again?

Don't think of it. Don't. He stepped off the chair and simultaneously gave it a savage kick, so there was no way to get his feet back under him, so his traitorous brain couldn't rebel and force his legs to find purchase.

What if it finds me?

Don't.

But what if it does?

Don't.

Oh please, please d—

SEVEN

Prisons were like hospitals and gas stations: No matter where they were, or what size they were, or who ran them, or who was in them, they always smelled the same. Cleaning products and sweat, with a slight aftertaste of urine and ennui.

"Urine and ennui"? Get a grip, Chambers.

Detective Jason Chambers put his book (*The Gashlycrumb Tinies: A Very Gorey Alphabet Book*)* aside to focus on the Drake contingent, who were nearly finished jumping through the bureaucratic hoops necessary to visit an inmate in the state of Illinois.

He'd inherited the Drake file from his predecessor, a dour grouch who had never warmed up to Angela Drake and didn't mind if she—or anyone within bitching distance—knew it.

---

*And it's not even the weirdest thing Gorey wrote!

"One of them Insighter freaks," Detective Kline had confided. "Had the fucking balls to tell me I was Joey Vacher!"

"Who— Oh. You mean Joseph Vacher?"

"Yeah, if you can fuckin' believe it."

"This was upsetting news?" Chambers guessed, barely making an effort to appear interested.

"Yeah, no shit." Kline had been packing his desk, an exhausting (judging by the moon-shaped sweat stains on his tan shirt) and smelly (going by . . . well . . . the smell) task he seemed glad to break off from. He slumped into his desk chair, which let out a wheeze as it took his weight. "Said it right to my face! 'Hey, Kline, you used to be some dumbass frog serial killer.'"

Chambers, who had spent far too much time with Kline in the last month, had an idea what the problem was. "Which you took exception to. Not the part about you being a killer . . ."

"No *way* was I ever that loser."

"Just not *that* killer."

"Damn right!" Kline rubbed his sweaty forehead, turning drops of sweat into dark streaks. It was amazing how filthy you could get just pushing files around.

"Your standards," Chambers guessed, "would have been too high in any life."

"Hey, if I was ever gonna kill myself like a pussy, I would have done it right the first time. Stupid SOB managed to fuck that up *twice*. Cut his own throat—lived. Shot himself—lived. In the face! Twice! Lived! How the fuck can you fuck that up?"

"I'll assume that's rhetorical." Chambers himself had taken a statement from someone who had jumped off a three-story building and lived (a quadriplegic to the end of her days, but alive) and met a teenager who had aimed for his own eye, but the bullet ended up plowing a path around the circumference of his skull, leaving him with a shocking scar and no loss of cognitive function. He hadn't even lost the eye. In other words: Such things happen, as any doctor, cop, or Insighter could testify.

Kline ignored him and plowed ahead. "Even setting aside that bullshit, if I was gonna be some creeper frog psycho—"

"Isn't your wife French?"

"Don't change the subject."

"I wasn't."

"If I was gonna kill anyone, I woulda stuck to one sex. This guy was all over the place—a woman, teenage girls, teenage boys. And shepherds! He's creeping around the countryside murdering friggin' shepherds! What the *fuck*? No *way* was that me."

"You would have eschewed shepherds," Chambers guessed. "And killed a higher class of people."

"Like hookers!"

"You think herding sheep is worse than prostitution?"

Kline ignored the question. "I wouldna been sloppy about it, either, I don't care if we're talking this month or fifty years ago."

"Or a hundred twenty years ago, since that's when Vacher was active."

Kline made a waving away motion with both hands. "Snatched his last victim in earshot of her family. She kicked up a fuss and *boom!* Fucker's caught. I wouldna got caught. And if I did get caught, I wouldna confessed. And if I did confess, I wouldna pussy out by trying for an NGI.* And if I did pussy out with an

---

*Not Guilty by reason of Insanity

NGI, when it didn't work I'd have taken my death sentence like a man. This guy, they had to drag his pussy ass to the chopper."

"Guillotine."

"I mean, fuck!"

"That sounds upsetting," he allowed as an alternative to *Kline, are you familiar with the theory about people who protest too much? And are you unaware that slapping on cologne isn't a substitute for a shower?*

"They're all fulla shit," was the closing argument. Kline meant Insighters, presumably, or killers, but the older man was sour enough that he could have meant mankind in general. And it wasn't the job. Kline had been a dour rookie and a jaded patrolman and, as a detective, was more or less dead inside. And clearly not at all pleased with his French wife.

Chambers figured that was about as good as it was going to get, so he left, but not before Kline got the last word (again): "We got the right guy, kid!"

Chambers turned back around. "This again? I'm thirty-two."

"Nobody confesses to murder and then calmly sits in a cell for over a decade without a peep if they're innocent!"

And there it was. One of the many things about the Drake file that bugged anyone who came in contact with it.

And here came one of the other things that bugged the hell out of anyone who came in contact with it: Angela Drake. She was doing what she usually did: pacing like a thwarted tigress as her cousin handed over the PVI forms crucial to IDOC procedures.

"How could I have forgotten how much fun this is? The only thing better than the body search is the paperwork," the man announced to the air. "That sounded sincere, right?"

"Archer, none of us want to be here. Least of all your father. I get that cracking jokes is your way of defusing the tension, but why would you want to defuse the tension? We're *supposed* to be tense and horrified to find ourselves here. We're supposed to feel that way so we fight hard to get him out," Angela snapped, veering off from her pacing long enough to glare. Then she grabbed the bridge of her nose and squeezed. "Argh, sorry. I'm a little jittery." She flapped a hand at him. "Sorry."

"Wow, you *have* changed," Archer Drake observed. In closer proximity, Jason Chambers could see the family resemblance: both tall and lean, long noses and mouths meant for smiling, though Angela's hair—shoulder-length strawberry blond layers— was much lighter than the man's. "You're still an uptight, controlling jackass, but now you feel bad when you behave like an uptight, controlling jackass. And that wasn't a joke to defuse tension!" he added as she took a few steps closer. "It was an objective observation. That's a legitimate thing, right?"

"Of course it's legitimate. But your cousin's right, this isn't a happy errand, so why pretend?"

"Thank you, Leah," Angela said, pointed and triumphant at the same time.

"Miss Drake."

Angela spun and smiled when she saw Jason had joined them, which was a rarity in his profession. If he thought about how often people scowled at the sight of a cop, he'd get depressed. Well. *More* depressed. Not for the first time, he wondered why he'd been drawn to a profession where every single day on the job, people were not glad to see him. "*Angela*, like I told you last time, and the time before that, please call me Angela."

Please call me Jason.

Please call me Jason.

Please call me Jason.

He opened his mouth.

Please call me Jason.

"Sorry. I forgot." *Not even close.*

Fortunately, the dazzling intense woman he'd been horrified to realize he had a crush on

(a crush! like he was sixteen! what next, the acne makes a triumphant return?)

was too busy with the introductions to notice his stilted delivery. "This is my cousin Archer and his fiancée—"

"Leah Nazir," he interrupted. He'd recognized her at once. "Hello. Detective Jason Chambers. I'd know you anywhere."

She shook his hand. She had long, wavy dark hair; wide-set eyes; and a pale, pretty face. Her hand was tiny. "Have we worked a case before?" It was a good guess—most local cops knew Nazir consulted with police departments all over the country—but wrong.

"No, I was a big fan of *That's My Mom.*"

Nazir's smile dropped off as if his hand had turned into a dead rattlesnake. She extricated herself from the handshake and managed a small, "Oh."

Mistake.

"Oh," Angela added.

Mistake. Why?

"Sorry," he said. Because for some reason he now had to apologize for the fact that Leah Nazir was once a household name.

DEJA NEW

"It's weird that I keep forgetting you were a child star, right, hon?" Archer asked.

"Why do you keep asking questions you don't actually want the answer to? And it's *not* weird, it's lovely." She managed to arrange her lips into a gruesome approximation of a smile. "I'd prefer everyone kept forgetting."

"Sorry," Jason said again. And then he could put his finger on what he'd overlooked . . . not just Leah turning her back on acting, but the eventual fallout from that decision: Her costar/mother had been murdered just a few months ago. It had made headlines in various entertainment sections of various papers. *People* and *Us Weekly* had each done a small article on the case. "Death of an Icon's Mother," "Agent Murders Former Client," "*That's My Mom* Costar Slain." It hadn't been his case, but when it came to gossip, cops put hair salons to shame. The murder had been exceptionally foul and violent; two rookies had gotten sick at the scene. It had been discussed. Frequently.

"All right." The brisk voice pulled Jason back to the present. "Your IDOC paperwork is all set, here are your IDs back." A corrections officer had looked everything over and fed copies into the great bureaucratic machine that was ICC (pronounced "ick" to nearly everyone's annoyance). This was a small relief, because filling out paperwork didn't necessarily guarantee entrance to Intake Processing.

And if you *were* allowed in, you weren't done yet. Such things took time: a minimum of two forms of ID for every visitor. Searches. Paperwork. No cell phones, no pagers, no smoking. No boxes, no purses, no bags, no books. No sunglasses, no keys, no drinks, no food. No money, no backpacks, no magazines, no wal-

37

lets. Lock them all away, but the State of Illinois is not responsible for anything stolen if someone breaks the flimsy lock and absconds with your purse, bag, book, keys, drink, food, backpack, wallet.

Diapers, tampons, medication? Determined on a case-by-case basis. (Hint: Take your meds in the parking lot.) Contraband? Illegal per the Illinois Code of Criminal Conduct. (Hint: Leave contraband in the parking lot unless *you* want to live in a cage.)

Clothing? Everyone must wear underwear. All females must wear a bra.* No tank tops, no shorts, no dresses. No hats, no gloves, no scarves.

All this to sit in a bare, sad room and stare at a loved one who, for whatever reason, now lived in a cage.

"Drake family." This from the intake processing officer, whom no one saw unless the paperwork was squared away.

"That's us," Archer said, and Jason saw Angela bite her lip.

"Come on," Jason said, and led them to the Visitation Room.

---

*Seriously. The bra thing? Required by the State of Illinois. Which makes me wonder about enforcement.

EIGHT

Angela could feel her pulse hammering away in her own ears, which was distracting. And what was worse, it wasn't because she was nervous about facing her uncle.

Jason Chambers. He was why she was especially grateful for the invention of antiperspirant. And why she was irritated to catch herself giving thanks to the good people at Degree.* Since they'd met a couple of weeks ago, she had found the sober cop in the understated gray suit (or black or navy) to be the human equivalent of catnip. There was just something she liked about him, every single time. He was a big bundle of contrasts: brutally short brown hair, bright blue eyes. Lines of wear bracketed his eyes, but a dazzling smile (when she could coax one from him). Underwhelming sober-colored suits, wild socks.

---

*I love Degree antiperspirant! I make no apologies for that.

Yes. She liked the man for his socks. She would admit it, but only to herself. Oh, *God*, if any of her family found out she had a sock crush she'd have to leave town. Perhaps the country. And then the planet.

But there was no denying it: She was hooked the moment she spied his *Mona Lisa* socks. Subsequent visits had revealed Vincent van Gogh's *The Starry Night* and Gustav Klimt's *The Kiss* socks.*

It was her fate to find such a man irresistible: The cop who knew just how fucked up her family was and thus, sensibly, would want nothing to do with her on a personal level. He kept her at arm's length, always, and she couldn't fault him for it. They'd never be more than coconspirators. Wait, that wasn't the right word . . .

Never mind. Focus.

Here, again, the visitation room: white walls, shiny white floor, long wooden benches with long tables, all set up (as comfortably as mass-produced benches and chairs could be) to seat fifty or so. The far wall had a line of chairs against the glass so people could talk to inmates who for whatever reason couldn't come into the visitation room itself. It looked like a well-lit classroom and smelled like a gym.

It was a large room that always felt claustrophobic. The first time she had visited her uncle years after the murder—since her mother had refused to give consent, she'd had to wait until she was old enough—she'd been terrified the guards

(correction officers, that was the phrase. just like it wasn't a prison,

---

*These exist! I am not making this up! Google it, or check Amazon.

it was a correctional facility; they're not guards, they're correction
officers who cheerfully work at a correctional facility—so it's not so
bad, it's not so bad, it's not so bad)

wouldn't let her leave. It seemed inconceivable that uni-
formed strangers could now tell her up-for-anything uncle
where to go and what to eat and when to sleep. And if those
people had control of him, surely they could easily take control
of her?

Even now, years later, a part of her brain frets until the gates
close behind her, until she's walked through the lot, until she's
gotten in the car and driven away. That small scared scrap of
brain finally, *finally* shuts up when IDOC is in the rearview.

'Til next time.

Here he came, her uncle, and she was struck all over again
by the irony: Prison agreed with him. Dennis Drake was in his
sixties, but other than de rigueur salt-and-pepper hair, cropped
close in a buzz cut, and laugh lines,

(are they laugh lines if they're caused by stress?)

he could have passed for mid-forties. She knew that Dennis
looked as her father would have if he'd lived long enough; born
thirteen months apart, they'd occasionally been mistaken for
fraternal twins.

Dennis was in a Minions-yellow IDOC jumpsuit, socks,
loafers. Clean shaven and pale, with the grayish complexion of
someone long years away from sunlight. His light blue eyes
scanned each of them and she could practically feel him adjusting to their new, adult ages in his head. Hell, when *had* he last
seen his son? Had to be . . .

"Hi, Dad." None of them had taken seats, so it should have
been the easiest thing in the world for Archer to take those

three or four steps and embrace his father. But it seemed to take forever for him to get there, and the hug was as impersonal as a hug could be: arms forming a stiff A-frame, nothing touching below their shoulders. "'S been a while." To put it mildly . . . This was Archer's third visit in ten years.

"Archer."

"This is my fiancée, Leah Nazir."

"Yeah, I remember her from your letters." Dennis nodded to Leah, who was probably the least uncomfortable person in the group,

(what a pleasant change that must be!)

and extended his blocky hand, the knuckles slightly swollen.

(he's getting so old in this cage)

"Nice to meet you."

"Thank you, Mr. Drake. It's nice to meet you."

A small, crooked smile. "Is it?"

Leah smiled and shrugged, and tightened her grip just a bit.

This. *This.* This was the moment. The Aimee Boorman of Insighting would, in this one grasp of hands, see something momentous from his past that would help them figure out what really happened. From there they could figure out how he'd ended up in that particular room on that particular night, and from there, they could deduce and find the real culprit and justice would finally finally *finally* be served.

It would work because the universe practically demanded it. It would work because it was no coincidence that Archer got involved with Leah at the same time the irritating jackass in charge of her father's murder case retired. Events such as those were too momentous and perfect to be written off as "random coinkey-dink," as Mitchell would put it.

But never mind Mitchell. Leah and Dennis were still shaking hands. Then they stopped shaking hands. And—and—

Nothing.

Wait! Give it a few seconds. It'll happen, THE UNIVERSE WANTS THIS TO HAPPEN.

Nothing. Instead they were shuffling around, finding chairs, settling in for their allotted time, trying to get as comfortable as possible considering the room

(benches!)

and the occasion.

(awkward!)

No, not entirely nothing. *Something* was happening, because Leah was looking at her, and there was something like resigned patience in her face . . . and . . . was that? Yes. Patience . . . with a dash of pity.

She knew, Angela thought, her throat closing in despair. *Knew what I thought. What I hoped. Knew it'd be no good. Came anyway. Will waste no time going back to her own life once we're done here.*

Shit.

NINE

APRIL 15, 1710
CONCORD, MASSACHUSETTS

So the dead would stay dead and she would marry. She was old for such things—she would see thirty soon, and felt a thousand—but, regardless, her father would see that she lacked for nothing. As he should.

Payment rendered for twenty murders. Although it could have been worse.

Even now, she had trouble believing it had all happened, all of it had *really happened*, it had been like a roaring conflagration, devouring lives and smashing families and leaving only useless stinking ash behind.

Useless stinking ash was her heritage, and never was one more deserved. And it could have been worse. That was what she told herself through every day and night of the horror: Twenty murders, yes, but seventy-two were tried, so it could have been worse. Twenty murders, but nearly a hundred accused, so it could have been worse.

Rebecca Nurse was bad enough. And Bridget Bishop. And Susannah Morse. And John Proctor. They were dead and everyone was safe. They were dead and everyone was safe and if other people now had Bridget's taverns, and Rebecca's vast acres, and Susannah's inheritance, and John's many properties, that was mere coincidence and certainly nothing that should haunt her, haunt her, haunt her.

It wasn't as though powerful men, intelligent men, men who knew a great deal more about the world than she ever would, encouraged her. Oh no-no-no. The dead were witches, and a danger to all of them and thank God and His Beloved Son they were now and forever casting their spells in hell. But she had heard her father's complaints about Bridget's brazen ways

("A woman should own nothing, and certainly not taverns or public places of any sort.")

and John's stinginess

("He could so easily be of assistance. And he won't; I truly believe the devil pushes out all his good impulses.")

and the Nurse family's land disputes

("We had an agreement. That particular plot of land is mine by rights. And they know it, but their greed smothers the voice of God.")

and they *were* witches, they *were* the servants of Satan, they had devils' marks on their bodies and spells in their lying, crying mouths and everyone was safe now, it was over and they were safe and she was to be married and it wasn't her fault and it was all her fault.

She would marry Benjamin Baron and bear him children

and teach them the Lord's Prayer, and warn them that devils were real and often looked like ordinary people and sounded like her father. She would live to be an old woman, too old to be afraid of ghosts and it would be all right.

Everything would be all right.

TEN

"No," Dennis Drake said for the fourth time.

Angela swallowed a groan and dropped her head; her forehead hit her outstretched arms with a dull *thud*. Which was exactly how she felt: dull, wrapped in cotton—and every time her uncle shook his head, the cotton pulled tighter. Pretty soon it'd be hard to breathe.

"Dad." From Archer, who, from the state of his eyebrows (who knew he could arch them so high? they were like fleeing caterpillars!), wasn't far from losing his temper. "C'mon."

Another head shake. Another "No."

This was nothing new, but she'd expected more. Like she'd expected Leah to instantly solve everything. Or at least come up with a new clue. Or a name. Or a plan. Or an insight, no pun intended.

Instead: The brick wall of Uncle Dennis's will was as flexible as a concrete bench. She'd been slumping lower and lower as her uncle dug his feet in further and further, but now she forced herself to sit up straight. "Ridiculous. This is ridiculous. You've been stuck in here *how* long?"

"Feels like years."

She made a great effort to not grab her own hair and yank. Or his. "It *has* been years!"

"Oh. Thought you meant stuck in this room."

Leah made a sudden noise that sounded awfully like she was choking down a giggle. In response, Dennis cocked an eyebrow at her and said wryly, "Glad one of us is entertained."

Detective Chambers cleared his throat. "Mr. Drake, in my professional opinion there are some real problems with what you said happened and what did happen, and likely to your benefit, not the opposite."

"Don't care. Go direct traffic."

"Maaaaaybe don't alienate the cop trying to help you?" Archer suggested.

"Ha! Tell that to her." He jerked a thumb in Angela's direction. "Before that other cop retired, your cousin called him a waste of space. To his face."

"I did not!" Angela replied hotly. "I called him a complete waste of skin cells." She paused, considered, and continued, "In hindsight, that wasn't smart."

Archer leaned over and whispered to Leah, "That's pretty much our family motto."

"It was accurate," Angela admitted, "but not helpful."

"And *that's* on the family crest. I'll show it to you later. You'll be horrified."

"It's nice to have new experiences to look forward to," Leah murmured back.

"Again: Don't care. Didn't care about the last one, don't care about this one." Dennis fixed his pale gaze on

(gulp)

Angela. "You hear but you don't listen. Are you having déjà vu* right now? Because I am. And the reason is because we have this exact conversation pretty much every year. Nothing's changed."

"Except some things ha—" she began, but he cut her off with a curt gesture.

"This was always my mess. I bought it; it's mine. I didn't take a plea for a lesser charge. I didn't take a plea to leave wiggle room if I got buyer's remorse." Her uncle's voice was calm, but his eyes had narrowed and he'd lost what little color he had. Some people flushed red when they got mad; Drakes went pale. "And I wanted to do it. But this is what that costs: seeing me here a couple times a year."

"For years, not even that! By your rule!" she cried. "This is the first time you've seen your son in years, you haven't seen me for two, but you must know we'd come more often if you'd let—"

"But I won't let," Dennis continued with deadly calm. "You're doing it again: You're hearing, not listening. I made it clear after my plea, I made it clear each time you came, I made it clear two years ago, I made it clear last month. Nothing. Has. Changed. I'm in, for the duration. Move the fuck *on*."

---

*Ooooh! Note the play on the book title. See that? See what I did there? #subtle

The appalled silence was broken by Detective Chambers's flat, "I don't know what they've got on you, but it must be considerable."

"Visit's over." Dennis popped up from the table so quickly Angela would have missed it if she'd blinked. "Now then," he continued with cool calm, "you guys probably know that IDOC gen pop gets six visits a month, four hours each. You guys are gonna push me over my limit, and for what? So you can keep not paying attention? So we're done. Archer. Leah. Detective Chambers. Angela."

He said my name last. Is that bad? I think that might be bad.

With that, he walked away and—as happened every time—he never slowed, or even glanced back. It always looked, to her, like he was marching back to war.

She put her face in her hands, then groaned into her fingers. "Waste of time. All of it. Son of a bitch. Sorry, Archer. Sorry, Leah."

"You've got nothing to apologize for," her cousin said. "You're a goddamned hero as far as I'm concerned, putting yourself through this for all of us."

Not really. I'm putting myself through this for all of me. But she could never say that. Would never.

And then, featherlight, she felt a touch between her shoulder blades, too brief to be a pat. She took the small comfort that had been offered, and cursed herself again for being such a shit to Archer when they were kids. This had to be as awful for him as it was for her, but he still took time to let her know with a nonverbal signal that he was there except he wasn't, he was sitting too far away, beside Leah, it was impossible for him to have reached across so who the hell . . .

Oh.

Detective Chambers.

Oh.

Meaningless, she reminded herself. But she could still feel that touch.

ELEVEN

"So *that* was a sizeable pile of nothing."

"Like the family Easter basket of 2013," Angela agreed. All jelly beans but no Peeps or Cadbury eggs. It had been a living nightmare.

They were trudging out to ICC's parking lot, and a glum group they were. Angela could just make out Archer's car; her spirits were so low, it looked miles away.

"I can't believe that was the first time I've seen my dad in years and . . . and it was just a whole lot of blah."

Angela winced. "At least now you see you haven't missed anything. I know you were down about it for a long time."

"Oh, the 'I forbid you to visit me, cherished eldest child' edict? Yeah, gotta admit, it was hard not to take that personally."

Angela had to muffle a giggle. Trust Archer to find a way to make the horrible seem almost hilarious. "Thanks for coming with me, anyway."

"Of course," Leah replied. "We were glad you called."

Archer coughed. "Um."

"And we were glad to come."

"Um— Ow!"

"*Weren't we?*"

"Oh, yeah." Archer rubbed the fleshy part of his arm where Leah had gently pinched the bejeezus out of him. "Super-duper glad. No question. Tons of gladness."

"And while the visit didn't have the desired effect," Leah continued, "we did learn a few things."

"Yeah: Pathological stubbornness is a Drake genetic defect."

Angela snorted. "No, cuz, we already knew that."

"This is just from my experience talking to people who are hiding horrible secrets," Leah admitted, "but I think Dennis Drake is hiding a horrible secret."

Archer nodded. "Oh, yeah. Did you see how fast he got out of there when Detective Chambers implied he was protecting somebody? That was it, that was the end of the interview, right then, just . . . *whoosh!* 'G'bye, don't call, don't write.'"

From behind them, quietly: "He's got guilty knowledge of someone."

"Ack!" From Archer, who had stopped short and then turned. "Sorry, Detective. You were so quiet. I might've forgotten you were still there."

"He gets that a lot," Angela piped up. She'd seen it before. Jason Chambers was so unassuming, people engaged in conversation with him forgot he was there. *Cops*—trained observers—forgot he was there.

And that's goddamned catnip to me. Nobody ever forgets a Drake is in the room. Though they probably want to. Why do I keep comparing him to catnip? I don't have a cat. Or nip.

"He lied, for one thing," Jason continued. He'd sped up a bit so he was now walking beside them. "And not for the first time. He claimed we were his last allotted visit for the month. But I checked when I logged us in . . . he had plenty of hours left for the month. He got rid of us simply to get rid of us. In fact, he still couldn't get rid of you fast enough."

"You, too," Archer said, but Jason shook his head.

"That's typical. That's normal. Nobody wants to talk to cops at the best of times, never mind when they're in prison. It looks bad. I'd expect him to want to keep away from me. But again, he wanted the whole group gone, *especially* you." He pointed to Angela. "And you." To Archer. "And that's very curious. Often longtimers will . . . Their lack of contact with the outside world is lessened by . . ."

When he paused again, Angela spoke up. "You're not going to offend us by pointing out something we all know. Usually longtimers can't get *enough* family visits. According to the ones I've spoken to, anyway." At Leah's sideways glance and Chambers's sigh, she shrugged. "What? Sometimes Uncle Dennis would change his mind and not see me. I'm there, I already made the trip, but I should instantly turn around and go home?"

"Yes, Angela. Those would be the actions of someone who isn't obsessed."

"Cram it, Archer. Anyway, sometimes I talk to the other prisoners, or their families. I ended up with a really good recipe for risotto that way . . ."

"Which is why," Chambers put in, "you're no longer allowed to clear Intake Processing unless ICC personnel *and* your uncle *and* someone working the case concur."

They'd reached the car by now, and Angela looked down at

her feet and scuffed a toe along the white line on the pavement. *You almost accidentally let one measly arsonist out and suddenly you're slapped with a lifetime label: SECURITY RISK.* The world was a cruel and unfair place. "It was one time," she muttered. "But anyway. That whole 'only the first year of your sentence is hard time, after that you adjust' myth is bullshit. You spend your first year, and a couple after, in deep, *deep* denial."

"It's all a mistake," Chambers said.

"My lawyer's going to fix this," Leah added.

"The judge will realize he was too hard on me and will reduce my sentence any day now," Archer finished.

"Right, we all know the drill. But Uncle Dennis . . . he never had that. He couldn't indulge in the luxury of denial because he went out of his way to make damned sure he was going to be locked up. And he went further out of his way to make sure he *stayed* locked up. So you'd think he'd grab for any chance to see any of us. But he never did. Does, I mean." Of course, that could simply mean her uncle wanted less chaos in his life, which was understandable. Or that he wasn't especially fond of any of them, which was cold, but also understandable. "But," she finished, "that still leaves us nowhere."

"Maybe," Jason said, nibbling on his lower lip. But instead of sounding discouraged, it almost sounded like he was . . . hopeful? Like he'd thought of something?

No, she was reading him wrong. Actually, she shouldn't be reading him at all. If her uncle could have taken the gold medal for stubborn, she could have for grasping at straws. Any straws. Even dirty ones. *Why am I thinking about dirty straws now?* She gave herself a mental shake and looked up to say good-bye to the detective, but he was already climbing into his own car, a practical and forgettable Ford Focus. Gray, of course. She didn't even get a last glimpse of his Van Gogh socks.

Archer had it right. All we've got is a sizeable pile of nothing.

She slumped into Archer's back seat and got ready to endure the two-hour drive back home. She was too downhearted to even give Archer shit for his habit of driving slowly through stop signs. Which was pretty downhearted.

TWELVE

When I finish my jerky and porridge and coffee, I will kill an innocent man.

For the first time in a long time, the hangman had no appetite. He had no fear of blood or shit or puke, of death or the things men did to deserve death. He'd been hunting since he could hold a knife; he had attended many funerals. He could not remember a time when he did not understand death was a natural end for all God's creatures, even when it was engineered as a tool of the state.

He had hanged a rapist when he was nineteen, then went home and devoured the last of the corn bread (his sister had gifted him with a twenty-pound sack of meal when he moved west, knowing his penchant for baking and eating it by the pan). Now in his early thirties, he had executed men for everything from stealing telegrams to patricide. His appetite had never flagged because punishment was a consequence of crime. Think of the chaos if it wasn't! Besides, *someone* had to do it.

So, no. He did not fear death. He feared hell.

Chief Leschi was a native, a war chief, a raider, and an instigator. A man who took a bad deal, then blamed everyone but himself for taking that deal.

But he wasn't a murderer. And most people knew that.

The chief kicked up a ruckus—you bet! He would tell anyone who stood still how the government tricked him, stole from him. He squawked often enough that Acting Governor Mason sicced the militia on him. Didn't shut him up, but *did* result in two militia fellas turning up dead. This horrified every white person in a hundred miles, and was enough for Mason.

First trial: hung jury. Second trial: conviction and death sentence. Because the second time, the judge did *not* explain that killing combatants in war did not meet the law's definition of murder. (The state occasionally learned from its mistakes.)

So, guilty despite a total lack of evidence. Guilty despite his fine lawyers. Guilty despite appealing to the Territorial Supreme Court. Guilty despite sympathetic coverage from the press. Guilty despite appeals to the governor. Guilty despite the local lawman's stunt: Sheriff Williams let himself be arrested so he wouldn't have to supervise the execution.

But the government couldn't back down. Not after taking the trouble to frame Chief Leschi for the murders. Not after terrified locals had shrieked for the chief's head for eleven months. So they maneuvered around the sheriff, moved the execution date, and then moved the locale to Lake Steilacoom.

And an hour from now, the chief would swing from gallows so hastily thrown together, the platform was still bleeding sap.

"Don't envy you this one," the sheriff had said, and it was true, today his duty was his burden. But the sheriff knew, and the prosecutors. The press knew. The locals knew. It was that lone fact that afforded him one comfort: This would not be his sin alone. They would all be complicit, and, one day, they would all answer to God for it.

Forgive us, Lord God, for we know exactly *what we do.*

He went out to do his duty.

THIRTEEN

Angela trudged into the house by the back kitchen door, to be met by Jack, who had just slid something wonderful (as was his wont) into the oven. He turned to face her and even after her exhausting afternoon, she had to grin at the black with white lettering on his apron: YOUR OPINION WASN'T IN THE RECIPE*.

He greeted her with, "I don't even have to ask. It's all over you. In particular, your face."

"In particular, you're right. Though I think you're guessing."

"Uncle Dennis was a wall."

"Yes."

"A scowling, stubborn wall."

"Times ten. Yes."

---

*This exists! Oh, Amazon, is there anything you *can't* do?

"But on the plus side, the weather was beautiful."

She burst out laughing, she couldn't help it. "It's raining, you goofus."

Jack shrugged and pushed a hand through his fringe in the zillionth attempt to keep his (sun-streaked shaggy brown) hair out of his (dark blue) eyes. The top of his head came to the bridge of her nose, when ten months ago he was only up to her chin. Their mother, in a rare moment of levity (and connection to Planet Earth), swore she could actually hear Jack growing at night.

"Like I said: It was all over your face."

She dumped her purse on the counter, took a whiff. "Such crap." *O heavenly air, redolent with the scent of brownies from Jack's Pinterest board.* "I'm the poster child for inscrutable. I take you at poker almost every month."

"Yeah, when we're *playing poker,* a game where a straight face is a necessity. We're not playing now. You just trudged into the kitchen."

"I didn't trudge. I slunk. What's that smell?" Because now she could smell something beneath the brownies. Something dark and disturbed, a scent that had no place in any kitchen.

"Well. Mitchell made brownies."

"Oh, my God!"

"Right? So after I put the fire extinguisher away—we need another one, by the way—*I* made brownies. They'll be out in twenty. And I'm making that frosting you like."

"With the honey?" She made no effort to keep the hope out of her tone. It wasn't like they were playing poker, right? She loved Jack's just-for-warm-brownies frosting and she would never apologize for that, dammit.

"Absolutely. Just as soon as I clean the eggs out of the toaster."

"He tried that *again*? That's our third toaster!"

"This season," Jack added. "Target loves all our asses."

"You're all horrible and thoughtful," she managed.

He blinked at her in his slow, sweet way, like an owl in an apron. *Slow* in this case was the opposite of an insult. Jack was always careful, even in the midst of plotting—and often masterminding—whatever Drake madness was on the agenda. "Yeah, well. You know. Family, right? It doesn't have to suck *all* the time."

"No. It doesn't." She toed off her flats and thought about what that could really mean. "Maybe going to ICC today accomplished something after all."

"Yeah?"

Let it go.

Give it up.

Live your own life.

Be happy.

"Yeah. It might be time to just . . . not give in, exactly . . ."

"Angela, there's nothing wrong with focusing on yourself for a change. You're almost thirty—"

"Hey! Years from now." Five, in fact. Half a decade. Way far away from now.

"And you've spent half that time digging through old police files and driving at least one cop into retirement—"

"Do not get me started on Detective Kline, and I didn't drive him anywhere."

"You skipped prom to track down a witness—"

"Just the junior prom. They were going to hold it in the gym, for God's sake. I didn't want to wear a formal dress in the same room where Chucky Lewitt threw up. And where Ron Milman threw up. And where Jill Barrett got a nosebleed. And where thousands of kids have sweated over the years. Just . . . ugh."

"Okay, I'll give you that one," Jack allowed. "But now there's a new guy on the case, so you're all over the files again, you're bugging the same people again, you're tracking down the same witnesses again, you dragged—uh, invited—Archer back home for another frustrating ultimately useless visit. And through it all you've looked after all of us and Mom, too, which frankly must be exhausting—it sure *looks* exhausting—and all this in the face of Uncle Dennis's total refusal to help you with any of it."

"Why are you narrating?"

Jack gave her what he thought was his severe glare, which meant his regular stare while wrinkling his nose. This accomplished nothing except making him look like a vaguely alarmed rabbit. "My point is, it's not giving up. It's moving on. And there's not a single one of us, Uncle Dennis included, who would ever dare blame you for it, judge you for it."

"But the bottom line—"

"Bottom line is, no one's gonna call you a quitter. And if anyone did, I'd lace their brownies with drain cleaner and then I'd get *really* creative."

She stared at him. He stared back with another slow blink, unwrinkled his nose, then turned to the cupboards and methodically began pulling ingredients for brownie frosting. "Sometimes it's hard to remember you're only sixteen," she said to his shoulder blades.

"We're *all* older than we are," he replied, without turning around, which shouldn't have made sense but did. "Heck, Mom lost the love of her life, and we—"

"What?" That was wrong. Her parents had been fuck buddies, not soul mates. When Emma turned up pregnant, Donald did the right thing and married her. Angela had always been a little embarrassed that she was six months older than her parents' marriage. "That's not quite right, Jack."

"Oh, c'mon, they were all lovey-dovey all the time back in the day. Don't you remember?"

No. And you're the one who doesn't remember. But why shatter an illusion? "Well, they were passionate, that's for sure." Lots of squabbles. Lots of arguments that flared into fights that flared into slamming doors, sometimes a car roaring out of the driveway. But Jack had been little more than a baby then, it was no surprise he didn't remember it the same way.

"However they were, it's sure moot now. But thanks," she said. "For all of it. I'll— You've given me something to think about." She could already feel her mind probing the idea of closing the file on her father's murder, this time permanently, like a tongue poking a loose tooth. Leave it alone? Or poke at it until you couldn't stand it any longer, and then just pulled the fucker out?

"I've also given you brownies."

"Yes! My eternal gratitude is yours."

"I'd rather have ten bucks."

She snorted. "I'm not paying a family member for baked goods made with ingredients I paid for."

"Cheapskate. Speaking of family . . . Where's Archer and the woman he was incredibly fortunate to knock up, ensuring she'll hang around for at least eighteen years?"

"Jesus." From insightful young adult to thoughtless teenager in less than ten seconds. *A new record!* "She has a name, Jack."

"I know. Her name's the Mangiarotti of Insighters. But who has time to say all that? It just makes everything take longer, starting with the 'Happy Birthday' song."

"It's disturbing that you've given this so much thought. I think they're still in the car. Leah wished to, um, discuss . . . uh . . . Archer's habit of . . ."

"She's busting him for rolling through stop signs!" Jack's blue eyes lit up. "And you *left*? You should have gotten it on video."

"Pass. I think it's their first big fight in a while. And it just whipped in out of nowhere. Makes me wonder if . . ." She cut herself off. She'd wondered if it was pregnancy hormones, to be honest. Leah had gone an alarming shade of red and laid in to Archer, who'd sat frozen in the driver's seat like a deer hypno-tized by semitruck headlights, but that was as patronizing as it was pat. Besides, Archer *did* run stop signs. Constantly.

Before she could pester Jack to just hurry up and make the frosting already—and also she had dibs on the bowl—the back door was flung open and in marched Leah, Archer in her wake.

"It's physics, you gorgeous dolt! *Stopping* is *stopped.* Move-ment is *movement.*"

"It's basically the same thing," he protested. To his credit, he wasn't whining. Much.

"Do you not understand basic physics?"

"He doesn't," Jack stage-whispered.

Leah made a sound Angela couldn't place at first: the com-bination of a yelp, a giggle, and a shriek of rage, all while simul-taneously grinding her teeth. "How are moving and stopping the same instead of being, oh, I don't know, *total opposites*?"

"This really isn't a big deal."

Oh-ho. Rookie mistake, Arch. Heck, even Jack knew that, and he was in high school.

"Do not presume to tell me that flagrantly frequently flouting the law—"

Flagrantly frequently flouting, can she say that three times fast? I can't even think *it three times fast. Fragrant flou— Nope. Not even once.*

"—is not a big deal. Especially given what we've been up to today. We just got back from seeing your severely incarcerated father and your go-to move once we left was to break the law? How did I miss the fact that the father of my child has a criminal mind?"

"I don't know," Archer admitted. "I did help you kill a guy, remember. After your dead mom hired me to spy on you."

Argh, don't bring that up! I warned the Horde not to ever bring that up!

"It's been his go-to for years," Jack broke in, possibly to shift the subject away from murder, or to stick it to Archer. Though there was no reason it had to be one or the other. "You know he did that the day after he passed his driver's test, right? Think about that for a second: The guy didn't even have the laminated license yet, yet his thirst to flout the law was *that* strong. Tragic."

Leah jabbed a finger in the boy's direction. "This brother or cousin of yours is helpful and makes a great point!"

"I have a name," Jack huffed. "It's Arianna Kissmybutt. The second 't' is silent."

"Get bent, Arianna," Archer snapped.

"Whoa! Do you kiss my mother with that mouth?"

Archer turned back to his fire-breathing fiancée. "Leah, you're acting like you've never been in a car with me before."

"Ha! I wish. And putting up with something isn't the same as condoning it."

"Those two things? Are exactly the same thing," Jack pointed out.

"Jack, enough," Angela muttered. "This is not the time to instigate loved ones into a full-blown WWE wrestling match."

"That's *never* true, cuz. Particularly now. It's the perfect time."

"I'm telling you right now, Archer Asshat* Drake, I'm not tolerating your— Oh shit!"

Wow! So irked she can't even finish sentences now! She just randomly swears. Jack was right: I should be filming this.

Leah had frozen in place, then looked down and grabbed her belly with both hands like she was trying to tickle herself. When she looked up, she looked astonished and thrilled and afraid. "There it is again! I felt her, she's kicking!"

"You can tell it's a foot?" Archer managed to look impressed and puzzled at the same time.

"Well, kicking or punching. It sounds malevolent if it's a punch, though, so I'm not sure that's fair."

"Wait, what do you mean 'again'?"

"I didn't know for sure the first time," Leah replied defensively. "I'd just had a *lot* of ginger ale. I didn't want to jump the gun."

Ginger ale = maybe not a kicking or punching baby. Got it.

---

*Not his real middle name.

"In that case, I'm thrilled you're temporarily gas-free." Archer reached out and pulled Leah to him, which was tricky since she was still frozen in the act of tickling herself and she'd set her feet.

"Hey!" she snapped, but let herself get grabbed. "You're not off the hook, you scofflaw bastard."

"I know, I know. I'm sorry." He gave up on the hug attempt and patted her stiff shoulders instead. "You're totally right, my first instinct after leaving a prison should not be to rack up misdemeanors."

"That's all I was saying."

"Because things are different now."

"That's all I was saying, too!"

"I'm agreeing with you."

"And apologizing."

"And apologizing," he soothed.

"Because you were totally in the wrong."

"One hundred percent."

"And this isn't about hormones!"

"Nope."

"Okay."

"Okay."

"It's great you two made up," Jack said, "but this is boring now."

Archer by now had sort of snuck an arm around Leah's shoulders in a stealth side hug, which didn't prevent him from frowning at the youngest Drake. "Why aren't you making frosting right now? Those brownies are brazenly naked. C'mon, Leah, let's lay—"

"Lie," she corrected.

"—ourselves down and marvel at your lack of gas."

"You're ridiculous."

"Irrelevant!"

Angela watched them go, not a little jealous. Not about the baby—there wasn't a single detail about pregnancy that didn't sound ghastly and she was in no hurry to experience any of it. But she was definitely envious of Archer's connection with Leah. They'd fallen in love while protecting each other. They had taken life, then made it. Made a person. Well, they were working on a person. They were workshopping a person. And yes, it was overly simple but no less true: Things were different now.

"So I can't," she finished aloud.

She heard twin clicks and saw Jack was fitting the beaters into his hand mixer. "Yeah, figured you'd see it that way."

"What way? I didn't let any details drop."

"Didn't have to, because you were thinking the same thing I was. You don't want another generation of Drakes growing up in ICC visitation."

"Damn right I don't."

"Not that we did because Uncle Dennis usually wouldn't let us visit, but you get what I mean."

"Yes."

"So you're still in."

"Yes."

"And we're all still in." He thumbed the power button and started whirring cocoa powder, powdered sugar, and vanilla together in the bowl.

"Yes!" she shouted over the mixer. "And you are way too young to have that much insight into people!"

"And I barely put any effort into it!" he hollered back. "Think about *that!*"

"I can't! It'll keep me up at night!"

Newly energized, and not yelling over the hand mixer, Angela headed for her laptop. There had to be something there. Or something that was already there would lead in a new direction. If not at first glance, maybe later tonight. Or later this week. Either way, her self-indulgent daydream was over, and it was past time to get back to work.

She'd come back later for the bowl.

FOURTEEN

"I picked up the mail."

"Okay," Angela replied absently, engrossed in the minutia of legal jargon.

"You didn't have anything. Just some catalogs."

"Thanks for the update."

"So. How was . . . everything? Um . . ."

Angela looked up. It had finally happened, the thing she had long foreseen: Her mom had forgotten her only daughter's name. *Dammit! Jordan wins the pool.*

"Angela," she prompted.

"I know that," the older woman snapped. "For heaven's sake." She was standing in the doorway to Angela's office in her long yellow robe, the one Jordan and Paul insisted made her look like a sleepy banana. Her short brown hair, streaked with silver, was damp from her pre-bed shower and she was in fret pose number two: one hand on her hip, the other reaching up to fiddle with the neckline of her nightgown (also pale yellow, so sleepy banana—times two).

Huh. Six p.m. already? And did she just snap at me? Careful, Mom. You'll sound engaged. What's next, raising your voice?

Mom coming in (well . . . not exactly in, since she almost never crossed the threshold) was a rarity. To be fair, all the Drakes respected Angela's office, formerly her father's office.

At first she'd kept it as a shrine: leaving his diplomas up, never switching out the old pictures of his kids and nephews, working around his paperwork rather than filing his away to make room for hers. She saved the chewed pens. She didn't empty the recycling. She left his coffee cup on the desk blotter for more than a year, and finally threw it away (coffee, she had learned, gets cold, scums over, shrinks, gets sludgy, gets moldy, and eventually disintegrates, ruining the cup in the process).

Now, years later, the room was well established as her office, everything in recycling was something she'd put there in the last two weeks, she drank hot chocolate and rinsed her mug every night, the bite marks on her pens all corresponded to her teeth. She'd kept her dad's diplomas up, but placed hers just beneath his, and as each brother/cousin graduated, she put theirs on the ego wall, too.

Everything else was hers: the laptop, the files, the printer that was broken and the printer that wasn't, the accordion Post-it notes Paul liked to steal, and, to her amusement (some of her clients were old school), the fax machine.

She'd gotten her bachelor's degree in paralegal studies, then sat for the NALA* and was certified by the Fourth of July. The certification was Mitchell's idea: He'd pointed out that since she spent most of her free time researching their dad's case, which led to other cases, why not get paid for it? "You aced everything," he pointed out, "because by the time you got to college you'd been doing it for ten years. There's gotta be jobs out there that fit those parameters. Also we're out of milk."

She'd thought about it for all of five minutes and realized he had a point. (She also wondered how the *hell* they could be out of milk when she'd bought two gallons the day before.) She knew she lacked the desire and discipline for law school (it took too long, and she'd have no say over the cases she got for years, if ever), and the selflessness to go through the police academy ($44,000 a year to get shot at? Pass). Research, she could do. Writing legal briefs, she could do. And she could do it from home, something that couldn't be said for patrol officers. So, yes . . . why *not* get paid for it?

Now she telecommuted for a number of attorneys and sometimes it was interesting and sometimes it was dull, but she made a respectable living and between her salary and the insurance/pension from her father's death and the fact that she lived at home and the mortgage was paid off, they were okay. Financially, anyway.

"I was wondering about your . . . ah . . . trip."

Right. Back to the present: Her mother had decided to spend a few minutes feigning interest in her life. In a way, this was worse than the indifference.

---

*National Association of Legal Assistants

"My trip?" *She never says the words*, Angela realized. *It's always "your trip" or "the errand."* "To the state prison my uncle's been languishing in lo these long years?"

"Well." The hand drifted up. Clutched the gown's neckline. Fiddled. "Yes."

"It was . . ." A rerun? A bust? A waste? Fun seeing Jason's socks? ". . . like it always is."

"So you won't need to go back anytime soon." When Angela said nothing, her mother continued. "There's—there'd be no point. Right?"

She closed her laptop to give her mother her full attention. *Oh holy hell. Let's just get to it, okay?* "Something on your mind, Mom?"

"I just think it's a waste of time, is all."

"So you've said. Many, many, many, many, many, many, many times." *And even that many* manys? *Not enough.*

"And now"—here came the vaguely hectoring tone she knew well—"you've dragged your cousin back into it."

Angela felt her eyebrows arch involuntarily. "'Dragged'?" Not the verb she would have gone with. And that her mother thought Archer could be dragged anywhere was laughable.

"He has a new family now," the sleepy banana masquerading as her mother went on. "He has . . . responsibilities. New things he should be focusing on, not . . . er . . ."

"Old business?"

"You make it sound like I don't care."

Because you don't.

"Of course I care."

Nope.

"But how long until you let this go?" Mom paused, like Angela actually had a time period in mind. Like she'd jump in with, *I thought I'd give it another three years and seventy-eight days, and if I don't have it solved by then, I'll hang it up forever.* "It's been a decade."

"Mom, I could understand your mind-set if it was one you had gradually come around to. But you've never liked me looking into Dad's murder." It was almost as if her mother knew more than she had told back in the day. Not guilty knowledge, exactly, but . . .

Wait. Why assume she doesn't have guilty knowledge? I've never understood her paralyzing grief. What if she had something to do with Dad's murder? What if it's not grief, but guilt?

Ridiculous. The woman had problems, but ascribing guilt was a big step too far.

Meanwhile, Mom's brows had rushed together and she nearly shouted, "Because you were a child!"

"Yes. But I wasn't for long. We all grew up pretty fast." Unspoken: *We had to, because you fell apart. You know who paid for that robe, right?* "After a while—and not a long while—I wasn't a child. I was a pissed-off young adult looking for answers and you still did everything you could to discourage me."

In response, a mutter: "Obviously not everything."

"And it's not just me." Here was a conversation they should have had years ago. Oh, well, no time like the present. *This'll teach her to hover in my office doorway.* "You've always been opposed to anyone researching the case, discussing the case, *thinking* about the case."

"That's not—"

"No. No denial this time. Let's try something different, okay? Just for fun. No denial!" Angela realized she was rocking back and forth in her agitation. *God, this ergonomic chair was the best gift to myself.* "Hell, when I was in college, my prof offered extra credit to anyone who wanted to help me. He was goddamned enchanted by Dad's murder and loved that I was working a 'real-world scenario.' And, yes, he was an insensitive boob, but half my floor took him up on it—free labor and a bunch of fresh eyes and you were *still* against it."

"That's not what college is for! It's for drinking too much and learning new things and making terrible decisions about your sexuality but coming to your senses in time for graduation!"

"I . . . Wow." *Where? Where to even start?* "If it's any consolation, I did all that other stuff, too." *Oh, my God. I did not just tell her that.*

Mom's hand froze mid-fiddle. "Oh. Well. Good for you, then."

I visited my imprisoned uncle in the company of the Andretti of Insighters and a detective wearing Van Gogh's Sunflower *socks and this is* still *the most surreal conversation I've had today.*

"Mom, something I've always wondered." *Bad idea. No, good idea. No, terrible idea. Fuck it.* "Why do you care? This . . ." She gestured to the files, the boxed files in the corner, the entirety of the office, which wasn't a shrine to her father but *was* HQ for catching his killer. "All of this, it doesn't affect or alter your life at all. Whether I'm working on Dad's case or writing a brief for Judge Shepherd, your day-to-day routine is exactly the same. So what's the problem?"

Her mother stared. "You really don't know?"

"I really don't know."

A long sigh, followed by, "The problem is, I don't want to see my daughter throw her life away like—" She cut herself off, so quickly Angela heard her teeth click together.

"Like my uncle?" she asked quietly.

"It should have been him."

As a revelation, this wasn't exactly shocking. Emma Drake had not kept that concept to herself. "But it wasn't. So we had to deal. Have to deal. I understand why you've never visited Uncle Dennis—"

A bark of laughter, quickly choked off. "Figured that out, did you?"

"Yes." *This is the longest conversation we've had since Paul accidentally sent us all to the emergency room. Soooo many forms. The paperwork was worse than the stitches.*

To Angela's alarm, her mother took another step into the office. "Okay. I'll reiterate, so there's no misunderstanding going forward. It should have been your uncle—"

"There's—"

"—bleeding out on that filthy floor—"

"—no misunderstanding—"

"—in that shitty little drug warren."

"—on my end. Any of our ends."

"Not your father."

"Yes. Got it. But, again: We have to deal with what *is*."

But her mom wasn't listening. "So that doesn't come as a surprise to you? That I wanted your uncle dead?"

"No, but it's good to receive confirmation. I guess."

"And now I've reiterated."

"But d'you know what else was a surprise, Mom? You taking Dad's death so hard. The others are too young to remember, but you guys used to fight. A lot."

"About your uncle! About how he was an irresponsible junkie shithead we all should have stayed away from."

"Not just about— Well, yes, you fought about Dennis. But I remember Dad wanting some space, and you weren't having it."

She snorted. "He wanted a lot more than that, but this isn't about him."

Um. It's not? Isn't EVERYTHING about my dead dad?

"It's about you wasting your life. It's about how even though you know how I felt back then and how I still feel, you're *still* trying to save Dennis! You've pissed away years trying to save someone who was always worthless. How can you *do* that?"

For several seconds, Angela could only gape at the enraged banana before her. "That's why you withdrew from me? From all of us? Even Jack, and he was little more than a baby at the time! You've been . . . what? Sulking? 'She's ignoring my wishes, I'll ignore hers'? For ten years? Seriously?"

The banana deflated. "I can never make you understand."

Back atcha, Mom. "Did you ever like Uncle Dennis?" Angela remembered very little of pre-murder Dennis. Whenever she thought of him, post-murder Dennis was always at the forefront. As best she could recall, he'd been the fun uncle, the guy who was always up for anything. But to a kid, that could mean going to Dairy Queen after 9:00 p.m. How wild and crazy had he really been when she looked at him through the lens of time?

As if her mother could read her mind, she said, "He was always a pain in your father's ass. And mine."

Yes. That message is loud and that message is clear. "I know . . . I remember you used to tell us how jealous he was of Dad."

Her mother shook her head. "It was more than envy. He wanted to *be* your father. And sometimes, your father wanted to be him, if you can believe it."

Hmm. That was a new take on the old story. "I remember

he was always happy to drop everything and have fun with us. Even when Jack was just a baby, he'd bundle us all in his car—"

"Your father's old car. Which he took. Often without asking."

"—and off we'd go."

"Yes. So he could pretend he had what your father did."

"Or maybe they were just brothers who shared their stuff?"

Mom shook her head.

"So all the fun things he did for us, they were only ever about him? Dennis never loved us because we were just symbols? Because that's harsh, even for you."

"No. Harsh is stealing what other people have and pretending it was yours all along. It's almost as bad as just coveting what others have."

Here was a well of bitterness Angela had never suspected. It was one thing to loathe your husband's killer. It was another to realize the loathing had always been there, long before the murder. "For example?"

"Well." Up came the hand again, fiddling, fiddling. The neck of her gown was starting to fray. "He—he ruined your father's credit rating!"

"Thank God they locked him away, then. I feel safer already. Why didn't you leave?"

"What?"

"You guys were fighting all the time about Dennis, why not pack us up and leave?"

"How can you ask that? I never would have left him. And he never would have left me."

Angela started to reply when she suddenly had—not a recollection, exactly, but a piece of memory: her father standing in his bedroom doorway, holding a bulging suitcase.

Where did that *come from?* But the more she tried to pin it down, the faster it faded.

"You know what?" her mother was saying. "Never mind." Her mother let go of the gown and held up her hands, palms out. "Forget I came in here. Forget we talked." And just like that—*poof.* Meaningful, painful, long-overdue family discussion over. Exit Emma Drake.

Angela stared at the empty doorway for several seconds.

No, Mom, I won't forget. That's what you've been trying to do. She got back to work.

FIFTEEN

Walk or die.

But he couldn't walk.

So.

He'd known there were risks. Of course he had; he wasn't born here, but almost five thousand miles away in Belgium. That journey had been fraught with peril and he had despaired of ever seeing land again. More than once he had dropped to his knees: *Please help me in Your wise compassion, O Lord, please spare me an ocean grave and in Your mercy, guide me to land.*

He had been heard and, at the time, was grateful to have been spared drowning, a bad death surrounded by hundreds of fellow passengers, all gasping and crying and praying, all fighting the sea.

Now he was surrounded by land stretching infinite miles in every direction, and he was alone. The Lord Almighty had answered his prayer with a vengeance that, under different circumstances, he would have found amusing.

He supposed he should pray and prepare for death, he supposed he should greet his Maker in as serene a state of mind as possible. Forgiving them—forgiving Lewis Keseberg—would be the Christian thing to do. It would prove John Snyder Hardkoop was worthy of a spot in heaven.

But.

John had spent hours trying to get serene, but every time he closed his eyes to pray, Keseberg was there, telling him to get out and walk, telling him the party in general and Keseberg in particular would not waste their precious, dwindling resources on a seventy-year-old immigrant. (An odd distinction, since Keseberg was himself an immigrant from Germany.) Warning him again when he collapsed beside the stream: Hardkoop would not be allowed to ride and no one would stay with him.

A true Christian would not ascribe sinister motivations behind Keseberg's exhortations that he rise, that he walk, that he keep going. A good person would assume Keseberg was being encouraging in his blunt way, was trying to save him.

But Keseberg couldn't hide the relief on his face when John didn't move. He might as well have scrawled it on his forehead: *More for the rest of us if he stays. More for me.**

Now, a day later, after he spent the night shivering and staring at the stars and mentally murdering Lewis Keseberg in sev-

---

*Fun fact: Lewis Keseberg was the only survivor at Donner Lake. He had eaten Tamsen Donner to stay alive. But Mrs. Donner had seemed as healthy as anyone could be in those circumstances, and it was a puzzle that she had mysteriously died just in time to sustain Keseberg. He was accused of murdering her for food; and to the end of his days, he told people that human liver was "the sweetest morsel."

eral satisfying ways, he'd propped himself up beside the stream and contemplated his ruined feet. *They've burst like overstuffed sausage casings*, he thought dispassionately. But here was a blessing at last: The colder he got, the more tired, the more hungry, the more the pain receded.

What didn't abate was his howling rage at being dismissed as a burden and abandoned. He simply could not get his mind serene. Dogs had been granted more dignified deaths than what he was facing.

He knew there was life beyond death. He knew that, one way or another, John Snyder Hardkoop would continue. And if it was the Lord's will that he be born again, if another life was his burden or blessing, so be it.

But he would take every care in the next life: He would make himself valuable. Irreplaceable. Someone who would never be abandoned in a vast wilderness and left to die.

And if he ever ran into Lewis Keseberg, he would cheerfully murder the man.

Yes.

He closed his eyes. It would be over soon, surely.

SIXTEEN

Leah snapped awake in the darkness. It took her a few seconds to remember

(it smells strange in here)

where she was

(streetlight's in the wrong place)

and then it clicked. Archer's old bedroom. Visiting his family, dealing with a multitude of Drakes. And the nightmares. Dealing with those, too. This was the second in two days, and they weren't hers.

That would have been frightening enough, even for someone in her line of work. She was used to seeing the past lives in her clients' eyes; she was a licensed Insighter (ID #29682), certified in Reindyne therapy,* and she'd been seeing far too much since she was a toddler.

But *these* lives. Leah knew them. They were the first she'd

---

*Reindyne is a hypnotic drug accidentally discovered in 1987; they were trying to develop a combination diet aid/heart medication. (Reindyne isn't real. I don't know if diet pill/heart meds are real.)

ever felt, some even before her own. They tasted the same, too: despair, grasping loneliness, the hard determination to never be forgotten, to never be ignored—with the underlying theme of look at me, *look at me, LOOK AT ME!* I am important, you CAN'T LEAVE ME.

She wasn't just pregnant. She was pregnant with her mother.

Beside her, Archer growled out another snore, then muttered, "Leave me 'lone with *all* the fish." Good. No point in both of them lying wakeful at oh-God-thirty in the morning. Nor was she ready to let him know she was going to give birth to his mother-in-law.

Let's think about that again. Really think about it. I. Am. Pregnant. With my mother.

???????????

All right. Try it again. We deal with the unknown (and the severely strange) by making it known, we deal by learning about it. So. In the history of humanity, this can't be the first time this has happened. There's precedent. There will be case histories you can look up. And even if there aren't, you aren't alone. Archer and a dozen Drakes will help you.

Nope. Still no good. Because it didn't matter if there was a precedent. It didn't matter if this happened to someone else three hundred years ago. It was happening to her, right now, and she was the one who had to face it. She was destined to swell like a bullfrog, endure edema and hemorrhoids and morning sickness, the tedium of multiple doctor visits, the cravings, the restrictions, the hormonal shifts, the stress and pain of labor and delivery. And at the end of all of it, she would give birth to her worst enemy.

She put her hands on her belly and laid awake until the sun came back.

SEVENTEEN

D eath, the last guest, was coming, but he'd been the one to open the door. He wondered if they would carve the truth *(here lies Hans Christian Andersen, who fell out of bed and never recovered)*

on his tombstone.*

He decided they wouldn't. Or, worse, they would carve *their* truth on his tombstone. People who read his stories thought they knew him. In the beginning, he had found it droll. But as time went on, it became less amusing and more depressing. And he had never been one to need any help succumbing to melancholy.

---

*Seriously! He fell out of bed and never recovered. And if he *had* recovered, the liver cancer he didn't know he had would have finished the job.

He imagined a conversation with the tombstone committee: "Let us keep things as simple as we can. Name and dates, I think." Then he imagined the gentle arguing that would ensue.

They would say, "So humble, even though you're of nobility," to the son of an illiterate washerwoman.

They would describe him as "A weaver of tales!" though it was nothing so profound (though in his youth he had apprenticed to an actual weaver).

They would say "A born scholar!" about a man whose school years were the worst, most hateful years of his life.*

And "A national treasure!" to a man whose works sold poorly until they were translated into other languages.

And "You would have made a fine husband!" to a man who only ever fell in love with women he could never have.

And "But such a gift with children! What a wonderful father you would make!" to a celibate.

Nobody knows me. Nobody at all. This thought, this yearning to be known, remembered, had been with him as long as he could remember. But nothing he did made any difference. They read his stories and created their own vision of him in their minds, one that bore little resemblance to the actual man. Perhaps that was a blessing. Was it the worst thing in the world that he had been turned into a character in his own stories?

Well. Yes. Because he *wasn't* a fairy-tale creature, damn it all, and he had no interest in disappearing into the pages of his own books.

---

*Fun fact: Not only did Andersen's schoolmaster regularly abuse him, he and his colleagues made it their business to discourage him from writing. Yeah. They told Hans friggin' Andersen to just stop with the stories already.

The bright spot in the mess was that he made time to meet with the composer to discuss the music for his funeral. The composer had been surprised—usually people consulted him *after* the death—and a little taken aback at his calm practicality. "Most of the people who will walk after me will be children," he'd told the bemused music teacher, "so make the beat keep time with little steps."

It seemed the least he could do, a phrase he normally detested (Nothing is the least one could do.). A last thing to do for children who were never his, honoring a life he never had.

EIGHTEEN

"Could you repeat that? You did what with his head?"

"I stuffed his mouth with garlic. Pay attention."

Jason checked his notes. Yes. He'd heard her correctly. His boss would scream, but his conscience demanded the next question: "Are you sure you wouldn't like a lawyer present?" *Because you need one. In five years on the job, I have never seen a suspect more in need of legal assistance. And I am including the guy who killed his accountant with a harpoon.*

"No lawyer!" The witness/suspect sat bolt upright, though that might have been because the chairs in the interview room were designed by masochists who assumed everyone loved back cramps. "I'm guilty."

It certainly looked that way. He'd come upon the scene and taken it all in before he even had his ID out. The victim, naked and in pieces. The witness, gloved and wearing old clothes she wouldn't care were ruined. The grave she'd been digging in the salsa garden. The blooming pink roses behind her, as well as the bright yellow boots on her feet (grave digging = muddy) had been the perfect surreal touch.

The matter-of-fact neighbor who'd called 911 summed it up quite well: "Y'know how when people find out a killer lived in the neighborhood, they're all 'But they were so quiet and nice!'? Yeah, not these guys. They're both fucking crazy. And loud. But mostly with the crazy." Jason'd written it down verbatim. Too good to paraphrase.

She'd certainly been chatty on the way to the station, waiving Miranda and bitching about the traffic. She was a petite brunette with hair that had been slicked back with so much product, he could almost see his reflection in the top of her head when he handcuffed her. Old jeans, faded paint-spattered T-shirt, no jacket, and those cheerful yellow boots. Hazel eyes, freckles. Small and wiry and she looked adorable, which made sense. Most murderers didn't look dangerous until they'd gone ahead and taken a life. Sometimes not even then. He'd learned that two weeks into the job.

"So there's no point in calling a lawyer," she finished.

"There is, because—"

"No lawyer, flatfoot!"

"What year do you think it is? That is not sarcasm, by the way. That's a legitimate question because I'm not sure you're, ah, cognizant."

"I'm plenty cognizant. It's 2017, which is just ridiculous given what I had to do this morning."

"Early this morning, in fact." He'd gotten the call at 6:37 a.m.

"Well, yeah. I couldn't kill him at night, *obviously*."

I can hear the italics when she talks. "Is that why you drove a stake through his torso?"

"No! I mean, I'm the one who staked him, but I was aiming for his heart. It wasn't like in the movies," she admitted.

He sympathized. "Few things are."

"It was really hard to get it in there."

"I hear that a lot."

"I practiced on all those mannequins for nothing!"

"That's a new one, though." Jason wasn't a doctor, but he was pretty sure her blade caught on a rib, which was great news since protecting the heart is their job. But in the end, it made no difference. Despite the miss, the victim had rapidly bled out.

"It was so fast! It was like his body was a garden hose and he was spraying his blood everywhere."

He checked his notes again. "And you did these things because you thought he was a vampire."

"Yes."

"Despite the fact that he had never, not once, per your statement, tried to suck your blood or turn into a bat—"

"Oh, please, that one's just pure myth."

"—or burn in sunlight?"

"I said he *was* a vampire, not that he *is* one." She was all irritability and wrath in sunshine yellow boots. "Don't you know anything?"

"Clearly not."

"He drank all my blood in a past life."

"So this was payback?"

"Yes." This with the expression of "someone's finally catching up" on her face.

"Which you understand has been illegal since Darrow vs. Henry VIII?" he persisted for the record. "Back in 1964?"

"*Yes.* It's why I had to take care of it myself." The suspect crossed her arms over her chest and gave him a smile almost as cheery as her boots. "There's not a jury in the world who'll judge me for it."

"By definition, every jury judges the defendant, even if the outcome of that judgment is positive."

She waved away his summary of the American legal system. "They'll get it."

"I have to say, you certainly have a positive attitude."

"Oh, yes." She uncrossed her arms and leaned forward, resting her elbows on the table. "I'm generally a positive person. Things will work out and if they don't, don't give up! You can fix it, you just can't be afraid of doing the work."

If she doesn't go to prison, this woman has a real shot at being a Hollywood spin doctor.

"You are by far the most cheerful person I have ever arrested."

The woman who had cut off her brother's head and tried to drive a chair leg (which she'd whittled to a point over the last three months) through his heart beamed. "Thank you!"

"Time to get photographed and fingerprinted," he said kindly, and she jumped to her feet, clearly ready for the next phase of her adventure.

"That's okay, why else d'you think I got highlights?"

"Why else, indeed?" he replied, and escorted her out.

NINETEEN

He was midway through his paperwork
(should I put in the thing about her highlights?)
when he saw Lassard making her way to his desk. Depending on what was in the folder in her hand, this could be terrific or terrible.

Captain Marci Lassard greeted him with, "Nice catch."

"No." This wasn't false modesty, or even actual modesty. He hadn't done any detecting, simply responded to a call and arrested the bad guy. That was fine. Most police work was strictly custodial. That was fine, too.

"But you could have shot yourself in the foot, Jason."

"Marci—"

"It worked out for you, it usually does, but it's not your job to repeatedly remind people arrested for homicide that 'no, really, you can still have a lawyer, are you sure you don't want a lawyer?' When they turn you down—and thank God she did—you focus on *your* job: taking statements, building a case for the DA."

"She was pitiful."

"Irrelevant."

"Wonderful attitude, though."

"I'll agree it's nice when they don't try to kill us, or worse, spit on us . . ." Marci Lassard, like most cops, had in her younger days been cried on, puked on, bled on, spit on, and shit on. Most of it barely made her blink, but she loathed saliva. She was a heavy hand-sanitizer user long before most people even knew there was such a thing. "But that's still no reason to sabotage your own investigation. I don't want to have this chat with you again, Jase."

"That's a relief."

"Hilarious." She slapped the folder on top of his copy of *Dancing Cats and Neglected Murderess.* Jason could actually feel himself getting pale. Not this. Not this again. No. "See this?"

Nooooo! "Oh, God."

"That's right."

"Not the chart again, Marci."

"Take a look."

"I am begging, do you hear me? Begging you. Look at my face, observe the stress."

"I *thought* you looked a little constipated."

"Listen to my voice, my pleading and pathetic voice," he whined. "Put the chart away. I see that thing in my dreams. I will obey you in all things. I will clean the lunchroom fridge every day for a month."

Too late. She slapped the Chicago Police Department—Organizational Overview Chart* in front of him. Her finger jabbed at a box about midway down. "I'm here. And I want to be . . ." The finger, having jabbed, moved on. ". . . up here." Superintendent of Police. "By way of here." Chief, Bureau of Detectives. "*You* want me to be somewhere down here." Records Inquiry Section.

"I promise I don't." He didn't. His predecessor did, which is why Kline was his predecessor and not a partner.

"I can't move from here . . ." Point. "To here." Poke. "Without the detectives under me making lots of arrests and closing lots of cases. Encouraging someone to call a lawyer when they've waived their rights is not helpful to either of our careers. And, sorry to sound heartless, neither are closed cold cases."

Thought so. "Has my productivity suffered since I took over the Drake case?"

The captain plunked down in the chair beside his desk. "You know it hasn't." She brushed her short, reddish-brown bangs back from her face. The fluorescent light bounced off her wedding ring; she and her husband were the rare "met in high school and still in love twenty years later" couple. Other than Mr. Lassard's belief that police work was exactly like what he saw on TV, and his insistence on using phrases like "we threw a real 415e last weekend!" around his wife's colleagues, Lassard was a good enough guy.

---

*You can get this on the Web. The CPD's website is very helpful!

Certainly his wife adored him; she'd asked him to change his name to hers and he had, without hesitation. All her life, she knew she'd be a cop, just like Commandant Lassard from the *Police Academy* movies. "It was a calling, and not just because I was Charles Rowan* in a previous life!" she'd tell rookies, eyes shining with a near-fanatical light. "There I was, watching the movie and my name was exactly the same as the guy in the movie. The boss with all the goldfish! The Lassard name up on the big screen! It was fate! The only reason we even watched *Police Academy: Mission to Moscow* was because Blockbuster was out of *Pulp Fiction*!" (Woe to the rookie who asked, "What's Blockbuster?")

"This really isn't about your productivity," his captain continued. "It's about you not burning out."

"Really? I thought it was about the chart."

"Everything leads back to the chart," she said solemnly, then grinned. "But enough on that for now—"

He nodded. "I've been punished enough."

"Hilarious. So you and the family went to visit Dennis Drake yesterday."

"Yes."

"He didn't give you shit."

"Not even the smallest trace of shit."

"So your next step . . . ?" Marci's delicately arched eyebrows were more for form's sake; she'd worked homicide longer than he had. She knew perfectly well what the next steps were. And weren't.

"The next steps. Right." Ah. Well. The Drake file's Closed

---

*See the Author's Note. I'm too lazy to cut and paste it here. Ugh, writing is hard.

status was problematic. The CC Division had their own budget, equipment, and staff, and as a detective with another bureau, he wasn't entitled to any of it. His captain, who wanted her detectives happily challenged because such people brought results, had given him some room to run. But nothing had changed in the month he'd had the file; the missing witnesses were still missing, Dennis Drake was as recalcitrant yesterday as he'd been ten years ago, Kline was still gone ("You grinning shiteaters can go fuck yourselves sideways.") and thrilled to be gone, and Leah Nazir hadn't been able to come up with a magic fix. He wasn't surprised by any of it; he'd expected all of it.

"You're my steadiest, least excitable guy," his captain was saying. "Not just in my division; you've got some of the lowest affection of anyone I've met who isn't a sociopath."

"Thanks." That was the appropriate response, right? Even if it wasn't necessarily a compliment?

"You're also methodical and you don't rattle. But that doesn't mean you're invulnerable. It doesn't mean you can't burn out, or snap."

"Because it's always the quiet ones?"

"Because I've seen you almost every day for years and I've never even heard you raise your voice."

Yep. Sounded right. Sounded like the feedback he'd been receiving since he was nine. He'd been tested for the spectrum, and had no idea if the negative results were a relief to his parents or bad news.

"What I'm saying is, there's laid-back, and there's comatose." Long, delicate pause. "Are the meds for your depression working out?"

There it is.

"Dysthymia."

"What's the difference?"

Normally he'd find this line of questioning irritating or, at best, pointless. But Captain Lassard never lobbed "So how're you feeling?" questions for the sake of small talk.

"Dysthymia is much like depression, the same general symptoms present for treatment, but they're not as severe and they last longer."

"Depression Lite."

"Close enough." Not as severe = the good news. Lasting longer = the catch. A lot of sufferers—himself included—would go years without seeking professional help, because they assumed being low, being sad, was just part of their character, and could not be fixed.

Jason thought the ancient Greeks had it right: The literal translation of *dysthymia* was "a bad state of mind."

"I'm on Paroxetine now. Sixteen weeks in." Citalopram had been a disaster. He didn't mind the decreased sex drive so much—he wasn't seeing anyone and the Angela Drake fantasies were exactly that: fantasies. Not being able to get it up or, when he got it up, not being able to finish wasn't *too* bad: It wasn't as though his penis's dance card was full. Nor was the insomnia the problem; he had always been able to function on four hours a night. But the shakes, the sweats, the having to take a piss every hour, and the explosive diarrhea had been deal breakers. "Copy that, dispatch, I'm en route as soon as I find a public bathroom and destroy their toilet."

Pass.

But the Paroxetine seemed to be working, and the side effects were nothing he hadn't dealt with when he wasn't medi-cated. The problem with any SSRI* was that it usually took more than a month, sometimes two months, for any change to be noticeable. You could diet down (or up) a couple of sizes before the meds kicked in, that was how long it took. You could get through half of a football season. You could put your house on the market, sell it, find a new home, pack, move. You could walk halfway across the country.†

"So the Paroxetine plus therapy equals life isn't terrible all the time," he finished, hoping Marci was going to get to it soon.

"Oh, yeah?" she asked. "You saw a professional?"

"Sure." *You know I did.* "Like you did." Insighter screening was standard for anyone in the academy; all recruits were re-quired to take two sessions, on the second day and at graduation. Depending on your department, you could also be required to see one whenever you were up for a promotion, if you'd had to fire your weapon, and (most puzzling) for off-the-job injuries. "All my past lives had some form of it or another."

"Didn't you head up to ICC with what's-her-face? The head kahuna of Insighters?"

"Leah Nazir."

"The one who killed her mom?"

"No, she killed the man who killed h—"

But Marci was already shaking her head, annoyed with her-

---

*SSRIs are serotonin reuptake inhibitors like Prozac or Zoloft.

†It's true! Thirty miles a day x 42 days = 1,260 miles.

self as always when she got a detail wrong. "Right, right, I knew that, it was all over the news . . . I saw her on TV a few times. The Brenner case, and *Lane v. Hitler.* What was she like?"

"Quiet and pointed. No wasted words."

"A soul mate!"

Jason smiled and shook his head.

(not in the cards for me . . . or my soul)

Marci continued, "She touch you?"

"Sure. We shook hands."

"She give you the rundown on your past lives?"

"No, of course not. That'd be like a doctor running into someone with a broken arm, examining them, and setting the bone on the spot."

"You're saying a doctor wouldn't do that?"

"Captain . . ."

"We're getting off topic," she said, which Jason knew wasn't true. Marci didn't start up random conversations and then let them roam far afield. She had wanted to talk about what was going on inside his head so she could decide on his workload. "We were talking about your next move with the Drake file."

"Yep. We were. My next move."

He had no next move. He'd never had a next move. How to explain that it wasn't so much about clearing Drake as it was about seeing Angela? Marci, a relaxed and tolerant supervisor in nearly all things—including encouraging the use of her first name—would bounce him off the case in half a second if she knew. It'd be re-filed in the tomb that was the CCD and that would be the end of it.

All this to scratch an itch (even without the Angela factor, the Drake file bugged him—there was something right in front of his face and he couldn't see it) for a woman he barely knew.

"I've got some new records to look over," he heard himself saying. *Bad idea. Lying to the police or your boss is always a bad idea. Particularly when they're one and the same. Bad bad bad.* "But if there's nothing there, I'm at a wall."

She was nodding. "Yeah. Well. Do the best you can, but you've gotta know there's a limit here."

He did know. A lot of superiors would have nixed it right out of the gate. Especially when most people thought the killer had been locked away. "I'm thinking we'll bounce it back to CCD by the end of the week. Sorry, Jase."

"It's fine."

"I'll tell the family if you want."

"Not necessary." *Hand over my last chance to talk to Angela unless she kills someone and gets arrested? Nonsense.*

"Good talk," she said, rising from the chair.

No. Not really.

TWENTY

"Hey! You, in the smiley face shirt! Which I hate, by the way."
Angela looked up from her computer to see Paul hanging in her doorway. Literally hanging; he was clutching the top of the door frame and his feet swung an inch off the carpet. He was shirtless; his right pec tattoo (plain black ink reading TATTOO) was showing. "Do I criticize your casual attire?"

"Frequently."

"That's fair."

Paul's feet swung and kicked. "I'm getting taller, I *know* it."

"You're twenty-three, little brother. You're done growing. Vertically, I mean."

He managed to cling to the door frame, swing, and glare at the same time. "Oh, what, you're a doctor now?"

"No, I just have a rudimentary understanding of human physiology. Nobody gets a growth spurt for their twenty-fourth birthday. Are those my sweatpants?"

"Well, yeah. Who else's would they be?"

"Yours! Because you have six pairs."

"Eight if I count yours."

"Then don't count mine! The thing of it is, I wouldn't even care if you did it because you were a cross-dresser or transgender or experimental or anything like that. But you're none of those, you only take them to bug me."

"Guilty."

"Bugging me makes you happy. Weirdly happy."

"You should be happy you make me happy. Make me happier and tell me where the tape measure is. I've shot up at least a sixteenth of an inch in the last fourteen months. I'll prove it."

"I'm not sure you know what 'shot up' means."

"Since I'm the one doing the shooting up, I know all about it." Pause. "That came out wrong."

"Paul, you see all the paperwork, right? And the spreadsheets? And my harassed face?"

"Your face always looks like that. Now stop earning money to keep me in sweatpants and measure me, dammit."

Wily to his ways, she had saved her document the moment he'd bellowed her name from the doorway—average height and build, but Paul had a voice like a bullfrog that swallowed a bullhorn—so she knew she could leap out of her chair without worrying about the half-finished doc. In half a second she was across the room and tickling his belly, forcing him to thrash, laugh, and let go, falling in a heap.

She stood over him in triumph. "Now that makes *me* happy."

"Cheat."

"You're insufferable."

"And you're popular," he informed her from the floor. He sat up and rubbed the back of his head, to no good effect since his dark brown curls always looked mussed. "The new cop on Dad's case—Chamberlin?"

She froze in the act of bending over to give him a hand up. "Jason Chambers?"

"Prob'ly. Plainclothes detective, super shiny badge? Anyway, he's in the kitchen. For you, of all things. Are you stuck? You're all hunched over."

"Oh, God." The potential for disaster was staggering. Least important, but the first thing that came to mind: *I look like hell.* Most important . . . "Where's Mom?" she scream-whispered.

"It's okay." Her irrepressible brother, the oldest of the boys, bounced up from the carpet and gave her a reassuring peck on the cheek. "She's lying down for her post-lunch siesta. Prob'ly in preparation for her predinner siesta."

"Thank God." Her mother did not care for the company of those in law enforcement. Not even those trying to solve her husband's murder. Sometimes *especially* those trying to solve her husband's murder. It was almost like, as bad as her father's murder was, her mother was afraid the police would find out something even worse. Just one more thing in the Drake dynamic that made no sense.

"Okay. I'll go talk to him. Okay. Oh, my God, I'm so . . . I'm wearing— Okay. No time to— Okay." She looked down at her T-shirt and leggings and swallowed a groan (the Horde must not find out about her crush). "Okay. He's in the kitchen? Okay."

"You're not having a stroke, are you?"

"No . . . no. No, definitely not. Probably not. Okay."

"Hey, it's not all bad. He liked our weird doorbell."

"He likes 'Chick Habit'?" She was already half running down the hall. "Okay."

TWENTY-ONE

She found Jason examining the papers all over the fridge and humming under his breath. Other families put up their kids' artwork. The Drakes left each other various ransom notes

Mitchell, you fuck, you can have your Cokes back when you return my Little Debbies.

death threats

When I find out who filched my baby spinach, I will END THEM. I WILL END THEM.

and various to-do lists in progress

Grocery list: Eye of newt. Unicorn horn. Skim milk. Arsenic. Toilet paper.

He turned at once when he heard her come in the kitchen, looking bemused, nodded politely, then his gaze flicked over her shirt. She was fully aware she needed a shower and hadn't run a brush through her hair for hours.

"That shirt," he said, "is just one big mixed message."

Said the sober-looking fellow in the black suit with the dimple and the crazy-ass socks. "Yes, it's an oldie but a goldie." Black T-shirt, large yellow smiley face, bright white lettering: I HATE YOU. "What can I do for you, Jason? Detective Chambers, I mean?" *Jason, I mean. Long, tall stud in a black suit, I mean. Take me away from all the weird, I mean.*

He smiled. "You were right the first time. I apologize for the pop-in, but I was reviewing the case with my captain a few hours ago—"

"Really?" In less than a month, Chambers had done more than Kline in the last five years. *That's not quite fair. Kline was CCD, Jason's not. Oh, fuck fair.* "That's great!"

He shook his head. "Not really. I had nothing for her. I wanted to stop by to warn you—"

"Cheese it, *le flics*."

"Detective Jason, this is my brother Paul."

"Did you just call him 'Detective Jason'?"

"And the guy next to him is my cousin Mitchell."

"Gentlemen."

"No," Mitchell said, shaking Jason's hand. "Not at all." He turned to his cousin. "I told you I heard 'Chick Habit'!"

"Can we assume you're here to tell us our dead uncle is still dead?"

She sighed. "And this is—"

"Your cousin Jordan."

She blinked at the detective, surprised. He not only knew Jordan's name, but he knew Jordan was a cousin, not a sibling. Dennis Drake had fathered three children out of wedlock with two different women, one of them a product of a one-night stand whom the family never met. After the trial, the cousins had to live with Emma, Angela, and her brothers. There hadn't been any real choice—the cousins were basically orphans at that point. Thus, the Horde was born (all villains deserve a backstory). "Yes, that's—"

Jordan was sizing up the sober man in the black suit. "Nice to meet you. But you've only met with Angela. How d'you even know who I am?"

The detective looked surprised by the question. "I read your father's file. I, uh, memorized it. Accidentally."

"Since you like memorizing reams of files, I guess you're in the right job."

"Yes."

"Impressive."

"No. Just my job."

Angela was thrilled/mortified Jason was there, but that last comment was puzzling. The Drake case wasn't his job; it had been closed years ago.

"What can we do for you?" she asked again. "And by 'we,' I mean 'I' because, I promise, the rest of them will bring nothing but chaos."

"And brownies," Jack pointed out. Angela smiled at him, she couldn't help it, her smallest, sweetest brother/cousin.

"Yes. And brownies."

"Brownies?"

Angela realized Jason hadn't meant to say that out loud, because he immediately flushed. The smile she'd given Jack she now turned on him. "Skipped lunch, huh?"

"Paperwork."

"Siddown," Jack ordered, already tying on his Darth Vader

apron.* "We have so much food, what with all the adolescents still growing and the adult male who thinks he's still growing."

A yelp from Paul: "Hey!"

"Won't take two minutes to heat something up for you. Five if you want it fresh."

"I'm aware that's my social cue to say something like 'Oh, no, I couldn't possibly' or 'I don't want to impose,' but your kitchen smells wonderful. Your whole house does. And I can linger. I went off shift an hour ago. If—if I'm invited." Jason immediately sat at the turtle table. "I may have skipped breakfast as well."

Jack looked delighted at the prospect of someone new on whom to practice his culinary wizardry and got to work. Paul gave Angela an inquiring look. "D'you need us?" and she shook her head so hard the room spun for a few seconds. *No. God no. Go away and let me gaze dreamily at Jason Chambers. I'll save you the leftovers from the leftovers.* "You want us back in, just holler." But they were already turning away, knowing the look of a cop who had no updates. Mitchell lingered long enough to lean over and murmur, "If Mom wakes up, I'll try to keep her out of here."

"Thank you *very* much," she replied, then turned to Jason. "Drink? We have milk, chocolate milk, iced tea, pop . . ."

"Chocolate milk would be great."

Gah, he likes chocolate milk. That is ADORABLE.

She brought two large glasses and sat across from him. *Choc-*

Luke, I am your father. Eat your vegetables.

olate mustache, here I come. Because as awful as I look right now, I can always look worse.

"Sorry about the Horde. They tend to descend, create chaos, abruptly lose interest, and then vanish, emerging periodically to feed or do laundry."

"Looks like a fun group."

She snorted. "Let me guess: only child, right?" She'd heard such mythical, blessed creatures existed.

"No. Well, now I am. My brother was murdered when I was in high school."

Shocked, she instinctively reached out, then remembered herself and yanked back her traitorous exploratory hand. "I'm so sorry. That must have been awful. Is still awful, I imagine."

He nodded. "Twelve years last month."

"Is that why you became a cop?"

"No, I entered the academy because I lost a bet."

She blinked. *Weird.* "Oh."

He quirked a small smile. "Kidding. Yes, that's why I became a cop. And your father's death was why you became a paralegal."

"Well, that and my obsessive love for files and piles of paper and legal jargon and briefs . . . Jason, can I ask you something?"

"Of course."

He leaned back in his chair and propped his right ankle on his left knee, which was the most relaxed she'd ever seen him. And she wasn't going to check out his socks. No way. "Please don't misunderstand, because we're all grateful you took an interest when Kline retired. And you're here on your own time—you could have been home a couple of hours ago—which is above and beyond and that isn't a criticism at all. I think—we think you're great to do this. But . . . why? There must be thousands of old cases. And you probably have a dozen open files at any given time."*

He laughed. "Only on my days off. On my days on, I have more."

"Right. So . . ." She spread her hands, palms up. "Why us?"

He answered at once, with zero hesitation. "Because your uncle could have been me. I was the druggie lowlife and my brother was the golden boy. Pure good luck that I'm not behind bars, and don't have an arrest record. Pure bad luck that my brother's in the ground."

I can't believe he told me that. I love that he told me that. What to say to that? That one, at least, she could answer. The Drakes tried, whenever possible, to ascribe to the K.I.S.S.† theory. "I'm so sorry."

"Thank you. To finish answering your question, my chart-obsessed captain likes challenged and productive detectives, and your family's history resonated. We had to share a floor with CCD when one of our detectives was accidentally exposed to—"

"Scabies!" she cried. *Ack. Don't sound so enthusiastic.* "I, uh, heard. It was the talk of the courthouse for a while. And it definitely wasn't funny."‡

---

*About five thousand, per the *Chicago Tribune*.

†Keep It Simple, Stupid.

‡This actually happened in New Jersey! Two men were caught in "a lewd act" on a display bed in a Bed Bath & Beyond. They were arrested and exposed the arresting officers to scabies. They had to completely fumigate the booking area! I don't know what happened to the display bed, though.

"No," he replied soberly. "It wasn't. They had to fumigate the entire floor as well as the booking area."

"Awful."

"The officer had to seek medical treatment."

"These kids today."

"It certainly wasn't funny." Maybe not, but he was smiling broadly at her. So broadly, in fact . . . *Gah, dimple alert!*

"No," she managed, then gave up and laughed so hard she was dizzy with it.

When they both calmed down a bit, he continued, "While we were sharing space, Detective Kline would com—*comment*. He would comment on the case. Frequently. Over time, I was intrigued. And I saw you once. When you came to express your dismay at Detective Kline's, ah, priorities."

She remembered. She had expressed a great deal of dismay. So much dismay that she'd almost been arrested. So much dismay she hadn't noticed the gorgeous Detective Chambers, doubtless a subtle and mature presence in the background. "Bad day," she said shortly. "And Kline and I didn't have a warm working relationship. Or even a cordial one. Or an effective one. Mostly because he didn't think we were working together."

"His error."

"*Thank* you."

"Your father's case intrigued me and my captain didn't mind me taking a look. But I'm sorry to say that, even with your help, I'm deadlocked."

She nodded. "So my dad's case goes back into the freezer, so to speak."

"Yes."

"I understand. I'm not thrilled," she warned, "but I get it.

And it was above and beyond for you to come by in person to tell me." Agh. Presumptive much? "Tell us, I mean. Keep us all in the loop. That's really all I wanted from Kline—to be in the loop, y'know?" *To not be forgotten, the way my father's been forgotten. The way my mother's been forgotten, even by herself.*

He nodded. "Understandable."

"My mom, she'll be relieved."

"Oh?"

"Yeah. She's been after me to let Dad lie, so to speak. She hates all the time I've put into it. She mourns him, of course. But I think sometimes it's more because she felt cheated of the chance to verbally smack him around some more. They had passion, but they weren't a love match and also, why am I telling you this?"

"Because I like to listen?"

She snorted. "Good thing you're a cop, then." She realized she was leaning forward, almost hovering over him, and forced herself to ease off. "I'm not entirely delusional—I didn't think we were in a seventies detective show, working together to defeat some nameless villain, evil is punished, roll credits, and cue the terrible soundtrack."

"Something like 'For What It's Worth' by Buffalo Springfield. Or Steppenwolf's 'Born to Be Wild.'"

She could feel herself light up. "Yes! Perfect."

"Your doorbell. I like it."

"Oh, God." She hid her eyes with one hand. "Blame my brothers."

"Or thank them," he teased.

"They're huge Tarantino fans. That song plays over the end credits of—"

"*Death Proof.*"

She dropped her hand. "Tarantino fan?"

"Not really. He's loud, and not subtle. But he thinks he is, which gets old."

"You've described almost all of my blood relatives."

He laughed again. "To be honest, his movies remind me of my job. So they aren't escapist for me. But I love his soundtracks. They're eclectic and, unlike virtually everything else he does, subtle."

All I had to do was invite him over and let him lean on our door-bell and I could have seen a dimple! Argh, so many missed opportunities. And the dimple.

"But we're getting off track," he reminded her. "As I was saying, I've got nothing new for the file."

"I know. It was beyond decent of you to come here and tell us yourself."

"But." He leaned forward, his blue-eyed gaze never wavering. "I would imagine you'll keep working it."

Angela could feel herself flush with pleasure. Kline had never, not once, referred to her assistance as "working the case." Unless "Jesus Christ, I don't need a civilian getting in my way!" was code for "working the case."

"Yeah, of course."

"Commendable."

She took a page out of his book and deadpanned, "No."

He laughed. Again! "Had that one coming. But listen, if anything comes up or I think of anything, I'll get in touch right away."

"Thank you so much!" *Why am I excited? It's not like he asked me out.* "And could I call you if I have a question or run across something new? Or should I pester CCD?"

"Please pester me. If it's beyond my scope, I'll be glad to hand you off to one of their detectives."

Again: Why am I so psyched? It's not like I asked him out, either. She knew why. It was an excuse to see him again, however slim. *My dad's killer might not ever be found which makes me happy because I can occasionally call Jason Chambers. That's fucked up.*

"Aw, you two are cute." Jack bustled over with armfuls of plates. "Soup's on. Not literally."

Jason inhaled. "Something smells wonderful."

Her little brother beamed. "That'd be my cologne, also known as Dawn Ultra dishwashing liquid. Or Angela's perfume, *Eau de Office Max.*"

"Angela wears *Dune.*" Jason paused. "Sorry. I think that might be one of those things I shouldn't have picked up on. Or, having deduced it, shouldn't have mentioned it."

"Not a problem," Angela managed, because all the spit in her mouth had dried up. *Drinks chocolate milk. Great socks. Wonderful smile. Hard worker. Atoning for adolescent bad behavior. Notices my perfume. I might die. I might die right here in the kitchen at the turtle table. I'm coming, Dad! Soon we'll be together!*

"Or maybe you're smelling . . ." Jack presented their meals with a graceful flourish. "Steak Diane with mushroom risotto. Those're reheated from last night but the endive and watercress salad I just made." He turned and shrieked, "Any of you useless fuckwads want to stuff your mouth holes, get your asses to the turtle table!"

Angela started to turn back to Jason to apologize, and almost missed his chuckle. He was already sawing into his steak.

"Thanks, Jacky." Angela managed—barely—to not clap her hands. "Oh, looks wonderful."

"Well, you liked it well enough last night, so." But he was pleased. *Whew!* Because there was a careful balance to complimenting Jack: too far in the take-him-for-granted category and your next three meals would taste like bacon mixed with paper towels and tears. Go too far in the other direction, he was too embarrassed to go near the kitchen for a day.

"Oh. God." Jason looked up, chewing furiously. His eyes were narrowed with pleasure. "Outstanding."

Jacky jabbed her in the ribs and muttered, "Marry this man."
Don't tease, Jack.

Paul chose that moment to breeze in. "Can I have extra meat? Instead of the salad? Or the risotto? I'd also like meat for dessert. *Two* desserts."

"I'm not giving you a big plate of steak as your meal again. And I'm not making beef crème brûlée again. Eat the sides," Jack ordered.

"Ha! You're not in charge of what I eat or what I don't eat but hide under the couch, shrinky dink." When Jack reached for a cleaver, Paul added, "Fine! But I'm doing it because I want to, not because I fear you."

"Whatever works."

"Hey, Chambers!" Mitchell had plopped down opposite them and started in on the risotto. "Bet you're wondering why we call this the turtle table."

"Why would anyone wonder that?" Paul demanded. "You always think we're more interesting than we are."

Jason glanced down at the shiny lacquered table, then back up. He had almost demolished his steak and was starting on the salad. "Because it resembles a tortoiseshell in color and pattern? Like a form of marquetry?"

"Huh."

Now I'm going to get horny every time I think of marquetry. Dammit.

The chaotic meal—especially with the addition of Archer and Leah—which should have been a fifteen-minute study in embarrassment, was great fun. Even more impressive, Jason held his own under the barrage of inappropriate questions and observations. She was sorry when the meal was over and everyone went back to what they were doing when not gulping down risotto. That was a first.

They

(kiss me! I'll also settle for a comradely pat on the boob. well, my under-boob)

shook hands at the door. "I'm sorry I couldn't bring better news."

She shook her head at him. "Nothing to apologize for. It was kind of you to take the time and let us know. I'll be sure to reach out if I find anything new."

"I will, too." He hesitated, like he was going to say something else, then just smiled at her and left.

"Nice enough guy," Jordan observed from over her shoulder.

"Uh-huh." *Nice* didn't begin to encompass the coolness that was Jason Chambers.

"Too bad about Dad's case," Paul added. "But this guy's a huge improvement over Klown."

"Kline," she corrected.

"Pretty sure it's Klown. And if it's not, it oughta be."

"He's wonderful," Angela declared. "Did you see his socks?"

"He had socks?"

"He had feet?"

"Monet's *Water Lilies*." She sighed. No question: Jason Chambers was making her care about art again. Hopefully it wouldn't turn into some odd, embarrassing Pavlovian response. Museum visits would be a nightmare.

TWENTY-TWO

S he had known when the contractions would not stop, even after her daughter had emerged, though in truth she had suspected for some time. She had gotten so big, every woman who saw her tried to smile and then looked away. A few pulled her aside: *Do not worry, your man is a big man, and you! So tall! You have a large son in there, I am sure.*

She had no sons in there. She had two girls. Twins, as she had been a twin seventeen years earlier.

We have to keep our ways, her mother had whispered, as her grandmother and great-grandmother had reminded their daughters, and back and back, all the way to their beginning, when Kutkh gave the Koryaks the moon and the sun. *Without the old ways, we are no better than the Cossacks. Without them, we would have lost one villager for every two.*

Pity the Koryaks on the mainland, who had suffered exactly that after enduring smallpox and war. She could almost feel sorrow for the Cossacks, who had never fought Koryaks and were amazed and fearful to see how her people waged war: with everything. Because their lives and their people were so, so precious, they set their homes ablaze to deny the Cossacks shelter. They killed their own women and children to deny the Cossacks slaves and the spoils of war.* Defeat was unthinkable, but if it came, there was nothing left for the enemy, and the price for all sides was high.

Her people's love was fierce and all-encompassing, and not just in times of war. "Save me," an elder would say, would demand. "I am sick, weak, show me my value. Did I not teach you the last blow? Do you not love me?" And so the mercifully quick death, rescuing a revered elder from the inevitable slide into the suffering of old age.

Twins? A double burden on mother and tribe. Instead of a strong, thriving infant, the village had to contend with two smaller, weaker babies who would drain resources. Twins were a tragedy.

"I love you," she whispered to the one, raising a work-roughened hand to press over the tiny mouth and nose. "As my mother so loved my sister." To the other: "And you in your love for me will someday do the same."

Without those acts of love, what were they but godless savages?

---

*The Alyutors pretty much set the standard for a "scorched earth campaign."

TWENTY-THREE

Jason blinked, disorientated. The village, the smell of smoke and suffering and pain, was gone in a moment. He was back in his room

(back? you never left. just a dream, just the same dream)

and a few seconds ago he had been a member of the Alyutors, his reindeer cloak spattered with muck and blood, *his* blood, and he was pressing his hand over his baby's mouth as an act of lo—

Oh. *That* dream again, the one where his sister had been killed and then, years later, he'd killed one of his daughters.

Stop showing the same slides, he thought irritably at his subconscious, the thing that never shut up. *I know all this. There's no need to keep hammering it home.*

He groped for his phone and squinted at it: 5:57 a.m. A new record for that month. Not hard to reason why, either. After he'd returned from the cheerfully chaotic Drake dinner, he'd actually felt . . .

. . . felt . . .

. . . good?

Not only good, and sated, but pleasantly tired; he'd crawled into bed just after midnight. And slept, undisturbed, for nearly six hours.

Huh.

And he was hard. Nocturnal penile tumescence had reared its mushroom-shaped head once again. *Like the groundhog predicting when spring will come*, he thought, amused. His erection was more a cause for puzzled bemusement than alarm. It was a universal biological phenomenon most healthy men experienced; it didn't mean that infanticide aroused him. As for what did . . .

Did the Drakes rekindle my sex drive?

Of course not, that was idiotic. *Angela* was rekindling his sex drive. Well, Angela and Paroxetine.

In fact, he'd been having a string of good days; his big black dog, it seemed, was going back to sleep.* It would lope back into his life soon enough, but as his mother had been fond of reminding him, even big dogs have collars.

He hopped out of bed and headed for the shower. He was halfway to the bathroom before he realized he was whistling "Chick Habit."

---

*Uh, that's not a euphemism for penis. Many who suffer from depression/dysthymia refer to their illness as a big black dog, taking a page out of the poet Samuel Johnson's book, and/or Winston Churchill's.

TWENTY-FOUR

Sherlock yanked John forward by his jumper and claimed
his mouth, his plush lips slanting over the smaller man's—

"No update, I assume?"

"I wasn't reading BBC's *Sherlock* fanfic!" Angela
slammed her laptop closed. "If. If you were wondering."

"I understand."

"Well, maybe just a couple of pages."

Leah smiled, one hand on a slim hip, the other holding on
to the doorjamb as if unsure of her welcome. Which meant
Archer had given her an earful.

"You don't have to hover, c'mon in. And you know Archer
has frequent bouts of clinical insanity so you should take whatever he says about me with a metric ton of salt, right?"

"Archer told me you work hard to take care of the family
and deserve your privacy."

"Sometimes his insanity is more benign," she admitted.

Leah laughed and let go of the door. "You're a bundle of contradictions, did you know?"

"I didn't, actually. What's up?"

"Several things, but I don't want to interrupt your—"

"Don't say 'work' with quotation marks, implying I wasn't working," Angela warned, smirking. "I won't have it."

Leah grinned back and took the chair opposite the desk. "Your disgusting* fangirl secret is safe with me. Surely you must know that as the Babe Ruth of Insighters, it's literally my job to keep secrets."

Angela groaned and buried her face in her hands. "I'm so sorry. They are awful. We're awful."

Leah waved that away. Though her tone was light, Angela thought she looked pale and strained. *Just the pregnancy? Or the stress of being in the vicinity of a murder of Drakes?*

"It's fine. Are you the only Insighter your family's produced?"

"Well, so far. We're not all done having kids yet. Heck, some of us haven't even started. You and Archer are way ahead."

Leah put a hand on her stomach for a moment. "Yes, well. It's not a contest. Or a race."

Angela snorted. "Good thing, because as far as I can tell, your fiancé is the only actual adult in the family. Besides my wrongfully convicted uncle . . . No, wait, he frequently throws 'I'm not speaking to you, so don't you dare come visit' tantrums, so I stand by the original assessment." *Who would have thought?*

---

*The views expressed by Leah Nazir are her own and do not necessarily represent the views of the author, who worships JohnLock.

"Paul was telling me about his girlfriend—"

"Oh, that . . . that won't last. He goes through women like a cat goes through cat litter. A *short* cat."

"Are you seeing anyone?"

"Not for a while." She held up a hand, traffic cop-style. "And before you say anything, it's not the work and it's not the murder. I've got other priorities, is all. So when I do date, they don't get my obsession and I don't get their 'but tons of people get murdered every day and this happened ten years ago, so can we fuck now?' indifference. Or the Horde runs them off. Usually both. It's too exhausting to fix."

"'Fix'?"

"Look how we live." She made a gesture encompassing the house. "More than a half dozen people in a 2400-square-foot house. Most of us are legal adults. None of us have lived away from home for very long. Or if we do, we always come back. Archer was the first who didn't. And before you blame my mom—"

"I wasn't going to," Leah said mildly. "Though it's interesting that you immediately went there."

"It's not just that she's . . . y'know, shattered."

"Is she? Forgive me, because I haven't known any of you very long, but her grief . . . it's almost vengeful in nature."

"That's just how she grieves. You didn't, uh, pick anything else off her after you shook her hand?" Like—ha-ha!—maybe she was the killer? Or knew who was?

Bad path to go down, so Angela got back on track. "Our mom doesn't want to be alone, and if it was just that, we could fight. But *we* don't want her to be alone, either. So we stay and get older and Mom never leaves the house, much less dates, and Mitchell handles the taxes and balances the checkbook and I'm the main breadwinner and Jacky's the cook and Mom's a ghost and the weeds grow up on our father's gr—" She stopped herself. "Sorry. You're probably as sick of hearing this as I am of talking about it."

"So you're all—"

"Trapped," she finished. "In a very nice cage that we locked ourselves. A comfortable cage with great food where we can be with people we love. But it's still a cage. Archer grew up. The rest of us are in limbo. By choice, but there it is."

"But what if you did meet someone? What if you wanted children, what if Paul got married tomorrow?" Leah was leaning forward, her small hands clenched together almost like she was at prayer. "Would you leave? Would your mom? Sell the house and start chapter three of your lives?"

Angela gave Leah a long look. Pale face, dark circles under her dark eyes—so her face was color coordinated, if nothing else. One of Archer's button-downs. Khaki shorts. Bare feet. Comfortable but tired. Engaged but holding back. *Where is this coming from? This is more than getting-to-know-the-in-laws chit-chat.* "There's no long-term plan here, Leah. I don't know what Mom would do if Paul stopped measuring himself long enough to get married. I don't even know what I would do. Jacky's going to college in a couple of years and he's leaning toward the University of Chicago. He won't consider anything out of state. He won't consider anything out of Chicago. This is nothing anyone asked him to do. Paul and I flat-out told him he had the grades to go anywhere in the country and we'd support wherever he wanted to go. Mom even weighed in. But as far as he's concerned, if it's not within a two-hour drive of the house, it's off the board. Because he grew up in the cage, you see? So do we kick him out? Force him to go to, I don't know, UMass? Dad's alma mater? Or fresh ground, a place that no ever Drake has even been near, help him make his own way? Even if he doesn't want to?"

Leah leaned back, loosening her grip on herself. "Your mother. When I shook her hand. She's—"

"Not there," was Angela's flat reply. "I know. I had to be around her for years before I figured it out; I don't get entire lives from a handshake."

"It's less fun than it sounds," Leah said dryly.

"Sure it is." Still. She couldn't help being envious, the way a minor league pitcher envied a big league superstar. "But Mom— she's lived before, like most of us have. At least three lives."

"Seven," Leah fake-coughed into her fist.

"Do you live in 1995? Nobody fake-coughs insults anymore."

"Smart-ass," she fake-coughed.

"God, stop it." *Whoa. Did I just giggle? I think maybe I did.* "But yeah, I get where you're going: In every life, she's always alone."

"In every life she's alone by choice," Leah corrected. "Which isn't the same thing."

"Choice or not, that's the reason *I* can't leave. I figure she deserves at least one lifetime where she's not totally abandoned by the time she's in her forties."

"So keeping her company . . . that's the purpose of *your* life this time around?"

Angela didn't know what to say to that, so she said nothing. Leah leaned forward again. "Please listen to me. And forgive me for talking to you like a client, when I've got no right to butt into your head or your life."

Oh, shit. "It's fine."

"It's not, you're just being polite." When Angela laughed, Leah smiled a little. "You are. You're also too hard on yourself, but that's an inappropriate chat for another day."

"Oh, boy. Can't wait."

The smile was gone. "I have done exactly what you're doing. It never works out. It *never* works out, do you understand? The end result is always two lives wasted, and then you're born again, only this time with a predisposed habit to put yourself second and you spend *that* life doing the same thing and around and around we go."

"It sounds like we're talking about my mom. But it feels like we're talking about yours."

"This may sound strange," Leah almost-whispered, as if confiding a great secret, "but being pregnant has made me ponder mother/daughter relationships."

"What an odd coincidence!"

"Right? What are the odds?" For the second time in ten seconds, the smile dropped off Leah's face as if it was never there. "Don't do it, Angela. You're not doing either of you—any of you—any favors."

Angela thought about that for a few seconds, and Leah let her. Finally, Angela said, "Thank you for the advice. I mean that sincerely. But what's this really about?"

"Mothers and daughters. Families—old ones and new ones. The ones you're stuck with and the ones you make."

"Funny you should say that," she said slowly. "I was giving serious thought to hanging it up earlier this week. Letting Dad's file go back into cold storage—not that it's up to me, but you know what I mean—and just . . . letting it all go. *Poof!*" She waved good-bye to the imaginary file flying off to CCD. "And I won't lie, the idea of doing that—it was as tempting as it was frightening. Like standing in the doorway of the plane with your parachute, ready to jump. You *want* to jump, you paid the instructor to bring you up there and you jump, but it's still scary."

"Ooooh, metaphor."

"You hush up." *It is weird and wonderful that I'm going to be this woman's cousin-in-law. That we're talking like regular people! Which I am, but she is not! Argh, stop fangirling, you've already been busted for that once today.*

She took a breath and finished, "But the day we got back from ICC, I got to talking with Jack and I thought—"

"You thought damned if the next generation is going to grow up like this."

"Yes. Exactly. But another way to look at it is: I saw the cage door start to ease open and I wasted *no* time slamming it shut again. And I'm fine with that." Well. "Fine" wasn't the right word, but she knew Leah would get it. "But my choices don't have to be yours, just like Archer's weren't mine. Whatever you're wondering, whatever's on your mind, whatever decision you're trying to make, I don't think Uncle Dennis should factor in. And he'd be the first to tell you that."

"Well." Leah was studying her the way you'd look at a book you weren't sure you'd like, only to find it was growing on you. *Or maybe I'm just projecting all over the place.* "I'm no stranger to family drama, that's for certain. But even if you won't take good advice, you certainly give it."

"'Family drama.' Yeah, that's one way to put it." Angela shook her head. "I can't imagine. I can't imagine what fighting your mother's killer was like. What? Don't you think it's strange that nobody's talking about this? Well, not strange so much as courteous—I kind of threatened the Horde with dismemberment if they brought it up. But it's just you and me now. And I don't like elephants."

"If you want to ask, then ask."

"I don't need the gory details. I'm just trying to wrap my head around having to kill someone to save your own life. Most people know about it but not someone who's done it."

Leah waved her hand in a faux casual gesture. "Oh, it was mostly terrifying with a dash of horrifying. I wish I could have saved my mom, though. Even after everything she did. You know how people say 'I wouldn't wish that on my worst enemy'? Well, she *was* my worst enemy. And I wouldn't have wished that on her. He sliced her up like a trout. And don't take this the wrong way, either." Then she stood, bent sharply at the waist, and threw up in Angela's recycle bin.

TWENTY-FIVE

"You're sure you're okay?"

"Yes, Archer." *Physically.*

"Maybe we should go see a doctor."

"It's just morning sickness."

"At night!"

"You know it's called that because for most women, it hits in the morning, right? It doesn't mean it's always exclusive to the hours between 12:01 a.m. and 11:59 a.m. and that any deviation from that means you need to live in your OB's waiting room. You're actually reading the baby books you keep buying me, right?"

"Something's up," he insisted, his face set in stubborn lines. His forehead was so laddered with concern wrinkles, a chipmunk could have climbed it. Easily. Archer's bad luck that his grim face was one of her favorites. "You're not sleeping well, you're having nightmares every night—sometimes twice a night—you're not keeping much down. And reliving what that shithead did to your mom? 'He sliced her up like a trout'? I

131

cannot fucking believe she asked you about it! Angela's ears are gonna be ringing for a while."

"Yes, I heard you 'discussing' your concern with her. As did the rest of the house. And it was unnecessary."

Archer's pacing sped up, which Leah hadn't thought was possible. She prayed he wouldn't trip; he was going so fast he'd probably get a concussion. "Don't care. She should have left you alone. I told them, I *told* them not to bug us—you—about that. You wouldn't believe the heinous shit I threatened them with if they disobeyed."

"If it was anything like the heinous shit Angela threatened them with, I think they were properly cowed."

"No! They were the opposite of cowed! The minute my back was turned they threw off being cowed! I am very angry and confused and thinking too much about cowing!"

Don't laugh. Don't laugh. Deep breath. "I sought Angela out, Archer. It's not what you think." She squared her shoulders and tried to look firm and uncompromising, which was tricky when you were prone. "Sit down."

He stopped and stared at her, his eyes so wide she could see the whites all around, like a horse that got a whiff of fire. "Oh, my God."

"Sit down, please."

"Oh, fuck. It's bad, isn't it? Just tell me." He whirled and paced faster, scraping his fingers through his hair until it was standing up in shaggy, aggravated spikes. "We'll figure something out. Whatever it is. Maybe you should go on bed rest? Let's go see a doc and ask about bed rest. I'm sure you'll be fine. The baby's gonna be fine, okay, hon? Don't worry. Okay? But just tell me. Whatever it is."

"I will. But first I want you to have a seat."

"Just tell me!"

She propped herself up on an elbow and glared. "I want you to sit down in this room's only chair, which is beside the bed, because it will give you proximity to me, which I will find comforting and also because following your pacing is making me feel like vomiting again. Now sit. *Down*."

He sat.

She lay back and looked at the ceiling. They'd been there a week, she'd had ample time to stare at it. To think about what to say, and when. Trust Archer to notice but give her time and space to broach the subject.

"We are having a daughter," she began carefully.

He was already nodding and she was already trying not to roll her eyes. The nod. The patented ArcherNod that said: *Everything is fine, you can tell by the way I'm nodding in agreement with you. I wouldn't do that if things weren't fine. So nodding is good, nodding is good.* The irony? It never calmed her down. "Okay."

"As far as I can tell, our daughter is perfectly healthy."

"Okay." Archer was already fidgeting in the chair, dread and concern fighting for pride of place on his face.

"She'll probably be beautiful. Not 'all babies are beautiful' beautiful. *Beautiful* beautiful."

"Okay."

"And this baby isn't tabula rasa. She's lived before."

"Okay."

"The reason I know this is because the baby is my mother."

"Okay. What?"

She repeated herself. *Better get used to that. You're going to be talking about this a lot.*

"You're pregnant with my mother-in-law?"

"Yes."

"Your mom's coming back."

"Yes."

"Through you."

"Yes."

Then he just sat. And sat. It didn't surprise her—she'd had the luxury of taking a week to adjust to the bombshell—so she stayed quiet.

Finally, he looked up. The concern ladder was back on his forehead. *Where's a chipmunk when you need one? Can I catch one? And train it to walk on Archer's forehead? Why am I now obsessed with chipmunks?* "How do you— I don't doubt you. But how do you know? And use small words, on account of my brain dumbness."

She smiled, as he'd intended. Because he didn't have "brain dumbness."*

Ugh, really not a fan of that phrase.

Archer was one of the few people who couldn't see his past lives, one of the few she couldn't read. He was an utter blank, but in the very best of ways, like a canvas that could be made into anything. Meaning he was either a brand-new soul

("At least I'm not a rerun like some people," he teased.)

or he'd lived so long and so well he had earned a clean slate. Archer didn't know, or care, which it was. She didn't know— ironic, and she was well aware that made him fascinating to her—and cared, a little. Out of intellectual and spiritual curiosity, if nothing else.

---

*Gotta side with Leah on this one.

"I know it's Mom because our baby is dreaming. But they aren't my dreams." She paused, trying to find the words to explain how sometimes You Just Know without coming off like a condescending jackass. "I've seen other people's dreams—their lives—when I'm awake. That's always true, you know that. I can see them even more clearly in therapy sessions after a dose of Reindyne. But never like this. Never while sleeping. In all my life, I've never dreamed anyone's lives but my own."

"So you knew *about* your mom's past lives but never *experienced* them. Which is how you recognized her in our daughter."

"Yes, exactly. And it's a problem. It's a problem on top of a huge pile of problems." She sighed. "One I'm not equipped to endure, much less solve. I never thought I'd find someone who would adore my extensive weirdness—and I'm not talking about the Insighting! I mean my weird B-list Hollywood career. My mom-baggage."

"You *never* thought?" He shook his head. "Because that's insane. I thought you were wonderful even before I fell in love with you. And don't take this the wrong way, but right now I want to focus on the impending reappearance of the star of *My Daughter, My Whore*. But I want to come back to this. Because you could have had a family with anybody you wanted anytime you wanted."

Wrong. But I love that you think so. "Well, like I said, I wasn't sure I'd ever find someone I could stand who could stand me, much less start a family with them. I knew I was in over my head *before* this week—"

"But lots of couples feel that way."

"Have you already forgotten the Walgreens pee-stick freakout?" Given his shudder

("If I have to pee on every pregnancy stick in the store, I will! This has to be a mistake, and I'll prove it! I would also like two candy bars! Anything but Milky Way!")

he hadn't. Though he would have been within his rights to repress the hell out of it. That had been an eventful weekend.

"But this?" She gestured to her stomach. "It's unprecedented. I've been all over the literature, and there's nothing documented. I'm not arrogant enough to insist no one ever gave birth to a parent or grandparent before—I'm a firm believer in 'there's nothing new under the sun.' But if someone did, they either didn't know or kept it quiet."

"So . . ."

"We're on our own," she finished.

He picked up her hand, kissed her palm. "See, that's another thing you've got wrong. We're not on our own."

A sweet thought. Inaccurate, but points for trying.

"But, hey," he continued, now mouthing at her fingers like a gigantic minnow looking for algae. She giggled (how did something so silly make her laugh every time?) and her fingers twitched against his lips. "At least tonight when you wake up from one of her dreams, I'll still be awake on account of my own impending nervous breakdown. We can keep each other company!"

She burst into tears and when his face sagged, she held up her hand (the one he wasn't nibbling on) to reassure him. "Happy tears," she managed. "God, I love your irreverence."

"I *am* pretty irreverent," he said modestly, and she laughed. The "laugh until you cry" cliché had never worked for her. The reverse, though?

Perfect.

TWENTY-SIX

"N o!" "Just once. Just to see if you like it."

"I don't have to eat mud to know I won't like the taste."

"But it's not mud," Paul pointed out. "It's salted caramel brownies. Look, I'm not saying your original recipe is bad . . ."

"Better not be. Because one, my original recipe is sublime, and two, there are several sharp knives within my reach. And you're not wearing a cup."

"Your recipe is transcendent! But maybe you could . . . just . . . kind of . . . mix it up a little?"

"Listen, you barbarian Horde of one, I have never jumped on a bandwagon in my life and I won't start now."

"You're wearing Crocs to cook! How is that anything but bandwagoning?"

"Bandwagon isn't a verb! And Crocs are classic! They're ancient, like the high-heeled shoe, Crocs've been around—"

Archer leaned forward, the better to murmur. "Prepare to feel ancient," he warned Angela and Leah.

"—since 2002!"

"Ouch." From Leah.

"Yeah, that one smarts," Angela said, then adding, "Paul, stop trying to fix something that isn't broken."

"Salted caramel frosting. Salted caramel cake. Salted caramel cupcakes. Salted caramel cheesecake. Salted caramel marshmallows. Salted caramel puppy chow." Jack threw up his hands. "Salted caramel bark! Salted caramel frappés! Salted caramel martinis! Salted caramel roasted almonds. Salted caramel candles. Salted caramel caramel. Boring, boring, boring!"

"See, you were droning on, but all those things sounded great," Paul said. He was in his usual Saturday midday attire: sweatpants, a faded green too-tight sweatshirt, bare feet, the red tape measure dangling over one shoulder (he occasionally used it as a belt). "Even the candle."

"No salted caramel in this kitchen! Unless you make it yourself. In which case, I will yield territory long enough for you to be a salted caramel *sheep*. Following along with the salted caramel *herd*. And God help you if you leave me a sink full of caramel-coated dirty dishes. God. Help. You."

Leah shook her head. "You guys ever notice that when someone repeats the same phrase over and over, the words lose their meaning pretty quickly?"

Archer was already shaking his head. "Leah, hon, all I heard, honest to God, the only thing I heard you say just now was 'salted caramel, salted caramel, salted caramel, salted caramel.'"

Angela swallowed a giggle. "And, of course, now we're all craving salted goddamned caramel."

"Not my problem," Jack snapped, turning back to his cookbook shelf with a huff. The brouhaha du jour had begun when he was flipping through his cookbooks to seek inspiration for a new dessert. Which, unfathomably, was Paul's internal cue to make the horrific, misguided suggestion that rather than try something new, Jack should jazz up an old recipe.

They were seated around the turtle table—most of them, anyway; Mitchell and Jordan were at work. Emma Drake was at the other end of the house, having completed her daily chore (the mail) and now doing who knew what. She tended to break her fast early, before most of them were up, preferring toast and coffee because anything else slowed her down. "If I eat all that, I'll get logy and just slouch around the house all day," she explained. Which was terrifying to think of.

Jack had prepared a breakfast (as was his wont) that was delicious but (as wasn't his wont) lacked his usual perfectionist/gourmet tendencies. Scrambled eggs but no dill. Bacon, but not thick-cut . . . the precooked kind you could zap in a microwave. Muffins, but not from scratch. Milk, but no lattes. Juice, but not fresh-squeezed.

Jesus. We really take this kid for granted. He's phoning it in and it's still a terrific meal.

"Thank you, Jack," she said brightly, then drained her glass. "It's all delicious as usual."

"Goes without saying," Archer said, his mouth full. He swallowed and added, "Leah, this kid, you wouldn't believe it, he's been good at this since he was *five*."

"It shows," she replied, smacking his hand when he went for

the last of the bacon, then wolfing it down herself. Every Drake in the room had the same simultaneous thought: *She's perfect for us! Uh, Archer. Perfect for Archer.*

Then. The fatal error. Archer, as he often did, kept talking. And, as often happened when Archer talked, disaster followed: "Jack, even on an off day your grub is outstanding."

Angela froze. Leah glared at the father of her child. Paul quietly backed out of the kitchen. Everything seemed to slow down and simultaneously get sharper and louder.

Jack slooooowly turned away from the cookbooks. "'Off day'?" he asked with deceptive pleasantness.

Archer was slooooowly getting out of his chair, doubtless ready to slip unobtrusively—or sprint—out of the kitchen. His exit was foiled when Leah seized his sleeve and yanked him back down. Her dagger-eyes were eloquent: *You said it. You stay and deal with the fallout.*

"I. Um. Yeah. You. I'm sorry? Jack? It was delicious and I attach no qualifier to that. Also, I'm sorry."

Jack just looked at him.

Archer shifted to full-on babble: "So very very sorry. Completely sorry. Just incredibly, very terribly sorry. It's a wonderful meal, look! My plate! Totally clean!"

Jack walked over to the turtle table. Archer did his level best not to cringe. "You're right," he said, inspecting Archer's plate. "That's pretty clean. *All* your plates are pretty clean." He gifted Angela and Leah with an approving smile. "So doing the dishes should be easy, doncha think?"

"I would be happy to do the dishes," Archer replied at once. This was a duty that rotated between Drakes; today was Paul's day. Paul, at least, would be delighted that Archer's mouth had once again raced ahead of his brain. "So, so happy to help any way I can with the dishes."

"Good." Jack looked at Leah for a long moment. "Are you . . . I should have asked this before. Is there anything I should be making for you, for the baby? I went online earlier and read up on prenatal nutrition—"

"Which is why you've been filling me full of vitamin C and green smoothies and whole grains and yogurt," Leah replied with a warm smile. "Among other things. That is kind of you, Jack. I've eaten better in the last week than I have in the last month. I have paid for meals in Paris that weren't as good as one of your midday snacks. Thank you."

Jack ducked his head, suddenly shy, and Angela was struck—again—by how young he was. "'S no trouble," he mumbled, and then went back to the cookbooks.

"Your youngest cousin is terrifying," Leah mock-whispered to Archer.

"He didn't scare me one bit. Now for the love of God, give me all your dirty dishes so I can start my soapy amends."

Leah looks better, Angela thought, watching the couple laugh. A little more rested, a little less pale. If anything, Jacky was the one who looked aggrieved and tired, and not just because of Archer's ill-timed idiocy.

Angela slipped out of her seat and went to him. "Jacky-oh, are you okay?"

"Course."

"Because you seem—"

"Aggravated because I'm surrounded by Visigoths?"

"Something like that." *Argh, too early. Can't remember what a Visigoth is. Sounds bad, though.*

"Haven't been sleeping well." This was a mutter directly into *Martha Stewart's Cooking School*, a hefty hardcover that could, if swung with enough force, kill a pony.

"For how long?"

A shrug.

A puberty thing? A stress thing? He doesn't study but he still gets A's and B's. I don't think it's school. Which means it's probably us.

"Do you—did you want to see a doctor? I'd be glad to make an appointment for you." He'd just gotten his license, so she added what she hoped would be an incentive to health maintenance. "You could borrow my car and hit DQ after, if you wanted. I would only ask that you bring me a banana split Blizzard. And maybe a Dilly Bar."

That earned her a faded smile, nothing like his usual wide grin. "You don't have to take care of me, Angela. I'm fine. You've got enough to worry about."

"That's not true, I can always take on more things to worry about. Worrying is practically my superpower."

He shook his head. "I'm okay. Uh. That cop, Detective Chambers? He had to shelve Dad's case, right?"

Is that what this is about? "Yeah, Jack, I'm afraid so. That's why he was over here the other night—he came to warn me it was likely, and yesterday he left me a voicemail to confirm." *That I definitely haven't listened to two or three or ten times.* "I hope I didn't get your hopes up."

"I didn't think that about you," he said quickly.

"I thought if we had a new investigator, and Leah, that the case might be— Well, it was a long shot. But I hope you understand why I thought it was worth trying." At his nod, she added,

"And don't worry, I'm not giving up. And Jason—the detective—he's going to keep me in the loop. If anything breaks, he'll let us know right away. It won't be like—"

"Klown." Jack smiled again, a real one this time.

"No, he's not like Klown." Damn. That was going to stick now. She hoped none of them ever ran across Kline again, particularly in public, because that would get awkward in a hurry.

"That cop. Not Klown. The other one. He's really sad sometimes."

Angela blinked. "Oh? I think—I think that's just the nature of his job, Jacky. He works homicide. He deals with dead bodies and grief every day."

Jack slowly shook his head. "I don't think it's because of his job."

"You're right, Jack," Leah called from the other side of the kitchen.

They both turned to her, surprised. Archer immediately pointed at Leah. "It was the Insighting eavesdropper! It wasn't me this time!"

"Eavesdropper? They're five feet away having a conversation in normal tones of voice." Leah turned back to them. "Detective Jason Chambers has depression. Or maybe dysthymia. He's had it for at least three lives."

Jack seemed to find that gratifying for some reason. "I knew he was sad, I told you!"

Archer shook his head. "Leah, I will never get over how creepy and impressive that is. Ow! Don't pinch. Fine, it's just impressive. Not creepy at all."

Angela realized she was gaping (her mouth had even fallen open a little, creating a sexy goldfish look, how embarrassing) and looked away before Leah caught her. The wonderfully be-socked Jason was coping with depression or—or the other thing Leah mentioned?

Mental note: Look up dysh—dys—find out how to spell that word and then look it up.

And he'd been enduring it for multiple lives? Was that why he was so composed and quiet and calm all the time? Was he trying to learn from his other lives, or just enduring until he got a reboot? She was dying to ask him about it. She was dying to ask him any number of things.

But. *Why did Leah do that?* Leah was a professional; she didn't diagnose near-strangers, especially out loud, especially when they weren't her client, and especially not with others in attendance. If she didn't know better, she'd think Leah was showing off. And since she *did* know better, what the hell was going on?

"What the hell is going on?"

"Gah!" Angela turned and saw her mother standing in the doorway. *Annnnnd my morning gets weirder. She's dressed! And interacting with family! At 8:00 a.m., no less. That's— Wait, why am I mentally bitching about this? This is great. I can actually discuss my concern for a family member with an engaged parent who is fully clothed.* She stepped forward and lowered her voice. "Mom, I'm glad you're here. Can we go into the other room so I can talk to you about J—"

"I don't want to talk about Jacob or Jason or whatever cop you've got fumbling around like an impotent idiot."

Angela blinked. *Okay. Lots of errors in that statement, starting with the fact that I wanted to talk to her about her youngest son.*

And "fumbling"? "Impotent"? That's a lot of rancor for someone she's never met.

"Well, then, I've got great news, Mom." But before she could finish

(cheer up, it's being shelved again! again)

her mother cut her off for the second time. "We talked about this."

"I know, Mom, and the thing is—"

"I said I don't want you going again."

Angela paused. "Careful, Mom. That was almost forceful."

Widow Drake's eyes narrowed. "Can't you see what it's doing to your brother?"

"Which one?"

"I'm fine!" Paul bellowed from somewhere in the house. "Leave me out of it!"

"Look at him!" Her mother pointed to a startled-looking Jack, who had moved on from Martha Stewart and was now clutching James McNair's* *Afternoon Delights: Coffeehouse Favorites* to his chest. "He's clearly not sleeping. This is a tough time of year for all of us, and you're making it worse."

Angela tilted her head to one side and studied her mother. "How am I, personally, making this time of year worse for 'all of us'?"

"He's dead. Let him stay dead."

Er. What? "Mom—"

"Your visits are a waste of time. I don't want you to go. *Dennis* doesn't even want you to go."

---

*James McNair and Andrew Moore are wonderful cookbook authors. Simple-to-understand recipes, gorgeous pictures, it's all terrific. Seriously, track them down and buy one of their books.

"Dennis," she said carefully, "is doing someone else's time. How can you be okay with that?"

"Because *Dennis* is okay with that."

"And how can you be against trying to get justice for Dad?"

"Your father already got justice."

"How— That makes no sense, Mom. At all."

But she was already shaking her head. "I refuse to let this go on. No more visits. No more files, no more crime-scene photos. Just . . . enough with the meddling. Enough."

"You know that whole 'quit meddling' thing is making you sound like a Scooby villain, right? It's a bit creepy. What are you afraid of? What could come out that's worse than Dad's murder?"

Creepy Mom didn't listen any better than Ghost Mom. "I'm putting an end to it, Angela."

Angela was still studying her like Emma Drake was an intriguing amoeba on a microscope slide. "Good thing I'm an adult, then, and don't have to tremble and obey."

She never says "prison," or "ICC." It's always "your visit" or "your trip." I used to think she did that out of grief, that Dad's loss was so painful to her, she couldn't bear to talk about her bro-in-law languishing in prison. But now I wonder.

Suddenly conciliatory, her mother laid a hand on Angela's sleeve. "I'm doing this for you, sweetie. You don't have the strength to stop this unhealthy obsession on your own, so I'm taking things into my own hands."

"Oh, is that what this is? You're—uh—saving me? From myself? And also from crime-scene photos?"

A nod. "That's exactly right."

"Mom, I'm not the only one of us who wants closure. With the notable exception of, well, *you*, the whole family—" She turned to gesture to them, only to realize that at some point they'd all stolen out of the kitchen with a minimum of noise, the bums.

"COW W W W W W W W WAAAAAARRRRR-DDDDDDSSSSS!"

By the time she'd calmed down, she realized her mother had left, too.

TWENTY-SEVEN

MAY 1985

FLORIDA STATE PRISON

S even minutes.

That's how long it took for Jesse Tafero to die.

If you're fucking someone you've been trying to get into for a while, seven minutes is no time at all. But if you're being electrocuted by the state of Florida, seven minutes takes a while.

He refused to go back to prison. So he shot two cops . . . and went back in prison. But it could have been worse. Sure. Could have been *him* in malfunctioning Old Sparky, six-inch flames shooting out of his head. The official story: A rookie had used a machine-made sponge instead of the standard sea sponge. Sure. Accidents happen. Even in prison. Especially in prison.

He wasn't sure he believed that. The rumor was, the legal system fucking hated cop-killers, and found new and interesting ways to torture them. Like "forgetting" to tell the new guy to use a real sponge, not something they picked up on sale from Walmart. That, he believed.

The guys close to Tafero's cell could still smell him for a week afterward. That smell—you can't ever get it out of your nose. Even if it's gone, it's not really gone.

So, yeah. Could've been worse—could've been him. And, yeah, Tafero's kids were pretty much orphans, because the lie that killed their dad had also put their mom—Sunny Jacobs—in prison. She was found guilty of capital murder and, like Tafero, got a death sentence, like Tafero. Unlike Tafero, there wasn't a death row for the ladies. 'Cause Florida was old-fashioned, maybe? Weren't up to speed on the equality thing? Anyway, she got solitary confinement. For five *years*. Death maybe would've been better.

No, he didn't believe that.

You gotta live, is all. No matter what you have to do. No matter what you have to say. Because when you were done, when God or the state of Florida put out your lights and burned you alive, that was it. There wasn't anything else. That whole past-lives bullshit? Pure goddamned fantasy, thought up by chickenshits: Oh, don't worry about dying, you'll be born again and you'll get it right next time!

What. Fucking. Bullshit.

So he testified *Jesse* had been the one to shriek about not going back to prison. He told the jury that *Jesse* had been the one to shoot Officer Black and Constable Irwin. That *Jesse* wasn't just a cop killer, he was an international cop killer—Irwin was Canadian, his bad luck to be visiting his pal, Black.

Walter didn't even know what the fuck a constable was; his lawyer'd had to explain it.

After condemning Jesse, Walter turned his attention to Sunny. Who'd let it happen, he testified, and she'd hadn't cared even a bit. Thought it was funny. And she wasn't trying desperately to calm her babies, and she sure never begged him to stop, to *Stop already, please stop. You're scaring them YOU'RE SCARING ME!* Naw, she was in on it. Or if she wasn't in on it, she didn't care when it all went wrong.

Just tell the truth, they prompted, though nobody in that room wanted any such thing. *Tell the jury what happened, that's all. Tell 'em and we'll talk to the DA. No problem. But you gotta do the right thing.*

So he did the right thing and his reward was second-degree murder and life in prison. And yeah, that was bad, but guess what was worse? Six-inch flames shooting out of your skull, that was worse. Stopping the execution three times to put out the flames, then starting it up again, that was worse. Your friends smelling you a week after your bad death, that was worse. Never a doubt in his mind. Nope. *He did it. Not me.*

Oh, sure, when it was all done, when the papers weren't writing about it anymore, when everyone was locked up and the cops were in the ground, he had his slipups. His conscience—miserable, useless thing—had prodded him to recant not once, or even twice. Three times he lost his guts, then spilled 'em: '77, '79, and '82.

But that worked out, too. 'Cause the guards, the cops, the DA—they didn't want the truth. Not on a closed case. Not after all the publicity. So he'd have an attack of conscience; but a few days later, sanity returned and he'd recant his recantation and the years slid by.

But then it was May 4, 1985, and the thing that hadn't seemed real, something to think about but unlikely to happen . . . well, it happened. They killed Jesse, and his bad death couldn't be undone.

So he'd fess up. Again. But he wouldn't recant recanting this time. Not because he was pussying out. Not because his conscience was the boss. It was because he hadn't had a good night's sleep in years. Because when he closed his eyes he saw Jesse burning and when he took a deep breath he smelled him. He got the shakes. His belly hurt all the time. He felt like puking all the time and when he did, there was red in it and he instantly flushed so he wouldn't have to think about it.*

It couldn't go on. He was disintegrating. He'd talk again. Not because it was the right thing to do; that was for fairy-tale suckers. He'd talk to save himself. That's what it was.

That's all it ever was.

---

*Walter suffered from a stress-induced peptic ulcer. Among other things.

TWENTY-EIGHT

"Agh, Jesus!"

Angela found herself sitting up in bed; the transition from dream to reality was so rapid, for a moment she still felt Walter's nausea. *Yes, yes, I get it, I'm compelled to work Dad's case because back in the day, I was a cowardly shithead. THIS IS NOT NEWS.*

At least it wasn't that memory fragment again, the one that kept bubbling to the top of her brain every other day or so. Dad with the bulging suitcase, but nothing before that image, or after. Her father holding an overstuffed suitcase, standing in the doorway and looking at her. Why was it bugging her?

She glanced at the clock and saw her alarm was going to go off in just over two hours. Fuck it. She'd hit the kitchen, make some mint tea. Try to get serene—as much as she ever could. Face the new day.

So she got up, pulled her robe over her opposite-of-sexy nightgown (faded flannel, sleeves too short, hem too short, cartoon penguin pattern), and started down the hall for the kitchen. Where there was . . . a light on?

To her surprise, Jack and Leah were also awake, sipping from mugs at the turtle table.

"What's this?"

Leah immediately looked guilty. "I didn't wake him! And I didn't ask him to make me anything." She pushed her nearly empty oatmeal bowl to one side. "I couldn't sleep. So I came down—"

"To see if you could snag the last piece of triple coffee cheesecake," Jack teased.

"Which was gone."

Jack, in his black boxers and faded T-shirt (MY GOAL IS TO BE THE CAUSE OF YOUR NERVOUS BREAKDOWN) giggled. "Rookie mistake, Leah. If you weren't an only child, you'd have known that that caffeinated sugary goodness was gone five minutes after I stuck it in the fridge. Why do I put any desserts in the fridge ever?"

"Four minutes," Angela muttered. It had been delicious: creamy and cool, sweet and smooth on her tongue, with the slightly bitter chocolate/coffee aftertaste.* Knowing she'd beaten everyone to it just made it all the more succulent.

"So insomnia's going around, I guess." She poured herself a cup of hot chocolate (whole milk, shredded Godiva chocolate, cinnamon, a drop of vanilla extract . . . Jacky's indulgent recipe had turned her off Swiss Miss for life) from the dispenser and sat across from them.

---

*That probably sounds weird, right? It's not weird. It works. Get some.

"So this is how we're all spending our Saturday night," she joked. "Such partiers."

"Sunday morning, technically."

"But you're okay, right, Leah? The baby's okay?"

"Yes. The baby . . . the baby's fine"

Jack's eyes widened. "Um, that pause was terrifying. Should we be calling an ambulance?"

Leah shook her head. Angela was amused to notice she was in one of Archer's old button-downs and a pair of gym shorts that had seen better days. "The baby's perfectly healthy. That's not why I'm up. But you're very nice to be concerned."

"I'm not concerned or nice. I'm just trying to avoid a lawsuit," Jack lied.

"I'm fine, the baby's fine. Besides, you wouldn't believe it if I told you," Leah said. "That's not a challenge. It's just a fact. There is no point in telling you. You won't believe me."

"If you're trying not to pique our interest," Jack said, "you're sucking at it."

"Do you make any caffeine-free desserts?"

"Yeah, that wasn't an obvious topic change. Fine, keep your secrets. That's what we do around here." He looked at Angela. "Right?"

He knows! He knows I have a crush on Jason Chambers and his crazy/cool socks!

"They're just socks, I don't care, they're not even sexy!" *Oh, my God. Here comes the most awkward pause in the history of human events. Say something. Either of you. Something.*

"I don't think you've had enough cocoa."

"Never mind." Angela pushed the thought of erotic socks to

the back of her brain. "Jack, I'm starting to think it's time for a checkup."

"Why? You seem fine to me. No more driven or shriller or controlling than usual."

"For you, dumbass. A checkup for you." To Leah: "Oh, don't laugh, you're just encouraging him."

"Can't help it." She giggled. "You're all adorable."

"That's a blatant falsehood. What lies has that lying SOB Archer told you when he lied about us?" Before she could respond, Jack held up his hands and made soothing motions. "It's okay. Shouldn't have put you on the spot. You don't have to pretend Paul and Mitchell are adorable. It's enough to acknowledge my and Angela's adorableness."

"Duly acknowledged."

"So the baby's fine." At Leah's nod, Angela continued. "And, Jack, you don't need an appointment." Jack nodded. "And I'm not obsessed." She nodded for herself. *If someone were to walk in—who wasn't a family member—they'd think we were all secret-keeping lunatics. Oh, wait . . .* "So we're all in the kitchen at 4:30 a.m. because everything's fine."

"Seems like."

"That's an accurate summation," Leah said.

"So none of us have anything to tell each other."

"Nope."

"What the chef said."

Delighted, Jack turned to Leah at once. "You think I'm a chef? Tomorrow, I'll make you oatmeal *and* porridge! Later today, I mean. But not triple coffee cheesecake. Because I'm bored with that one now and we're out of coffee."

"I could buy you more coffee," Leah said hopefully.

"Bring me all the coffee," the teenager declared, "and I shall visit upon you the most divine Chocolate Coffee Cardamom Layer Cake you've ever had."

Leah beamed into her cup of cocoa. And Angela, who was still uneasy from her dream/flashback, couldn't help smiling. Because, yeah, something was up with all three of them. But Jack had made it clear he wasn't ready to be forthcoming, and Leah's health was, frankly, no one's business but hers and Archer's.

And that was . . . that was all right, Angela decided. Sure it was. She could feel herself prodding that new idea. *So . . . DON'T be a controlling jerkass in this instance? Hmm. Radical thought. Am I on board? This one time I might be on board. I'll be more controlling tomorrow to make up for it. Promise.*

"Angela?"

I wouldn't have been capable of this five years ago. Or maybe even last year. Maybe Archer isn't the only one who grew up.

"Helloooooo?"

"I'm here," she said automatically.

"Sure you are."

Sometimes, she was coming to learn, you didn't have to spill everything and then talk it to death. You could just . . . be together. Even if it didn't solve anything.

Or maybe she was just tired. Either way: "So, who wants a refill besides me?"

Turns out, they all did.

TWENTY-NINE

Angela had missed the same spelling error three times in a row

(no more 4:30 a.m. hot chocolate for you, missy! at least not this week)

and when her phone rattled (Mitchell's suggestion that she download a rattlesnake rattle* for her ringtone was genius), she was glad for an excuse to take a break. To her surprise, Jason Chambers was calling. The chat had been short

("Of course you can come over.")

and sweet

("It's nice to hear from you!").

Also: ugh. *Nice to hear from him?* She sounded like someone's aunt. And not a cool aunt, the way Dennis had been the fun

---

*These exist! (Shudder.)

uncle. Somebody's grumpy aunt, the kind who kept all the balls that dropped into her yard and wrote bitchy letters to the editor about how noisy the downtown area was.

When Detective Chambers turned up a half hour later, she was ready for him. She'd put on makeup, run mousse and a curling iron through her hair, picked out appropriately sober-yet-stylish clothing that flattered and covered at the same time.

And then she undid all of it because good God, who dresses for a date when a homicide detective was giving you an update about your murdered father?

So she brushed the curls out of her hair, blew her bangs out of her face (her hair was always in one of two stages: "I'm growing it out" or "I need a haircut"), and slipped into black leggings, a thigh-skimming cranberry-colored long-sleeved tunic, and plain navy flats. She looked in the mirror, pronounced herself as not trying too hard, and went to the kitchen to wait.

Minutes later, she opened the kitchen door before he had a chance to knock and saw at once that she wasn't the only one low on sleep: His kind eyes had shadows beneath them. The navy blue suit was clean but rumpled, like he'd napped in it. And the dark stubble blooming along his jaw wasn't sexy *at all* and, oh, God, why did she lie to herself? She wanted to give herself beard burn. He wouldn't even have to do anything. Just stand still while she grabbed his head and rubbed his face all over her.

Archer had come in behind her and shook hands with Jason. "Hey, Detective, how's it going?"

"Fine, Mr. Drake. Could you come with me now?" he asked Angela. "I've got something I think you need to see."

"That sounds like every *Star Trek: TNG** ever," Archer declared. He had a point. They were a Trekkie household, always had been (nothing against the *Star Wars* franchise, they were fine if you liked glorified soap operas whose characters all had daddy issues[†]).

They'd all noticed that no one ever gave Captain Picard specifics. Ever. It could be a bomb, it could be a spy, it could be a bomb made of spies, and all Riker or Geordi would ever say was, "Captain, I think you should see this" or "Captain, you'd better get down here." As Paul had pointed out when he was a wee lad (a wee-er lad), "They're all terrible at debriefing their superior officer. Did they all flunk military protocol?"[‡]

(This had the unfortunate side effect of sparking the "Resolved: That the United Federation of Planets is the galaxy's military, not the galaxy's Peace Corps" debate again. No one got to bed before 3:00 a.m.)

"Why? Do you have an update?" she asked. "A new witness?" A new witness would be wonderful. The old ones were dead or had disappeared or had refused to talk in the first place. A new witness would be Christmas.

He shook his head. "I don't know if it's related to the case or not."

Okay. Is that disappointing? Am I disappointed?

---

*The Next Generation

[†]Yeah, that's right. I said it. And I'm not taking it back because *you know I'm right*.

[‡]It's true! Watch any *Star Trek: TNG* episode. They *never* give Picard a heads-up, they never warn him. They just lure him planet-side and hit him with the shock of the day. It's weird.

MARYJANICE DAVIDSON

"Will you come?"

Not disappointed. "Of course, I can go right now. I— Wait." She turned to Archer. "What's Mom up to?"

"Dunno. Jack said she's in her room with the door closed."

"Fine."

"But she knows he's here," he added, jerking his head toward Jason. "She asked who was knocking."

"Okay. So it's unlikely she'll come out anytime soon."

"Based on my lifetime of observing her behavior . . . yeah. Pretty safe bet."

Fine. Better than Widow Drake storming into the kitchen, insulting Jason for reasons only known to her, then vanishing for hours, maybe days. She remembered her uncle telling Jason to go direct traffic last week and wondered what caused the older generation of Drakes to have so little respect for law enforcement. She hoped, very sincerely, it skipped a generation. Preferably two or three generations.

Paul had once pointed out that living with Emma was like sharing a house with the Phantom of the Opera: You knew she was creeping around somewhere behind the scenes, wanting everyone to remain in the house, but she was hardly ever seen.

Jason was probably a bit weirded out by the exchange. Suddenly Angela was too tired to go into it one more time. "It's complicated," she said, and shrugged.

Jason pointed to himself. "Homicide detective. I know all about complicated."

"That's true," Archer cheerfully acknowledged. "You've seen shit that would horrify even us. Probably. Well, maybe not Leah. But the rest of us?"

160

"Maybe," Jason replied, deadpan.

"Possibly," Angela added, and then giggled, because why not? It was turning into that kind of day. Week.

So that was that.

❧

"THIS WILL SOUND strange," Jason Chambers began stiffly, "but I find cemeteries relaxing."

"I feel the same way about KitKats."

That startled a laugh out of him. "I knew I should have brought something to bribe you."

"You don't have to bribe me," she said quickly. "I was glad to hear from you."

"That may change," he said quietly, shutting off the ignition.

It was late afternoon and she would have loved a nap. But her fatigue had taken flight when Jason called. They were in his

(boat, carriage, train, car, who cares?)

car at a

(grocery store, gym, library, AA meeting, who cares?)

cemetery she was more than familiar with: Graceland.

"Okay, this I didn't expect."

"I wasn't even here for your case," Jason said as they got out of his car. "Like I said, I like cemeteries. They're beautiful and quiet. Sometimes the precinct . . . it's all noise, and most of it doesn't make much sense. I like my work, but some days . . ."

"Jason, you're talking to the woman who studied for finals in a prison visiting area. You don't have to explain one thing about yourself to me. It's fine."

"Thank you."

"For what? Not judging the hell out of you and then running away screaming?"

"Yes."

So out of curiosity, how many people have done that to you? Two? Five? Enough to make you feel bad about enjoying gorgeous landscaping, that's for sure. Morons.

"Did you know," he began, "they used to bury bodies on top of each other? It never occurred to them to spread out, so they packed them like sardines."

"Annnnnd now you've ruined sardines for me."

He smiled at her. "Sorry. But as I was saying, back in the day, Graceland was designed the new way, with more space and better maintained tombstones. They even set aside space for families to have picnics. So the grounds weren't just beautiful, they were practical. I think that's lovely. You know the saying: 'In the midst of life, we are—'"

"'—having picnics.' Yep, got it." But it was interesting. Visits here had always been more of a duty than a pleasure, but she had to admit it was peaceful.

"Do you have family here?"

"No."

"I mean—are *you* buried here? One of your past lives?"

He smiled and she caught a glimpse of that enchanting dimple. "No. I just like cemeteries. Especially their histories."

"Well, Graceland's got a lot of that. It's a who's who type of graveyard." *A who's who type of . . . Gawd. Stop. Talking.*

Luckily, Jason picked up the conversation slack. "Did you know George Pullman's here? His family was so worried about activists and former employees wreaking havoc on the corpse—"

"'Wreaking havoc on the corpse,'" she repeated, delighted. "I really like the way you talk. It's friggin' poetry."

"Thanks." Was that a blush? Surely not. "His family buried him in the middle of the night, in utmost secrecy. They lined his coffin with lead and sealed it up with reinforced concrete."

"Those wacky anti-industrialists."

Jason grinned. "It worked. But even if it hadn't, my thinking is: If you were prepared to go to all that trouble, and actually broke through to the coffin, take the body. It's yours. You've earned it."

They giggled guiltily, like kids who were talking about something so awful, it was actually funny. Or seemed that way.

Jason pointed out a few monuments. "They also had to move quite a few bodies here after the 1871 fire."

"Yeah, I read about that somewhere. It always gave me a creepy *Poltergeist* vibe."

"Sorry?"

"'You left the bodies and you only moved the headstones! *You only moved the headstones!*' You know. *Poltergeist*? Not the remake. The good one from the eighties. No?" She shook her head. "Terrible. Your habit of lurking in cemeteries is fine—"

"*Lurk* is an exaggeration."

"But your inability to see *Poltergeist* despite having had decades to do so is gonna be a problem."

"I would never want to be a problem for you," he replied seriously. "I'll see it."

What? He will? Just like that? Naw. Really? Is it possible this crush isn't just one-sided?

Naw.

"It's right over here," he added, gently taking her by the elbow (*!!!!!!!*)

and leading her past the imposing mausoleums. As always, she averted her gaze from the *Eternal Silence* statue. A bronze sculpture (oxidized, so it shone green, not brass) with a black base, the thing was ten feet tall, a sinister robed and hooded figure holding one arm across its face like Dracula fending off sunshine.

She'd been amazed and a little frightened (in her defense, she'd still been a kid) to find out there was a legend about the statue: If you looked into its dead stony gaze, you'd have a vision of your own death.* For years afterward, Mitchell always blindfolded the thing when they visited.

Should've taken a page out of Jason's book and just gone on picnics instead.

Wait. She knew this path. She recognized everything. "We're going to my father's grave, aren't we?"

"Yes."

That . . . that couldn't be good. She couldn't think of any instance in which a concerned cop taking her to her father's grave would work out for her. Not one.

Then she saw it. And instantly knew why she was there.

My God.

---

*This is true! That's how creepy the thing is, it inspires legends about seeing your own death. Yeesh.

THIRTY

She couldn't stop staring. Her father's grave consumed her world, which was probably a metaphor for . . . something. "Jesus. And you don't think it's random."

"No. I don't think it's random. I think it was specifically targeted."

Her father's grave had been—there was no other way to put it—brutalized. Someone had come along and smeared black paint over the name. Then they'd hit and gouged the hell out of it with a hammer or hatchet or something—and had shoved it off the base so it was off-center but hadn't fallen over.

"Any other graves? Or just my dad's?"

"Just his. As I said, I think it was targeted." He pointed at the scrawls, the signs of violence. "They weren't just after any random gravestone—we had to walk past, what? A few hundred others?"

"At least."

"There are hundreds of graves closer to the entrance, or concealed better so the vandals wouldn't be as exposed. But they walked past all those for *this* one. And see the name? Completely and deliberately obliterated, but they left the dates alone. And when they'd made as much of a mess as they could with the paint, they started kicking it—see the tread marks? Kicking the name over and over? That's focused negative emotion, not 'Jeepers I feel destructive, let's go trash a random tomb.'"

"Okay, first: 'jeepers'? And second, good point. And third, what the hell?"

"That was my literal thought when I saw it: What the hell."

"And you just happened to be here and found it like this."

"Yes." She saw his shoulders stiffen. "I understand why you might wonder if I have anything to do with it, but if you'll notice the soles of my shoes—" He hiked up one pant leg and she grinned to see *Mona Lisa* staring back at her from his ankle. "There's no paint. Of course, I could have changed shoes, but if you check with the dispatcher, I can prove I was on duty—"

"I like your Monet ones the best, but these are pretty good, too."

He froze in the act of rolling his pant leg back down. "You noticed. My socks?"

"Yeah." Busted. "It's unsettling, right? Me noticing them and then creepily commenting about how I stare at your legs a lot? Yeah, it is. Forget I said anything. Your socks are boring and even if they weren't, I sure didn't notice them."

"The Monets are your favorite?" He had an odd expression; part surprise, part hopeful.

"Well. Yeah. He's my favorite artist, though, so that follows. Right? But listen, I don't think you did it. I certainly don't think you did it on purpose so you'd have an excuse to call me because you're secretly a stalker." *It's wrong that I would have no problem with that. Very, very wrong.*

"I would— I would never do something like that to you. To anyone," he corrected. And yep, he *was* blushing. No question this time. *Eh. It's a warm day and he's in a suit.*

"I know." Wasn't that strange? She barely knew the guy, but she would have bet five figures he had nothing to do with blacking out her father's name. "But the timing is interesting, don't you think? Dad's case is back in storage. You're turning your attention back to your regular workload and buying weird socks. And I'm only working Dad's case part-time."

"So why do this now?" he finished. "Yes. Those were my thoughts also."

"Well, thank God you found it first. I'd have hated for Jack or Jordan or any of the others to see it like this. And we're gonna have to clean this up, I'm not sure the cheapie package covers it. I'll check with the office."

"That's another thing. I don't understand why the office didn't call you. The paint's dry, it doesn't even smell. This happened at least two days ago."

"I can tell you why—my mother. She told Graceland years ago that she was paying for minimum coverage and didn't want updates and don't call her, she'd call them." Which, again, Angela had chalked up to the pain of widowhood. How it had hit her so hard she couldn't bear to be reminded of it by anyone, and certainly not the boneyard where her husband rested.

Again, she wondered if she hadn't been reading Emma Drake completely wrong all this time.

Stop it. Your mother did not murder your father. Okay?

Okay?

"Are you going to notify your mother?"

That brought her back. "No. And she'll never find out, either. She's never been here."

"Your mother strikes me as a rather vengeful mourner."

Angela laughed, a short humorless bark. "That is the perfect phrase."

"I think it might be time to visit your uncle again."

"You think he knows who did it?"

"He might. Or he'd know why it was done."

"And if you know 'why,' you know 'who'?"

"Yes. Or he might be able to point us in a new direction. It's worth a discussion."

"In the loop" is a glorious place to be. "Agreed. I'm going to tell Archer what happened, see if he and Leah want to come with us—when?"

"Tomorrow, late afternoon," was the prompt reply. "I'll have to put in the request and take care of a few other things first. Can you keep your family away from the grave for thirty-six hours?"

She sighed. "That won't be a problem at all."

Which was, in itself, a problem. One she was ill-quipped to solve. But then, that had always been the case.

THIRTY-ONE

They're terrifying but likeable, Leah decided. Which was pretty fine for a family motto. Certainly better than the Nazir motto: *Quid de mi residuals?**

It was late. Angela had come back from her mysterious errand with Detective Chambers, pulled her and Archer aside, and in a low voice explained what Detective Chambers had shown her at the cemetery.

"Are you fucking kidding?" Archer hissed, mindful that the house was full of ears, even in the guest bathroom they'd crammed all three of themselves into (one of the few rooms in the house that locked). A toilet, a tiny sink, and three adults in a three-by-five bathroom made Leah grateful Jack had taken it easy on the garlic for dinner. "They wrecked your dad's *grave?*"

---

*"What about my residuals?"

"I'm so sorry," Leah added. "That must have been a horrible sight."

"Why didn't you call us, cuz? We'd have come to help. We'll go right now if you want."

"Archer, it *just* happened. And I don't want your pregnant fiancée scrubbing paint off a gravestone and helping us shove a two-hundred-pound stone back on its base. Jesus."

"Okay, good point. I didn't mean to jump on you, I was just surprised. So what'd you say? What'd you do? Are you going to tell Aunt Emma? Do you want me to?"

"Are you kidding? It's all Mom can do to handle the mail."

Leah had been unsurprised when the answer was nothing, nothing, no, and no. Emma Drake had a Ph.D. in a peculiar kind of grief that was, at times, more selfish than suffering.

There was a selfish side to grief, but no one talked about it because it was such tricky ground. It sounded heartless: *I'm* mourning. *I'm* suffering *without him/her/it. How can you say that's selfish?*

That was true as far as it went. But when are you finished? *Well, it's different for everyone. It's grief! You can't put a time limit on it!* Sure you can. Six months, a year? Five years, ten? When will you come back to life? When does mourning become hiding? And for how long?

I didn't get to say good-bye! was a common theme. And it was understandable—but what they were really saying was, *I wanted them awake and aware—and yes, given the injuries, he/she/it would have been in tremendous pain but I needed this, dammit! Sure, he/she/it would have been racked with pain and terrified to know death was coming, but I wanted my good-bye!*

*I deserve closure!** was another one. An understandable instinct, but ultimately futile, since there really was no such thing. Not even in a world where you could meet up with your loved ones in another life.

Emma Drake was displaying all the symptoms of grief-turned-selfish. Even without Insight, Leah likely would have figured it out.

Be fair, she told herself. *If it was Archer who went out one night and never came back? And Jack or Angela or Paul got life imprisonment for it, though you knew they were innocent? Are you sure you wouldn't instantly morph into your mother? What makes you think you wouldn't spend the rest of your life mourning your glory days?*

But thinking about what Nellie Nazir would do just made things worse. Because in about six months, her mother would be here. There'd be no more speculating about what she would do, because Leah and Archer and the world would be able to *see* what she would do.

What if she wants to be an actress again?

What if she does? Is that the worst possible scenario?

Yes. And what the hell are we going to name her? Nellie 2.0? Nn-nellie? Nellie Squared? Nellie "I'm Back" Drake? What? Whaaaaaaat?

Which is why Leah tried not to think about it.

After further whispered updates, and an attempt by Paul to get in the bathroom,

("C'mon, I just need the spare tape measure! It's right there under

---

*There's a clever, funny piece on this: "5 Ways the Grieving Process Turns Us Selfish" by Dennis Hong, on Cracked.com. Worth a look!

the sink! What are you weirdos even doing in there? You'd better all be fully clothed!")

she and Archer agreed to meet Angela and the detective at ICC tomorrow afternoon.

Later, they were treated to another fine meal by Jack, who had little to say, despite Paul's attempt to wriggle out of doing the dishes. As it happened, Leah was in a generous mood and was happy to clean up. The Drakes had asked nothing of her in more than a week, and if their noisy squabbles and power plays sometimes made her feel invisible, she reminded herself that once upon a time, all she'd wanted was to be invisible. There were worse things than being the quiet weirdo in the crowd.

She also thought helping in the kitchen might be a way to coax Jack into telling her what was on his mind (though she had a good idea), but he didn't linger once the table had been cleared. So: The kid was tired or he wasn't feeling forthcoming or both. *Or it has nothing to do with you, or what you think*, she reminded herself, *and you're projecting.*

Now it was late, close to midnight. Archer had dropped off to sleep after a bout of energetically tender lovemaking. It had started innocently enough with Archer blowing raspberries on her belly.

"Stop that."

"She's gotta learn the world is a cruel place full of raspberries. Pppphhhhhhhbbbttt!"

"Idiot!"

"Raspberries to the right of us! Raspberries to the left of us!"

"'Half a league, half a league onward.*'"

---

*Leah is quoting "The Charge of the Light Brigade" by Alfred, Lord Tennyson. It's going over Archer's head because he's an idiot.

"What?"

"Idiot."

Then he went lower. And stayed there for a while.

A few minutes later, she was reminded that Archer might not be up on his nineteenth-century British poetry, but he was an expert in how to make her gasp and shake and want him. Pregnancy hadn't dampened their sex drive, though she wondered if that would be true five months from now.

She'd cleaned up, then came back to a snoring Archer; he'd dropped off before she could offer him a washcloth. Normally Leah would have followed suit, but too much had happened in too short a time. She'd start thinking about Dennis and the tombstone and then would wonder about Jack. Then she'd think about Angela, who, for all her controlling ways, was quite pleasant and to be commended, partly for her own talents but also for being the head of the family since she was a child. Then she'd start wondering if there was any juice left and what it would taste like with a tablespoon of mustard stirred in.

The cravings. They sicken me even as they delight me.

Enough. One thing she knew about insomnia: Making yourself stay in bed when you couldn't sleep was not a good plan. All you did was lie there and think about the time. *I have to get up in six hours. In four hours. In two. In ninety minutes.* So she slipped into Archer's robe and padded out of their room, kitchen-bound. For orange juice and what might be even better: If her suspicions were correct, she could finally be of some real help to this nutty, exhausting band of charmers.

That was worth some lost z's.

THIRTY-TWO

She found Jack, as she'd hoped she would, sorting through what looked like hundreds of cookbooks. She found that equal parts commendable and exasperating. *How many books about pudding does any one family need?*

He turned his head—his back was to the kitchen doorway—and nodded. "Hey."

"Hello, Jack. Please don't leap to your feet and prepare me a nutritionally sound prenatal snack. I'm just here for the orange juice." Which was one of the silliest things to drink when you wanted to sleep—hospitals kept it on hand because it got a patient's blood sugar up in a hurry—but oh, well.

"Wasn't gonna," he muttered.

"Oh. Then this just got awkward."

A muffled snort. She stepped to the fridge, got the juice, ignored the mustard (the poor boy was going through enough without having to witness *that* horror show), poured herself a glass, sipped, set it down, went to him, touched his shoulder. After a moment, he looked up at her. He was sitting cross-legged in front of the jam-packed bookshelf, and it might have been the overhead lighting, but he looked haunted. "Shouldn't you be in bed?"

She smiled. *God, the bags under his eyes.* "That's my line, Jack. Can I help you? Will you tell me?"

"I'm okay."

"Bullshit. Which I say with deepest respect as a guest in your kitchen."

He blinked up at her. "I'm okay. You're the one who should go and sleep, you're making another person."

"I can do more than one thing at once. Well, sometimes. I'm sorry to pester, and I know we only just met, but I'd like to help you."

"I'm o-*kay*."

Sure you are. "If I can guess what's bothering you, will you confirm?"

A shrug. But this time, he didn't immediately go back to pretending to read a cookbook.

She sat on the floor beside him. "It's not that you can't sleep. It's that you're afraid to sleep."

Silence.

"You don't want to sleep because you're having bloody, violent, terrifying dreams. So being awake is good, right? But it's a problematic long-term solution."

"Everybody has nightmares."

She nodded. "Oh, yes. And lots of people fight them the way

you are—by trying to avoid them. Or they go the other way, self-medicating with Ambien or alcohol so they go down deep and don't dream."

"I can't do that, though." He immediately went red, like he knew he'd showed his hand and was now resigned to her taking advantage.

"That's right, you can't. And you're clever to know it. Access, for one thing, is a problem. You're the youngest in a house full of people who'd bust you in a cold minute, that's another one. So you're stuck with coffee, which is why you've slipped caffeine into every dessert for the last three days."

"Everybody likes triple coffee cheesecake. And mocha brownies with coffee frosting. And coffee meringues. And coffee cinnamon rolls. And—"

"Sure, Jack. Please don't misunderstand; I'm not criticizing you. I think you're to be commended." She nudged him gently with her elbow. "You had me buying you more coffee—you got me to feed your habit right under my nose, that's how long it took me to catch on. You made me your dealer, dammit!"

"Kinda," he mumbled. "But I usually made two batches of desserts, so I've actually been feeding you decaf."

"Huh. Well. That's something to be proud of, you duplicitous jerk."

He giggled, but immediately sobered. "I wasn't trying to trick you."

"You literally just explained how you tricked me. And how you tricked anyone who had one of 'my' desserts and thought they were getting caffeine."

He shrugged. "I just needed it."

"I know. But it's just another stopgap measure. It's not a

long-term fix. And other problems are cropping up, too, aren't they? Because the more exhausted you are, the more the world seems bigger and louder. Things that didn't bother you before are bugging the hell out of you now."

"But again, that happens to a lot of people."

"Here's what doesn't: You're starting to get pictures in your head, but they're not *your* pictures. They're not your thoughts. They're about people you don't know . . . Except you can't shake the feeling that you *do* know them. You were gray as a ghost when you and Paul were done wrestling for who had to paint the deck."

"Only because he forgot to put on deodorant."

"Or because you realized he was born in 1934 and his name used to be Yuri Gagarin, the first person in space. And the shortest person in space," she added under her breath, and managed to lock back a snicker.

Leah waited while Jack looked away and fiddled with his shoelaces. Then: "Yeah, exactly. That's exactly right and I shouldn't know that so why do I know that? I don't want to know that."

"No, I imagine you don't."

"So why?" His voice cracked on "why" and he flushed red.

"Oh, Jack. You know why."

"I don't want to know that Mitchell starved to death in a potato famine or that Angela has a history of getting innocent people killed or that Mom ends up alone in every single life," he cried. "When I was little—"

"When you were little," Leah said quietly, "they chalked it up to a vivid imagination. If you talked about it at all. In this house, it's easy to get lost. If someone said 'Insighter,' they were talking about Angela. Right? So you didn't say anything to disabuse them. And that worked for a long time."

"Yeah, but . . ."

"But puberty often kick-starts the ability, or gives it a sizeable boost—you can blame that on the pituitary gland. The same thing directing your body to grow several inches got your Insighting going, too. Because ordinary puberty isn't horrifying enough."

It fell flat; he wasn't in a joking mood. "I don't want a biology lesson and I don't want other people's lives in my head! I've got enough trouble juggling my own. Did you know I drowned in molasses in 1919?* I mean, what the *fuck*?"

"If it makes you feel better, my mom killed me in several past lives."

His eyes almost literally bulged. "Why? Leah? *Why* would that make me feel better?"

That brought her up short. "Well. When you put it like that, I have to admit, that was a dim move on my part."

"I don't want to be an Insighter," he said, lips trembling. His gray green eyes filled and she knew he would be embarrassed and angry if even one tear fell. "No offense."

"I'm not offended. I wasn't happy about it, either. And my mother . . . my mother was horrified."

"Well, yeah." Jack sniffed and raked his forearm across his face, dashing away tears. "Because she wanted an easier life for you."

"You're adorable," she said dryly. "Because she didn't want

---

*In 1919, near Boston, Massachusetts, a molasses storage tank burst, which unleashed a twenty-five-foot wave that traveled thirty-five miles per hour. Since people can only run at about eight miles per hour, twenty-one people were killed and 150 were injured. Like I needed another reason to hate molasses.

anything that might take the spotlight off her. She insisted it was just my overactive imagination. She spent years denying it."

"That's when you tried to get emancipated?" When she raised her eyebrows, he added guiltily, "I Googled you."

"Oh. No, I tried to get emancipated because she was making me work—shows, movie cameos, endorsements, all of which I hated—and keeping all my money."

"But your mom banged the judge so you were stuck."

"Uh, yes." *I should probably look myself up online.*

"But then you got famous. Famous-er. You were always in the news, but not because of TV anymore. Archer was super excited when he got to meet you, he told us all about it."

Got to meet me. Well, that was one way to put it. "Was hired to stalk me" would have been a tad more accurate.

History. Focus. "Yes, I was famous. On quite my own merits." Leah smiled, but it wasn't a happy one. "The unforgivable sin in Nellie Nazir's eyes is that I wasn't even on TV anymore and I was still more famous than her. Her only focus from the time I was seventeen until I—until last year—was luring me back to revive her career with '*our* comeback.'" Leah still couldn't say "our comeback" without a shudder.

"So you left to get out of the spotlight, but took a job that put you right back in it, and kept you in it."

She shrugged. "There wasn't a conscious plan, that's just how it worked out. And urgh!" She stretched and rubbed the small of her back with both hands. "Come on. Unlike you I'm a pregnant crone and this floor is hard."

"You're not a crone and you're not even showing."

"Irrelevant! Help me up and we'll sit at the turtle table and you can ask me anything you want while I drink juice and don't stir mustard into it."

"Anything? Really?" Then: "'Mustard'?"

"Less asking, more pulling."

When they were at the table and Leah was sipping her mustard-free juice: "Yes. Anything. But I warn you, any sex-related questions will be awkward and we'll probably have to avoid eye contact for a few days."

"Just . . . gross. No." He leaned forward. "Did you ever like it?"

I'm going to assume he's talking about Insighting. "Sometimes," she admitted. "I've been able to help a lot of clients." She thought of Chart #6291, formerly Clara Barton, currently chief of neurosurgery at Massachusetts General. And Chart #5272, formerly Ludwig van Beethoven, currently the author of *Musical Anhedonia Hath No Charms* ("How can I be him? I hate classical music. And concerts. And my hearing's fine."). The actions and consequences from their past lives bled into their present ones, paralyzing them. Leah had helped with that.

It wasn't always about making a mark, she'd explained to a construction worker who used to be Albert Einstein—the month before she met Archer. "You don't have to live up to your last life. You love being an electrician. That's great. Do you know how many people I meet who hate their jobs? Do you know how many people *anyone* meets who hate their jobs? To be honest, I'm a little envious. You make good money, you and your husband are raising a beautiful family, you love your life, what's the problem?"

"Well, after my folks had me tested . . ."

"Can I tell you something? Pretexting often brings more problems than it solves. It's like an IQ test: It narrows everyone's expectations. 'You have a genius IQ so you'd better invent something wonderful. Or cure something terrible. Make your mark or you've wasted your life. No pressure.' Expecting children to live up to that is begging for trouble.

"Pretexting does the same thing: 'You used to be Alexander Graham Bell, so we're already talking to MIT since you'll have an incredible life and become world famous by your thirtieth birthday.' It's crap. It's a straitjacket."

Other patients had the reverse problem, and she had helped them understand they didn't have to live *down* their past lives, either. "So you were a necrophiliac who targeted landladies until you were hanged in 1928?* You're not compelled to kill, you don't have to write letters of condolence to the victims' great-great-grandchildren. And if you're *that* worried your past will bleed into your present, buy. Don't rent."

Well, that one was perhaps oversimplified. But never mind. The bottom line is . . .

"Sometimes the work is beyond rewarding. Since most people only ever hear me complaining, it's only fair to mention that there are many days when I like what I do. It goes beyond helping people in their day-to-day lives. I've been able to work with the police and attorneys to put away some utter degenerates. There's satisfaction in that."

Jack was nodding. "Okay. Sure."

"It's a little like being a world-famous baker who doesn't like cake. Possessing the skill doesn't mean you love it. People de-

---

*Earle Nelson, aka The Gorilla Man, born 1897, died (the first time) 1928.

manding your cake doesn't mean you actually like baking." *Not my best metaphor. Well, it* is *past midnight.*

"But you're different from me. Just like Angela's different from me. What works for you might not help me."

"I'm not sure I follow."

"Because you're—I dunno—the Bette Davis of Insighters. Or something."

She groaned. "Oh, my God, you've all got to stop that. Not least because you've got it wrong. Davis had natural talent that she built on. She was relentless and fearless about her craft—she liked playing monsters—and the work was always, always her number one focus. It's why she was so mesmerizing on-screen. If you go back and watch the early films, you can almost see how each picture is a stepping-stone to the deeper characterization she found for the next."

"Oh, my God."

"I know."

"Film geek."

"Yes, well, Hollywood childhood. Those movies were my homework. And the best part—" She laughed a little, remembering. "My mom was furious when I told her she'd never been famous except for that time she'd been a serial killer—"*

"Wait, *what*?"

"—and she certainly wasn't the reincarnation of Davis. Or Garland. Or Hepburn. Or anyone of note."

---

*In *Deja Who*, we found out Nellie Nazir was once the Countess of Báthory, a Hungarian noblewoman who was thought to have tortured and killed more than six hundred girls and women. She was eventually tried, found guilty, and kept in solitary confinement, bricked into a room with walled-up windows, and died five years later.

"Can we circle back to your mom the serial kil—"

"The thing is, Jack, if I was the anything of Insighters, I'd be Greta Garbo: skilled, but ultimately resentful of the attention it brought and constantly tempted to exile myself."

"Um . . ."

"Sometimes I can barely be bothered to try. Which makes me the jerkass of Insighters."

"You're not making me feel better about being a freak."

"Ah, but as I remind my clients, my job isn't to make them feel better. It's to help them see. What I'm trying to explain is, it doesn't have to define you. It doesn't have to be a career. You don't have to end up—" *Like me.* "For most people, like your sister, it's just something they have a knack for. Like being great with numbers—the fourteen-year-old kid taking college trig, for example. Or like knowing what spices go together with what food even if you've never cooked. It helps—or hinders—exactly as much as you want it to. What if that same math whiz decides on medical school? It doesn't mean they're not a math genius, they're just putting their focus elsewhere."

She cleared her throat. "Wow, I'm talking a lot."

"Uh-huh. But, Leah, the thing is—" In his anxiety, Jack grabbed Leah's hand, squeezing for emphasis. "That's why Angela's always been so obsessed with Dad's case."

Unspoken: *And I don't want to be like that.*

"Is that what you think? That it's about her gift, and not her personality?" *Is that what you all think? That explains quite a bit, come to think of it.* She shook her head. "No, Jack. Your sister's obsessed—and I don't think she's clinically obsessed, by the way. We throw that word around *far* too often, so many people use 'obsessed' when what they really mean is 'focused' or—"

"Argh."

"Sorry. Your father's murder is a constant, strong issue for her because that's her nature, and it's nothing to do with Insight. Her attention to detail, her reliance on being in control—"

She was delighted when he snickered; it was an improvement over tearful despair. "Soooo tactful."

"Yes, well, I've got skills. Angela's personality traits have little to do with the ability. The way she looks after all of you— do you think that's because she knows Jordan died of gangrene after biting his tongue?"*

"What?"

"No, it's because something in her compels her to take care of all of you. Your sister isn't driven to spend years researching a murder because she can see other lives. She's driven to research it because she knows something's wrong and she wants to fix it."

"Okay. That's—okay." He sighed. "Can we stop talking about this for now? I'm not trying to be mean. It's just, there's a lot to think about."

"Of course."

"I don't feel . . . better, exactly? Just less bad, and I don't think that's the same thing. But I'll take it. To be honest, I'm so tired I feel like you wrapped a brick in cotton and whacked me in the forehead with it."

"That's what I'm here for."

He started to get up from the table, then paused. "Don't tell anybody, okay?"

---

*Allan Pinkerton (of the Pinkerton National Detective Agency) tripped on a sidewalk and bit his tongue so hard, he developed gangrene and died in 1884.

"Of course."

"And thanks. For talking to me."

"Of course."

"You want some more juice?"

"No, I thought I'd go back to bed and try to sleep."

"Me, too." He headed for the doorway, then paused and turned. "Y'know, you're really screwed up," he said cheerfully. "Your family's worse than mine, which I sort of thought was impossible. But think about it!"

"I have."

"Your mom killed you a lot—"

"I remember."

"—and was a serial killer—"

"Yes, I'm aware."

"—and you're pregnant with a Drake baby—"

"For Christ's sake. I get it."

"—and you have to go back to prison again."

"All true. Not sure what your point is."

"There's just so much madness wrapped up in all that. It's kind of glorious, you know?"

That made her laugh. Hard. And why not? The kid had a point. He'd also reminded her that helping clients see themselves gave her perspective into her own brand of insanity. She still didn't know what to do about The Return of Nellie Nazir, but it was a problem she didn't have to solve on her own, and remembering that was always valuable.

THIRTY-THREE

A lighthearted fact about chronic depression: One of the first things to bid you adieu is your sex drive. When you don't have the energy or drive to get out of bed, the last thing you want is someone in the bed with you, especially when they're advocating a vigorous skin-to-skin workout.

I am in a cemetery (aboveground, fortunately) pondering my sex drive. This is probably one of those thoughts to keep to myself.

He finished sorting the items in his trunk and turned when he heard the car roar in past the gates, dart around the parking lot, swing into a spot, and there was Angela, trying to get out of the vehicle before she unbuckled her seat belt. Or turned off the ignition.

How can you help but admire the woman's drive to vindicate her uncle? She nearly strangled on her seat belt in her rush to get to the truth. Outstanding.

She waved and came over in a hurry, blowing her delightfully tousled bangs off her forehead. "Good morning almost afternoon."

"Angela." *Ah. She's here, so it must be time for me to stiffen up and display my lack of interpersonal skills.* "Hello."

"Not that I mind, but why did you want to meet here?" She looked around the beautiful cemetery while simultaneously avoiding the gaze of the *Eternal Silence* statue. "We're not due at ICC until four o'clock."

"I thought—"

She had slowed as she got closer and was only a couple of feet away. "Oh. Hey! Oh."

He blinked, glanced down. He was in jeans and a short-sleeved dark green button-down. Loafers with socks. Most definitely with socks. "Something wrong?"

"No-no-no. I've just always seen you in suits. It's nice. You're nice. It looks nice, is what I mean. You do. Look nice." She smacked herself on the forehead. "Oh, my God, I've got to start getting more sleep."

He laughed. "That seems to be a common theme this month. I suspect the only one getting a full eight hours per is your uncle. And possibly your mother."

"I promise I don't always babble this much." She looked down at herself. "But now I'm wondering. Am I overdressed?"

"Not at all."

In fact, she was perfectly dressed in crisp black capris with a white blouse and over that, a deep rose sweater with whatever those wide necklines were, the cut that showed off her slender shoulders.* Shiny black loafers completed the look, which was practical and lovely for the mild summer weather.

---

*Boat neckline with dropped shoulders.

"You look—" Beautiful. Perfect. Cemetery-friendly? No. "You're fine." *Oh, for . . .*

He pulled his keys out of his pocket and hit the button to open the trunk, then stepped aside so she could see. He'd asked for, and gotten, permission to bring his car through the gates and park on the side road less than thirty feet from Donald Drake's grave.

She looked. And looked. Five seconds in, his nerves started to jangle. *Does she think I'm going to kill and bury her? Which is why we're in a cemetery? That would be disastrous.*

"This is—" She stopped, then started again. "It almost looks like you brought a lot of cleaning supplies and brushes and paint remover and garbage bags and the like. To my dad's grave. Which was defiled. And which no one's had a chance to clean up."

He looked at her. Well. Tried. She was still staring into his trunk. "You said, 'We're gonna have to clean this up.'"

Her pale cheeks were flushed. "I didn't mean you and I should clean it up. I meant the Drakes."

You overstepped. Again. "Oh."

She must have seen something in his expression because she reached out at once and seized his hand, then stared up into his face. This was startling and wonderful. She had never touched him outside of a handshake; she had never looked at him so intently. "You set up another visit with my uncle where he's likely to insult you, and then you arranged to meet me here so we'd have time to clean up my father's grave so my little brothers and cousins wouldn't see it."

"Yes. But I see now that—"

Her small hand clamped down on his, and he swallowed a yelp. *Yeow! Stronger than she looks.* "This is, no shit, one of the nicest things anyone's ever done for me."

Oh, thank God. "It is? Really?" He could hear the delight in his tone and resigned himself to constantly making an ass of himself whenever he was in Angela Drake's presence. "I mean, that's nice. That you like my idea. And don't feel I exceeded boundaries."

"You're not exceeding anything, I promise." She paused. "Uh, I'll rephrase."

"And after, if you like, I was thinking we could have a picnic. If you want." *If you don't think I'm a presumptuous freak with lustful designs on your body. Only one of those things is true.*

Her grin was sunshine bright, and almost as warm. "Jason, I would love that. Which is weird. But I don't give a shit. Also, I swear more when I'm nervous."

"I make you nervous?" That came out pretty neutral. At least he didn't say "*I* make *youuuuu* nervous????" with an accompanying flabbergasted expression.

"You, cemeteries in general, pending trips to prison . . . y'know, the usual." She released his hand and he massaged the feeling back into his fingers when she wasn't looking. She rummaged around in the trunk and brought out brushes, a pair of bright yellow dishwashing gloves, and one of the buckets. "Well, then. Let's get to it. Also I might use one of those big Hefty bags as a smock."

She did.

It was adorable.

THIRTY-FOUR

Ninety minutes later and the stone, if not good as new, looked a lot better. The gouges couldn't be fixed, but you could read Donald's name. It no longer looked like a nutjob had gone to town on it, just that time was doing some aggressive damage. That was more than Angela thought two people could get done in under two hours. Especially when one of the two was trying not to stare at the other one's butt in jeans.

That. Ass. It's not fair, it's really not.

They cleaned up and packed everything back in Jason's trunk. He went around to the back seat and pulled out a light green backpack with tan accents; there was a wine bottle strapped to one side and a rolled-up tan blanket on the other. He slung it over one shoulder, smiled at her, and said, "Shall we?"

Damned right. She was famished. Jack had slept late, but when he didn't make a big family breakfast, she tended not to bother, and if that occasionally led to her wolfing down a bowl of dry cereal at her desk (or wet cereal over the sink), that was her business. Even if she'd shown up with a full stomach, scrubbing a tombstone for ninety minutes would kindle anyone's appetite. Probably. Maybe a normal person would *lose* their appetite after scrubbing the graffiti off their dad's gravestone. She honestly had no idea; "normal" was beyond any of them.

But now what? Was this a date? Or just a relaxing post–tombstone cleaning ritual between colleagues who weren't actually colleagues? Maybe he had planned to have an alfresco lunch all along and invited her to be polite. They weren't holding hands. But it wasn't uncomfortable, either; they were walking—strolling?—together. Her controlling nature was baffled: It couldn't qualify what was going on, so she kept getting more and more confused. And the longer they were quiet, the harder it got to say something.

Luckily a small child had been struck by lightning a hundred years ago; it was the perfect icebreaker. She pointed out the statue of poor Inez Clarke, murdered by Mother Nature at age six. Her heartbroken parents had commissioned a statue of her exact likeness and sealed it in a glass box on the grounds. The thing was more than a century old and looked like it had been up less than a year.

"Your standard sad story," Angela said. "Except."

Jason smiled. "Always an 'except.'"

"Except when there isn't an except. Luckily that's not the case this time. Except they say that when it's a stormy night, she leaves."

"'Leaves'?" Jason was now standing in front of the glass box encasing the statue, one hand holding the picnic backpack, the other fiddling absently with a belt loop. "What, she takes her show on the road? Runs away? Teleports? Goes on strike?"

"Dunno. At least one guard quit over it. He was doing his walk-around in a rainstorm at midnight—"

"Have you ever noticed these stories never take place in bright sunshine at 10:00 a.m.?"

"Quiet, you. Anyway, when he got to her box, it was empty. He quit on the spot. Left the cemetery, never even went back to the security office. Just walked out and never went back."

"He went home without his car?"

"Jeez, Jason, I didn't take down the incident report. Anyway, the next day the statue was back like it never left."

"Possibly because it hadn't," Jason said dryly.

"And the legend grew," Angela finished. "I'll take a vanishing statue over the friggin' creepy *Eternal Silence* ghoul in green. Who wants to see their own upcoming death? Bad enough most of us see the ones we already endured. 'Oh, great, look at that. I've drowned twice, but apparently I'm due to be trampled by elephants this time around.' Blech!"

He seemed to falter a bit, but perhaps that was because they'd gotten to the footbridge over Lake Willowmere to Burnham Island. Even the most sedate walkers sounded like horses galloping across the small wooden bridge.

He cleared his throat. Angela tried to think of a single instance when someone cleared their throat and it *wasn't* to broach a difficult subject. Maybe the last time Jordan had a head cold . . . "Speaking of past lives, and endurance, you should know I've been diagnosed with dysthymia. It's—"

"I know what it is." She'd looked it up after Leah told her

how to spell it. To her credit, Leah hadn't asked questions. Just said, "D-Y-S-T-H-Y-M-I-A," from her side of the bathroom door. (Reason #262 to never ever gestate: You had to pee every sixteen seconds.)

"Oh. Well." He paused and she had the sense he was mentally squaring his shoulders. "You should know I take medication for it, I'm currently on—"

"Sorry to interrupt. Again, I mean. But it's fine. And—don't get mad—but I already—don't be upset, please, but the thing is, I already knew about your depression. Dysthymia."

He *stared* at her. "How could y— Leah Nazir." He frowned as he worked it out. Hopefully it was a frown of concentration as opposed to a "I never want to see you again" scowl. "She shakes my hand every time she sees me. She probably knows my life history."

"All seven of them. That was a guess, by the way. She didn't say seven. I don't know how many lives you've had. It's none of my business."

"But you've got the same ability."

"No. I have a sense of your past, but not the details. And I didn't want to pry. I *wasn't* prying," she rushed to assure him. "She just came out with it."

"When?"

"The day after she met you."

"You've known for over a week?"

"Yes." He seemed puzzled, and she wasn't sure why. *Better explain. Try to, anyway.* "Leah wasn't—y'know, she didn't say it like it was a negative. Because it's not. A negative, I mean. She said it to cheer up my brother, Jack. He said he thought you were sad, and she backed him up. Which is all kinds of weird, now that I think abou— Never mind. It's none of my business anyway."

"And if it was?" he asked quietly.

What? How could it ever be my business? He's making it so easy for me to read more into this. If that's what he's doing. I'm confused, and it's barely noon, I haven't even had any wine yet. "If it was, I'd be glad you got a diagnosis. And I'd be extra glad you're getting help. And I—I'd consider myself lucky. That you thought something that personal was my business. That you trusted me with that."

"Oh." The frown was gone, replaced by his slow

(dimple!)

sexy smile. "Well. That's all right, then."

"Right?"

"Right."

"Okay."

They got to the other side of the bridge, and Angela was determined to fill the silence before it got (more) awkward. "Did you know, a guy's whole family is buried on this island? How do you even broach that subject? 'Kids, we're all mortal and death is relentless but we'll eventually be together on our own private island. We can have Family Game Night for eternity!' Is that great or disturbing?"

He appeared to give the matter serious thought. "That would depend on whether or not you were a fan of Family Game Night."

"Yeah, I suppose." *I can't take it. And I'm not fourteen, for God's sake. It's ridiculous to be agonizing over this. Just do it. At least I'll know.* "That's it," she announced, then seized his hand and laced her fingers with his. "If you don't like this—"

"It's fine."

"—no problem, just tell me and I'll drop you like a hot rock. I might drop you like a hot rock either way, I'm freaking out a little, this has been a confusing month."

"I like this."

"But the thing is, I've been dying to do this all d— You do?" He did? "Great. Okay."

They walked for a few seconds in silence and then Jason made the oddest noise, and she realized he was giggling. "You're right," he managed, "this is much less awkward."

"Oh, shut up. I'm kind of clueless about the etiquette here." *Among other things.*

In next to no time, she was shaking out the blanket beneath a gorgeous willow tree while Jason unpacked a tremendous amount of food. "I'm not much of a cook," he warned her. "Most of this is store-bought."

"I'm not, either. My whole family's going to lose weight when Jack goes to college," she predicted happily. "It'll be a disaster."

He chuckled. "You seem rather cheerful for someone expecting a disaster."

"Drakes fending for themselves because Jacky's at school forging a new life will be a good thing, believe it."

"Does he know where he'd like to go?"

"He *thinks* he's staying in Chicago," she replied, eyes narrowing at the thought of it. The only thing Jack loved more than cooking was chemistry. UMass offered a fine food science program, one of the oldest in the country, and was in close proximity to Pioneer Valley, which was Foodie Central. The University of Minnesota was another example, and offered food science majors the chance to study their craft abroad in France, Thailand, England, etc. Cornell, Purdue . . . plenty of good programs Jack had the grades to get into.

And they were all a minimum of a two-hour flight from the sprawling red ranch where he'd grown up.

"Pardon me," she said. Jason had pulled out plates, cutlery, a tiny cheese board, a tiny cheese knife, sturdy wineglasses, napkins, a corkscrew, and a tiny black Hefty bag for the scraps/garbage. Then he moved on to food and had just pulled out the fourth—fifth?—plastic container. "Is that a magic backpack? It's like one of those clown cars. Or a bag of holding."

"'Bag of holding'?"

"Paul and I went through a D&D phase . . . Wow! Everything just comes piling out."

"I wasn't sure what you'd like." *So I bought the entire store* was probably the end of that sentence. Rare roast beef sandwiches with watercress on crusty baguettes. Tiny packets of mustard and mayonnaise. Tiny salt and pepper shakers, no bigger than her thumb joint. A Caprese salad with fresh basil. A Ziploc bag stuffed with peeled eggs she assumed were hard-boiled, with a teeny-tiny packet of seasoned salt. Two layered cobb salads in Mason jars. Four chive biscuits. A small selection of cheese (cheeses?), a waxed roll of crackers, a pint of blackberries. A small container of Kalamata olives. Chocolate chip cookies the size of her hand. Chocolate-dipped strawberries. An egg carton with a macaron nestled inside each little cup. Wine. Sparkling water. Half dozen nectarines.

"This . . . looks . . . ggnnn." Drooling. She was drooling like a farm animal. "Really good. Is what I meant." She managed (barely) not to snatch the plastic plate Jason was offering, and had it loaded in no time. She politely declined the booze. "It looks great, but I'd rather not rub the whole 'the cop you've got no use for and I enjoyed a wonderful picnic on my way to visit you in your cage, sorry about my booze breath, how was your horrible day?' thing in his face. Especially since we need his cooperation."

"A fair point," he conceded, and the wine went back into the backpack, to be replaced with the sparkling water. "Perhaps next time." Pause. "Unless you feel I overst—"

"Pass me another egg and enough of the overstepping fretting. This is wonderful. It's all wonderful—all the macarons are different colors! Agh, so cute! This is turning into a great, great day."

He lobbed an egg at her which she snatched out of the air and—miracle of miracles!—it didn't squirt through her fingers and slither off the blanket to land on the grass (bad) or ricochet off her fist to smack him in the eyeball (worse). He shifted around so he was leaning with his back against the trunk, then stretched out his legs, giving what he probably thought was an unobtrusive twitch that hiked up his pants leg, displaying his socks.

Monet's *Water Lilies*.

"Brilliant," she pronounced.

"I have several," he murmured in a voice so intimate and confiding, he might have been coaxing her to let him take her to bed and ravish her. "Monet. Van Gogh. Picasso. Munch. Klimpt. Degas. Botticelli."

"The rampant eroticism of Jason Chambers's barely contained sock drawer." She couldn't say it with a straight face, and by the time she got to "barely" he was laughing so hard he choked on a biscuit.

When neither of them could eat another crumb, he packed everything away. She stretched out on her back, staring up through the feathery willow fronds to the clear blue sky beyond. Even though they were in public, they were nearly invisible to anyone walking by. She liked that. It was like they were on their own private planet. A planet littered with buried corpses, but still.

"Angela."

"Mmmmm?"

"What does this mean?"

"It means it's a great, great day. Beyond that, I don't know."

"I don't, either. Though I enjoy seeing you in a social context as opposed to a work context. Not that I mind the latter," he assured her.

"So you like hanging out with me even if you don't have any crime-scene photos to show me?"

"Miraculously . . ." His tone was so dry, he could have used it to make beef jerky. "Yes."

"What if you came over for dinner again?"

He flashed the dimple. "That would be my pleasure."

"Or you and I went out somewhere. Would you get in trouble?"

"No. Your father's case was never mine to begin with, and it's not open."

"Oh. That's good." *Argh.* "You know what I mean."

"Yes." He was wriggling a bit, trying to get comfortable—the blanket was a good idea, but it was thin and scratchy. She finally reached out, gently grabbed his ear, and tugged until he was lying down with the back of his head on one of her thighs. "Thank you. I wasn't sure—"

"I know. It's fine."

"A great, great day."

"Yeah."

Later, she'd be grateful. It was the last "great, great" thing to happen for a *long* time.

THIRTY-FIVE

They made it to ICC by four o'clock. Barely.

"I can't believe we both fell asleep," she muttered as they hurried through the parking lot and into the building.

"I can. We were tired, we had a good meal—"

"A delicious egg-laden meal."

"It was a beautiful day." He showed the guard his badge, she showed her ID; they were allowed to go back. "It would have been odder if we hadn't dozed off."

She laughed. "Only you can make *not* falling asleep in a cemetery seem weird. And I've got to get a haircut." She was trying to scrape her bangs out of her eyes (fashionably long and too long were not the same thing) and repeatedly failing.

"Your hair is lovely."

"Drake genes—we're all shaggy. Like bison!" Stubborn, willful, argumentative, meat-eating bison.

Archer and Leah were waiting for them. They must have just

gotten there, as they were still holding the forms ICC needed to authorize their visit. *Whew!*

"Mr. Drake. Ms. Nazir."

"Hello again," Leah replied. "I almost didn't recognize you in jeans."

Archer was staring at Angela. *Don't squirm. Don't fidget. Don't look away. Drakes can smell fear, and also eggs.*

"Sorry to keep you guys waiting."

"We only just got here," Leah assured her, but Archer was having none of it.

He took a step closer. "You look great. You're glowing."

"That's a disgusting lie and you know it."

His nose was five inches from her own. "You're *glowing*."

"You're wrong. That's not my glow. It's Leah's! Because, y'know, the pregnancy. Right?" *Not my best off-the-cuff defense.*

"What, because one of you is glowing that means nobody else in the vicinity can? And then there's this clump of"—he reached out and brushed his fingers over the top of her head—"bark?"

"So?"

"In your hair."

"So?"

"And you seem so . . . Hmm, the word's on the tip of my tongue." He rubbed his forehead and gave the impression of someone thinking hard, which was annoying. "What's the opposite of grimly driven and obsessed?"

"Happily comatose?"

"Happy!" He snapped his fingers. "That's what it is. You're glowy and smiley and happy."

"So?"

"You're never happy here. None of us have ever been hap—

Oh. My. God." Archer seized her elbow and hauled her a few feet away from Leah and Jason.

She shook free of his grip. "You know they're only five feet away, right? If your goal is not to be overheard? Because they can hear us."

"You got laid!" he hiss-screamed.

She crossed her arms over her chest. *Wait! Not so much with the defensive body language.* Then she dropped her arms and just sort of stood there. *Oh, yes, very natural. Cripes.* "I did not."

"I can't believe this. It's almost unprecedented. Your sex life—"

"Which I won't be discussing with you today or ever, so put that thought out of your teeny-tiny mind forever."

"—is your business."

"How wise of you to know it."

"But is he *such* an improvement over Klown that you banged him within days of meeting him?"

"Technically it'd be within a month of meeting him. And I didn't bang anyone! In the last month, I mean." There'd been the lawyer who was clerking for Judge Finney last spring, but Angela had made the classic American error of mistaking an accent for a personality. He had Benedict Cumberbatch's voice, Moriarty's conscience, and Mycroft's bedroom skills: chilly and to the point.

Archer pointed to her head. "Your post-sex hair says otherwise."

"My hair isn't post-sex. And even if it was, my hair wouldn't say one damned word to you."

"So does your pleasant expression. And the fact that you're not looking around for a brick to hit me with. You definitely slept with him *ow-ow-ow!*"

She'd reached out and pinched him on the bicep and, when he jerked back and rubbed his arm, she hissed, "I did not!"

"My fault, I shouldn't have used the past tense. You *are* sleeping together."

"We are not sleeping together! In the present tense or otherwise. We are napping together."

"Spare me the lugubrious details, pervert."

"We cleaned up Dad's grave and had a picnic and fell asleep under a willow tree on an island full of dead Burnhams and then had to sprint to his car so we weren't late. Which is why I'm a mess."

"Wow."

"Yep."

"So much to process."

"I'm not asking you to process."

"Well, you're a cute mess," Archer said, smiling. "Listen: I couldn't give a shit who you're banging." When she opened her mouth, he added, "Or nap-banging. I just want you to be with someone who gets how great you are."

"You take that ba— Oh. And?" She braced herself for the punch line. Great at nagging? Great at obsessing over a decade-old murder? Great at hiding the tape measure from Paul? Great at designing a chore board they all loved and hated in equal measure? What?

"And nothing. You like him, he likes you and gets you, that's all I'd ever want for you."

"Oh. Well. Thanks."

"And I'm not going to ask, because I already know the answer."

"You're losing me. Ask what?"

"If you're nap-banging him because you think it'll help Dad's case."

"Oh. Good call on not asking." She gave him a narrow look. "I'd hate to break your nose."

He nodded. "But you know who *will* assume that. Right?"

She sighed. "Mom."

"Auntie Em, yup. She's always so weird around cops, it's almost like . . ." He trailed off.

"There's no need to cut yourself off. I've been having the same thought lately: It's almost like she's afraid they'll discover a deep, dark secret. But what could be worse than Dad's murder?"

"That's nuts and you know it," Archer told her bluntly. "She was home with all you kids that night, the cops checked her alibi first thing."

Relieved, she nodded. "You're right, I remember."

"For whatever reason, she won't like you going out with a cop. So here's some unsolicited advice—"

"Most of what comes out of your mouth is unsolicited. I'll put it at eighty-five, maybe ninety percent."

"Keep it to yourself for a while."

As it happened, she was on board with that advice. Although . . . "Archer, there's really not anything to keep to myself yet. It was one date. I think it was a date. Maybe it was an outdoor luncheon?"

"On an island of dead Burnhams, yeah, you said. Did you guys really clean up Uncle Donald's gravestone?"

She nodded. "It was his idea. We met at the cemetery and he had all the stuff with him. Plus a bottomless backpack of food."

"Hmm. Why *aren't* you sleeping with him? I think you should move past naps."

She had to laugh. "Two minutes ago you were freaking out at the thought of my less-than-vibrant sex life."

"Two minutes ago, I wasn't sure if he was taking advantage. Or if you were. C'mon, Angela, you grew up with cousins and brothers. We've always been wrathfully, irrationally overprotective of our lone lady wolf."

"Don't remind me. Now if you're finished invading my privacy, let's go invade your dad's privacy."

"Sure, why not? You're on a roll," he teased as they came back to Leah and Jason. "Maybe you'll crack the case."

She snorted and was about to retort when Leah held up their paperwork. "We've got a problem."

"What? Are they backed up?" Angela looked around; there was only one other family in the area. "Did you not have enough time to finish the paperwork? Or forget your ID? Not enough money for a flimsy lock to protect documents someone could use to steal your identity?" With all the hoops, it was a bit of a miracle that anyone was able to visit a prisoner.

"It's been finished for ten minutes. The paperwork's not the problem."

She looked from Leah's sober expression to Jason's and back again. "What? Is Uncle Dennis sick? Or unavailable?"

"He's refusing to see us."

"Oh." A setback, but not entirely unexpected. "Well, sometimes—"

"Ever again."

Okay, that was new. "What?" she asked, in case she hadn't heard right.

"He struck all Drakes from his visitors list. We're permanently banned."

"Except we're here on a sanctioned trip," Archer pointed out, but Angela was already shaking her head.

"No, we're not. We're not even here for an open case. If he won't cooperate, we can't flash a badge and press the matter. So . . ."

"Roadblock."

Shit.

THIRTY-SIX

"Sorry, Detective." The correction officer who couldn't process their paperwork looked authoritative and sheepish at the same time, which was a good trick. "You know the rules."

"Yes," Jason acknowledged.

The CO, over six feet tall with the shoulders of a swimmer, had dark skin, mild brown eyes, and a soothing speaking voice. Even though he was full of bad news, Angela could have listened to that voice all day. "And y'know Drake fired his lawyer right after the sentencing and reps himself." He spread his hands. "So it's like a lawyer not authorizing contact with a client—we can't do anything."

Angela opened her mouth, ready to try any number of arguments: But we have new info. But someone recently committed a crime that might be related to the case. But all of this can't be for nothing. But why aren't you doing podcasts with that voice?

"I would never sanction flouting the rules," Jason began,

which sounded promising. Nobody started like that unless they were about to sanction flouting the rules.

"'Flouting'? We don't sanction doing anything to the rules," Archer added.

"But my understanding is that sometimes ICC personnel have been able to work around visitation rules. Under special circumstances."

What could be more special than our special circumstance? Angela wondered. At times it was like they were all stuck in a soap opera.

"Yeah, but . . ." The officer lowered his voice and took a step forward. *What is it with people moving a foot away because they think they won't be overheard? Does no one understand acoustics?* "For this case? C'mon. You know he won't cooperate. You know there's nothing new. So what's the point?" Officer Maller looked at Angela. "No offense."

She *was* offended, as a matter of fact, but couldn't deny Maller had a point. And the fact that his attitude mirrored her mother's was just the frosting on the dog turd they were pretending was a cake.

"I'm not sure what we can . . ." She trailed off. Ten years of this, and it wasn't getting any easier. How could it not be getting even a little easier? *Fight! Think of something. Or get shrill. That doesn't always help, but it's a real stress-reliever.* "What if we . . ." *What? Come up with a last-minute idea no one thinks will work until it does? Why can't real life be like* Law & Order *sometimes?*

"Officer Maller, I think I can help you with your gambling problem," Leah said out of nowhere, startling everyone (but no one more than the CO).

"I'm sorry?"

"Your gambling problem."

"I don't, uh, have that." Maller cleared his throat with an uneasy rumble. "An addiction. To gambling, I mean."

"You're right. It's not a full-blown addiction yet, so there's time. I've got an idea how you can get rid of it. Could I speak to you over here, please?"

Blinking like he was in a windstorm, Maller meekly followed Leah through a door that opened to a small private office off to the side. At the *click* of the door closing, Angela turned and said, "See how she wanted to talk without being overheard so she left the room and went into another room and then closed the door to that other room? That's how you do it."

"It's not easy being in love with a legend," Archer said with a fond smirk, "but somehow, I manage."

"With respect to your fiancée," Jason said, "this is not an episode of *Law & Order*. She's not going to come up with a last-minute fix that will solve our—"

The door opened and Maller stuck his head out, spotted the officer behind the counter, and yelled, "Amy! Process these visitors, please!" Then he disappeared back inside the office.

Jason's rebuttal was succinct. "Huh."

Angela could feel the unbelieving smile cross her face. "This has been a weird day."

"A great, great day," Jason reminded her.

She hadn't dared try to hold his hand again once they were inside ICC. He might be confident that picnicking among the dead with a Drake wouldn't get him in trouble at work, but she didn't want to risk it just yet. *This . . . whatever it is . . . it's new and tender, like a fly larva, vulnerable to any outside forces that, oh jeez, my metaphors are getting worse.*

So though it'd be the nicest thing ever to reach for his hand and hold it while Archer said stupid things that were alternately aggravating and hilarious, she didn't. And she might have been reading too much into it, but from the way Jason was looking at Archer with a thoughtful expression, he might have been pondering the same thing.

Or he could be thinking about the next pair of socks to buy.

The oddest thing of all? Before meeting Detective Chambers, Angela would never have described herself as timid.

The door opened again and Leah came out with Maller on her heels. He looked dazed and pleased. "I heard everything you said. Thank you, Ms. Nazir."

Leah shook his offered hand. "Worth a try, right? At worst, you're only out half an hour of your time."

"Yes, ma'am." Officer Maller looked over their small group. "Let's get you inside, okay, folks?"

And that was that.

THIRTY-SEVEN

Except not really.

"C'mon, Leah, it's not like he's a patient."

"Client," she corrected. "We call them *clients*. Which I know you know, Archer."

"Well, he isn't one. So spill."

"'Spill'? What, you're a tabloid journalist now?"

"Those two things don't actually go together," Jason pointed out.

"Fair enough, Detective." To Archer: "No."

"Spill pleeeeeease?"

"This is not something you can get by using the magic word."

"*Pleeeeeease?*"

"You recall we share a bed, yes? And I can do any number of dreadful things to your unconscious body?"

Archer's eyes went wide. "You probably didn't mean to make that sound hot, but . . ."

Angela groaned. "This conversation actually makes me sorry Leah was able to work her magic on CO Maller."

"Excellent," Jason replied. "I thought I was the only one having regrets."

They were back in the large visitation room that always felt claustrophobic. And now that they were all trapped with an aroused Archer, it felt even smaller. Though it was nice to have most of the place to themselves. There was only one other family in there with them, likely because these weren't standard visiting hours. Visitor etiquette involved pretending that though you could see and hear the other people, they weren't really there.

Like we're not really here.

There were a number of reasons a family would be allowed contact visitation (the most desirable, obviously, though there was also video visitation or noncontact visitation). If someone was moving, or dying. A new trial, or the cancellation of same. Or when your cousin's fiancée figured out a CO's deep, dark secret.

Angela reached out and tapped Jason's shoulder to get his attention, which came with the added benefit of touching him. "How do you want to do this? Tell him what happened to his brother's grave and see if—"

"I would think if we— Sorry to cut you off. You were saying?"

"No, no, you go—I mean, it's your case. Well, it's not, actually, but you're the one with—"

"I think the best way— Sorry."

"No, no. Please. Go ahead."

"Jesus Christ." Archer groaned. "This is by far the worst moment of the entire trip. No contest. It's not even close. If this was a race, you two lovingly interrupting each other and then sweetly apologizing for lovingly interrupting each other would be so far ahead in the Worst Part of the Trip race, it would—"

"What did you do?"

Startled, they all looked up. Dennis Drake, who last week had seemed far younger than sixty-three, now looked a hale and hearty ninety. He had a crop of beard stubble; his bright yellow jumpsuit seemed muted and tired.

"Uncle D—"

"Don't call me that! Stop pretending this is about family!" he roared. COs were running toward him and the other family was shrinking back from the shrieking demon in yellow. Angela felt like shrinking back herself. Even his hair seemed outraged, standing stiffly in a prison buzz cut.

"I can't see you! I cannot make it any fucking clearer and you *still* won't listen!"

"Mr. Drake, step off." Angela realized that Jason had moved in front of her and that Archer had grabbed Leah's elbow and yanked her behind him. *"Now."*

"Let me *go!"* he screamed. "Drop it, all of you, drop it and let me go! *Don't."* He shook off the first CO and Angela was sorry to see it was Maller. *Oh, hell, he might not have gotten in trouble for letting us in before, but now . . .*

"You nosy bitch." *Is he talking to me? He's never said anything so awful. Yes, he sure is. My uncle has qualified my efforts to help him as the actions of a nosy bitch. A lot of firsts this month.*

"Please," was all she could manage. Could that thin, thready voice be hers? And please *what?* Please stop? Please be nice? Please go back in time and don't kill your brother?

She didn't know.

"If you don't stop." He cut himself off, making a visible effort to get control. But the rest of it came out through his teeth. "I will fucking stab somebody and get sent to solitary, do you understand?"

"Dad!" From Archer, who had been so shocked his vocal cords had temporarily locked. Which was shocked indeed. *Jacky won't believe it when I tell him. Also I will never tell any of this to anyone.* "You ungrateful piece of shit!"

Dennis had no eyes for his son, only for her. "Are you listening, Angela? Because you *never have.* I will kill someone to stay in solitary if you don't back off. Then it won't matter who pulls what strings. It won't matter how much more of your life you've pissed away, you won't be able to see— *Funnnkkk!*" That last was muffled, as three COs had piled on and Dennis was now howling into the floor.

It was quiet. No, it wasn't. The COs were talking to each other; the horrified other family were backed in the corner, whispering; and Archer was saying something—of course. Oh, and Jason's lips were moving. And his face was pointed at her. So he was probably talking to her. Might be time to tune back in.

"—all right?"

"Fine. I'm fine." Nothing but the truth. She'd been shouted at before. By experts.

"I take it back," Archer managed. "*That* was the worst part of the trip. But the lovey-dovey stuff was right up there. So, y'know, just to keep that in perspective."

Angela made a sound that was probably a laugh, if crows could laugh. That's what Archer was going for and she wanted to oblige and also, what was wrong with her legs? They were slacking off, that's what. They were trying to take a break, but no time for that. She had stuff to do. Right? Research? Or something? Maybe she'd sit down. Yes. Oh, that was much better. She could use a break. And she wasn't the only one. They should all sit down. Right?

"Angela?"

"I'm just fine. How are you?"

"Easy," Jason was saying to her temple. She could feel his arms around her and it should have been wonderful. "I've got you. It's all right. Let's get you off your feet."

"I'm not off my feet?" That was problematic. "Yes, let's get me off them. Leah? You okay?"

Cool fingers were on her wrist. "I'm fine, Angela."

"Why are you doing that?"

"I'm worried you might faint."

"*You* might faint." Lame. Best she could do. Plus it was a lie. Leah would never keel over because someone yelled at her. She'd fought off a murderer, and exposed lots of others. Clients who didn't like what she told them sometimes tried to attack her. So this was nothing by comparison. Nothing.

The more she thought about it, the more the differences between them were glaring. Leah Nazir wouldn't be a trembling wreck if someone yelled at her in a Visitation Room. She wouldn't feel like a wonderful picnic lunch was going to put in an abrupt reappearance. She—

"Oh, hell," Angela managed, somehow making it to the garbage can in time.

THIRTY-EIGHT

SEPTEMBER 1949

CAMPDEN, ENGLAND

On Sunday, Augusta Harrison read about her own murder in the paper.

It must be a joke, was her first shocked thought. *Like those fake newspapers you can buy where the headline proclaims you King of the Universe. Or perhaps it's someone with the same name as me.*

As it turned out, it wasn't a joke and it wasn't a case of mistaken identity. A year after she'd moved to Paris, then London, a man named John Perry found a pile of her bloody clothes in the living room of an abandoned house, and promptly contacted the authorities.

The police went looking for her and, of course, she could not be found. Augusta had only lived in Campden for a few months before moving on; her mother used to claim she had Gypsy blood. She hadn't formed any real ties and did not notify anyone of her departure. She had gone to Paris—delightful, but ultimately too expensive—and then London, settling into a rented townhouse in the West End a few days past. Only half of her belongings had been unpacked when she read about her murder.

The clothes Perry had found weren't just bloody; they had been repeatedly slashed with the kind of knife found in Mr. Perry's kitchen. When Mr. Perry's lawyer pointed out it was the kind of knife found in nearly *every* kitchen in England, the jury had not been swayed.

Worse still, Mr. Perry had been convicted of assault three years earlier at age nineteen (for which he served twenty-seven months), and had an IQ of seventy-eight. Once the bobbies had finished with him—which took days—he implicated not only himself but his mother and brother. The entire family had been convicted and would hang in a matter of days.

She sent a telegram to the Gloucestershire police.

Nothing.

She packed, bought a train ticket, went back to Campden, a town she had ardently hoped never to see again. Walked into the constable's station. Announced herself.

Nothing.

Found Mr. Perry's lawyer, who was engaged in dying from sepsis after his appendix burst and was, understandably, distracted.

She went back to the police and explained again. And as she perhaps should have foreseen, rather than admitting a mistake had been made, they decided that, somehow, the mistake was hers.

Because—and was it not absurd that this would cost a man and his family their lives?—she wasn't like other girls. She had a history. She didn't like staying in one spot very long, that was one thing. The thought of binding herself to a man and a house and his children for decades was horrifying, that was another. And she liked to drink. And she liked the *idea* of men, and the things an open-minded couple could do in a bedroom with the blinds drawn. Only the daily domestic details smacked of tedium.

Like this: She was small and red-haired and fair-skinned and dark-eyed and pretty and looked sweet, but wasn't. Men wanted to take care of her, and were piqued when they discovered she neither wanted nor needed them. She liked to fuck and she liked her freedom, not always in that order.

Much of the time, this worked well for her. But sometimes those things combined in a most disagreeable way and she had to leave town earlier than she planned. But there were always new places and new men, and if she wasn't hurting anyone, what was the harm?

She tried to explain this to her stone-faced audience, men who didn't understand why a woman would want to be in charge of her own life, men who found the idea as repellant as it was incomprehensible.

But how to explain her bloody clothes?

"I have no idea! Before I moved away I donated a number of items to the church. I did the same in Paris. Anyone could have picked them up, and they could have blood on them for any number of reasons."

But what were the odds of *her* clothes turning up soaked with blood?

"A good way to determine that the blood isn't mine would be to note that *I'm still alive*."

That was another thing. Her temper.

At least one suggested that she wasn't who she said she was. "You don't look like an Augusta," one of them said, eyeing her riotous red curls and freckles. "You look like a Sally. Or a Bridget."

It was all she could do not to fly at him and tear his face with her fingernails.

When, incredibly, it appeared the execution was going forward, she started talking to the press. "The press" in town consisted of an older gentleman in his forties, who was much more interested in her legs than the pursuit of justice. He, too, seemed to think the entire affair was a darkly hilarious misunderstanding, one it would be too much trouble to correct.

"But I'm here. I'm *right here*, I'm not dead. They didn't kill me."

A shrug. "Well, they killed someone."

"How does that follow? As I told the police, that blood could be on the clothes for any number of reasons. And, once again—I do hate to belabor the point—I am not dead!"

"Perry has a violent history, he confessed, he's too stupid to have done it alone, which means his family helped, that's all."

That was not *all*. "So you won't report this. You won't write about it." Cajoling hadn't worked. Getting angry hadn't worked. Perhaps shaming would work. "You won't lift a finger to save an innocent man? To expose a shoddy investigation? You won't take the trouble?"

"Oh, that's not my place."

She blinked. "Not your— It *is* your place. It's your essential function, what you are paid by Gloucestershire County to do."

"I'm not paid to make enemies of the constabulary. And I'll take their word over that of a drifter."

"Oh, I'm a drifter now? Is that right? Because during the trial, you wrote that I was a 'poor beloved local girl, brutally murdered by a monster who will face God's judgment thanks to the tireless efforts of our heroic Campden constabulary.' 'Brutally murdered' is redundant, by the way."

He had been fool enough to be complimented when she quoted his words back at him, but had no use for her editorial opinion, if the ugly flush spreading from his eyebrows to his chin was any indication. "Perhaps you've made it all up, then."

She clenched her teeth so her jaw wouldn't drop. She had been doing that with such frequency, she had a constant head-ache starting about an hour after she woke up until, after fretting in her bed for hours, she finally fell into an exhausted asleep.

"Made it up? To what end? What possible reason would I have to leave my life in London to return to this wretched town and pretend to be a murdered woman?" She had no chance of swaying him to her point of view, which she should have seen earlier, and was done holding back. "Why would I—or any sane person—do something so daft? Please. Enlighten me. Please, dazzle me with your journalist acumen. I'm sure I will be fascinated instead of repulsed."

"Girls like you," he said, gaze flicking again from her face to her chest and back up, "like attention."

"Men like you," she said, standing, "don't know the first thing about girls like me. And your office reeks of grease. You might try eating something besides chips. You'll lose weight and your breath won't smell as bad. Regrettably, you'll still be bald."

Then it was execution week: John tomorrow, his mother Wednesday, his brother Thursday. They anticipated her plan to disrupt the proceedings

(disrupt? I'll torch the building if I have to, they'll see a firestorm)

by closing the executions to the public, and forbidding her access to anyone in the station.

She packed. Again. She couldn't save them, and was afraid to stay. Her resolution to tell the truth coupled with her waspish tongue had made her more enemies than usual; this town was no place to linger. She genuinely feared a late-night visit from any number of disgruntled men. Especially since she was already "dead." Whatever they did to her, there wouldn't be a trial.

The worst part for her (the worst part for the Perrys was entirely different) was that unpleasant things like this had happened to her before. She couldn't remember her earlier lives, exactly, except in dreams that faded the longer she was awake. All she knew was she had betrayed the innocent and they always paid for her lies, while she never did. Her first memory was helping her mother making her third birthday cake. Her second was the strong sense that she must always take responsibility for all that she said and did. She made it a point never to lie, something that frequently brought her trouble, and never wavered from that conviction. But a clear conscience was worth the trouble, and she had thought that this time, this life, she had it licked.

I did the right thing, she told her diary. She had been keeping one since she was eight, but wouldn't for much longer. What was the point of being careful, of never lying, of being sure of all sides before picking one?

Later, when she was writing it all down, she laid it out, almost as if someone who wasn't her would be reading it:

From the moment I read about my murder, I did the right thing. How can it count for nothing? How can they all be executed?

I don't understand it.

I'll never understand it.

THIRTY-NINE

Archer and Leah had the house to themselves when they got back from the disastrous ICC visit. "Probably to ourselves," he amended. "No telling where Auntie Em is. Her room. The basement. Dante's Vestibule of Hell, which we also call the basement . . ."

"It's so quiet," Leah marveled. "Except for you talking." She was surprised to find it made her uneasy. A Drake throng was many things, but dull wasn't one of them.

"Contrary to what it might look like, they've all got lives outside of my dad's case. Oh! Say! Speaking of ungrateful assholes, I'm so sorry you had to witness that—that whatever-it-was today."

She took his hand and squeezed as they walked through the empty kitchen and down the hall to the bedroom. "Hardly your fault. All families fight." She paused. "I'm pretty sure. According to my clients, anyway."

He snorted. "That was a little more than a fight."

"Granted, but . . . Oh, hell, I'm talking through my ass."

"In your defense, it's a wonderful ass."

"Insatiable idiot," she said fondly. "You know this is all new territory for me."

"My uncle threatening to murder someone just to get out of our semiannual visits is new territory for everyone."

Leah had to smile. "Fair enough. And poor Angela."

That was something she hadn't counted on: being fond of Archer's cousin, who had held his lack of lives over his head like it was a shameful thing, and didn't get around to apologizing for any of it until a few months ago. Who, it must be said, was controlling and, it must also be said, shrill, and stubborn, and volatile.

But those words described every single Drake in existence, and Leah had more than a few of those qualities herself. Angela, at least, was *trying*. And she never quit. Even when her uncle was being wrestled to the ground by a flurry of corrections officers and screaming about how much he loathed her visits, she stood her ground.

Which was more than could be said for the "adults"—the one who landed them in a ten-year mess, and the one who hid from that same ten-year mess—Dennis and Emma Drake.

It came down to roles, Leah decided. Self-assigned and otherwise. If Jack and Paul and Angela's mother was a ghost, Angela was everyone's big sister. Even Archer's. Even hers.

"You know what's odd?"

"Knowing you, darling, it could be anything."

"Touché. There's something poking at my brain and I don't know why," he admitted. "I was a little uneasy after our first visit, but I figured that was because I hadn't seen Dad in years. But it's worse now. I can't shake the feeling that whatever-it-is, it's right in front of us. We're just so used to seeing it, we're not noticing it. Or something. Hell. I don't know."

Leah had paused at the door to their shared bedroom and Archer absently reached out and rubbed her shoulders. A sucker for any kind of massage—she was a bit touch-starved, legacy of her odd upbringing and odder line of work—she let her head fall back and moaned, a sound that always elicited a Pavlovian response in her fiancé. But who wouldn't make appreciative noises beneath Archer's hands? The man was so skilled, he could have been a masseuse to the gods.

"What, Leah? Why'd you stop?"

"Just thinking ahhhhhh right there . . . mmmmmm . . . wondering when we should go back home. There doesn't ummmmmm seem to be ahhhhh much more we cannnnnnnmmmm . . ."

"Do you mind if we stay 'til Friday? Two weeks chock full o'Drakes is more than enough to ask of anyone, never mind the mother of my mother-in-law."

She groaned and it wasn't at all Pavlovian, she sounded like a sleepy bear trapped in a well. "Argh, *gah*, don't put it like that." She shrugged so his hands dropped away. "Arrgghh."

"Sorry." Archer kissed the tender spot just behind her ear. "But y'know, if you set aside the horror and the years of psychological damage and the unprecedented new territory we're stumbling through, it's kind of funny."

"No."

"A teeny-weeny bit funny."

"Not really, no." She opened the door, stepped inside, then stopped short. The bed was neatly made and on her pillow was a small blue dessert plate, and resting atop the plate was a cream puff swan.

Archer's eyes went big. "Whoa. He never makes those! He says swans are mean* and *pâte à choux* is overrated.† How come you rate so high? And yes, that's petty jealousy you hear in my tone."

"I have no idea," she lied.

Archer was cautiously approaching it as if it was a real swan that would fly away if he startled it. "Leah, I'm not sure you understand the significance here."

"Why don't you try patronizing me? That's bound to help me figure it out."

"This is the Holy Grail of pastry! You know how many of those tiny, delicious-yet-mean swan puffs he's made me in twenty-some years?"

"Archer, Jack's only been alive for—"

"Two! You're here a week and you already have one? The world just doesn't make sense anymore!"

"So *this* would be the worst part of the trip, then?"

"Yes! We have a new winner. Dammit."

She walked to her side of the bed and studied it: light golden brown with pastry cream nestled beneath the wings and a beautifully arched neck. And best of all . . .

She picked up the plate and sniffed her swan, then showed it to Archer. "It's not coffee flavored."

"Which is making you smile because . . . ?"

---

*True.
†False.

"Because Jack's trying new things. That's all. And if you stop pouting, I'll share it with you."

"Okay. You should eat the head first—chomp!" Archer mimed savagely decapitating a bird shaped from pastry. "It's deeply satisfying."

"You can devour the head."

"I love you so much right now."

"As you should."

FORTY

Angela Drake was kissing him and he had no idea why.

At her subdued request, he had driven her to his town-house on Canal Street; neither of them had much to say on the way over. This made a forty-minute drive seem a lot longer than it was. *Angela Drake wants to come home with me. I should be as happy as I am nervous. But I'm more confused than anything else.*

The silence was broken when they pulled up to the low three-story brick building (which was only low in contrast to the skyscrapers in the distance). "This is nice."

"It's not home, but it's much," he replied, hoping for a smile. Alas. Thwarted hope. *Sorry, Olivia Goldsmith. Your wit was not up to the task. Although it might have been my delivery.*

He parked in his spot, got out, pulled the backpack full of leftovers and dirty dishes from the back seat, and walked her across the street and up the front walk.

The weight of the pack felt like a reproach. *So you scrubbed a gravestone and indulged in roast beef sandwiches and Caprese salad. You didn't think it would be that easy, did you? That everything would be fixed—for both of you—and you would date and fall the rest of the way in love and live happily ever after?*

No. Not for one moment. He had never fooled himself that anything about Angela Drake would be easy. But he wasn't in it for easy, and it had been a wonderful day. Not just a wonderful day with Angela, a wonderful day in his life.

Up to a point.

And though he was furious with Inmate #26166, he thought his time was better spent trying to help Angela calm down after she threw up. He had a hunch that her male relatives would attend to that other matter, regardless.

When they got inside he saw her looking around appreciatively and decided to get a crucial detail out of the way. "I inherited this," he explained. "My grandmother left it to my brother and me. By the time she passed away, it was just me."

"Okay." She was examining the books in the shelves to the left of the fireplace. "Gorey fan, hmm?"

"Yes. Also Wilkin, Hiaasen, McNair, Kinney, Iggulden, Miller, Gaiman, and Branch."

"Eclectic," she murmured, examining Susan Branch's homey, watercolor-illustrated *Vineyard Seasons* shelved beside Frank Miller's *Sin City*.

"Yes. And, again, I inherited this place. I wanted to be up front about it."

She gave him an odd look, and he was amazed at how quickly he'd blown it: within twenty seconds of putting his key in the lock. A new record.

"The reason I'm telling you this—"

"Twice." She softened that with a gentle, "You don't have to explain."

"—is because the last woman I went out with used real-estate listings to select romantic partners."

That got her attention, and even better, the odd expression morphed to interest. "I guess that's my cue to say 'no way' but . . . y'know. Chicago real estate."

"Remarkably, that is exactly how she explained it to me," he replied. "Once I realized why she asked me out, I told her I inherited this place. I didn't earn it. Didn't buy it. I'm a cop. I've always been a cop." *I'm not rich*, in other words.

"She dumped you."

"Unfortunately not. She told me that inheriting it wasn't a deal breaker, because 'no matter how you got it, it's still a terrific piece of real estate, we should go out some more.' Quote unquote. So I ended up dump—uh, breaking it off."

She brought up a hand to cover her grin. "Jeez. I'm sorry. That's awful."

"That's Chicago," he deadpanned, because Richard Gere in *Chicago* had been a tap-dancing demigod. He loathed all musicals save that one.

He led her through the short hallway and the two steps down into the sunken living room. His furniture consisted primarily of classic dark wood and muted colors: a tan love seat, a deep brown couch, dark patterned throw rugs, lots more bookshelves. The reddish-brown hardwood floors glowed. He had an unnatural fondness for waxing them: It was tedious and he could shut off his brain while sinking into the task. It was much like meditating.

"Something to drink?"

"Please."

"White wine? Red? Water? Tea?"

"Water is fine."

She followed him into the kitchen, which was small and sleek with dark wooden cupboards and black appliances, and took a seat at the butcher's block.

"Angela, you don't have to eschew wine because I can't drink with my medication."

"I don't think I was 'eschewing' anything. And you *can*, but . . . you probably shouldn't."

He laughed. "Excellent point. But please, have whatever you like, truly."

"Water really is fine, sparkling if you have it."

"Oh, I've always got some of that on hand. I have an unfortunate addiction to chocolate egg creams."*

"I've got no idea what those are."

"Too bad, because I am sworn to guard the family recipe—also from my grandmother—for life. But they're wonderful, trust me." He pulled out a small bottle of Perrier, made use of the ice dispenser in his fridge, and poured her a cold glass. She drained it right away—stress was a notorious dehydrator—and he promptly refilled it.

"So." He paused. He waited for his brain to spit out the right thing to say, something that would fix everything and make her smile and reassure her that her uncle might not give a shit, but she was surrounded by people who cared about her. *Think of something. Anything. An affirmation of life. A knock-knock joke. Something.*

---

*Join the club, pal.

Drawing a blank here, his brain replied. *Sorry, old friend.*

He cleared his throat. "So. About what—"

But she was already shaking her head. "Nope."

He took the cue and backed off. "As you like." But now what?

Angela, thank God, seemed to know. Of the two of them, she was definitely the least jittery. And the most dehydrated. She drank half her second glass, got off of the stool, and walked to the fridge, where he'd been stuck as he begged his brain to cooperate.

"Tell me to stop," she said, "and I will."

Then she kissed him.

FORTY-ONE

They'd staggered up the stairs and careened down the hallway—he bounced off a wall at least twice—and finally *finally* made it to his bedroom. Because life occasionally wasn't shitty, he'd changed the sheets the morning before and was caught up on his dry cleaning.

"Oh, my God," she panted, hands busy at his belt. "Immaculate fireplace. Gorgeous kitchen. A zillion cookbooks. More bookshelves. Mint green walls in your bedroom. Tasteful curtains and thick cream carpet. Were you Chuck Williams* in a previous life?"

"No." Jesus. Her hands. She was divesting him of clothing like a focused, sexy octopus. His one contribution was to nearly tear her sweater getting it off her; he wanted her so badly his hands

---

*The founder of Williams-Sonoma!

were shaking. A significant part of his brain had decided this was a fever dream. It couldn't actually be happening. *Ergo* it wasn't.

She gave him a gentle shove and his back hit the bed as she shimmied out of her black pants and made short work of her coral-colored bra and panties. Her hair was a rumpled cloud of reddish-blond waves and her breasts were small and sweet and plum-sized. He was surprised to see she was short-waisted; her long legs distracted from that, and she was speckled with freckles down her neck and across her chest.

"You are *really* beautiful," he managed, perhaps the most inadequate statement in the history of language.

"You're pretty cute, too." She kicked her clothes away, then climbed on the bed, crawled over him, bent down to kiss him

(God her mouth, I love her mouth)

then pulled back. "Is this okay?"

Was this okay? The woman he had dated eighteen months ago had taken his occasional impotence as a personal challenge, so sex with her was a bit like being caught in a rowing machine.

This? This was hot and sweet and fumbling and wonderful. Was this okay? Was he a carbon-based life-form? Would the Cubs win the World Series again? Did Angela have a delightful constellation of freckles he wanted to count and map?

"I—I'm hard-pressed to think of anything more okay."

"Hard-pressed," she teased, and her hand was on his stomach and then sliding down, and then her fingers curled around his cock, the part of him that currently had no idea what dysthymia was. "Oh, my. Should have guessed. I mean, you're tall. And you've got these wonderful big hands." She leaned down to kiss him again and her grip tightened at exactly the right time and exactly the right pressure, and he gasped into the kiss.

"What do you want?" he managed, his hands coming up to settle at her waist. "Tell me. I want to touch you, tell me what you want."

"Beard burn."

He blinked up at her and saw she was trying—unsuccessfully—to hide her grin. The thought that this was a lurid fantasy was getting harder to shake. "Er, what?"

"It's out there, right? But last week, when you showed up at the house all rumpled and stubbled, it really, um, did something. For me."

She wanted stubble? He would oblige and grow stubble. He would grow anything she wanted. She could have his beard stubble, she could have the breath in his lungs, the blood in his heart. He felt his jaw. "Unfortunately, I shaved for our da—for our tombstone cleaning."

"Just do the best you can."

So he tightened his grip and rolled her over until he was on top, and rubbed his cheek against her neck and the tops of her breasts while she giggled and squirmed beneath him.

"I'm gonna have beard burn in the most interesting places."

"This is already the oddest and most wonderful sexual encounter of my life."

"Oh, please. You ain't seen nothin'."

She was right. Minutes later—seconds? hours? his sense of time had vanished along with his underwear—he was inside her slick heat, one hand gripping the headboard, the other fisted (carefully!) in her hair. He was using the headboard to hold himself back as well as give himself some brace. He was afraid if he let loose he might shove her through the wall.

"Jason." She groaned, her long legs coming up and tightening around him with marvelous strength. "That's—ah—*Jeeeeeezus* that's—more."

"*Really?*" *Please don't let that be an auditory hallucination.*

"Yeah, c'mon, I won't break. Fuck me. Harder. You can—oh *fuck*, that's good, that's perfect, please don't stop—"

(oh, thank God, I'm not sure I could)

"Just—let me—I need to—almost—" He could feel her legs loosening their grip around his waist as she reached down between them, between her legs, and he took the hand out of her hair and caught her wrist.

"Show me. What you need. Put my fingers where you want them. Please, I have to touch you."

So she did and he brushed his thumb around and over the slippery button.

"Easy-easy, light and fast, that's nnnnnnggggggggg oh more please more like that please that's just right ah . . . ah . . ." And then she was arching beneath him and everything got almost impossibly tighter and hotter and at the peak of her pleasure he buried his face in her neck and counted back from one thousand by sevens

(1,000, 993, 986, 979, don't come don't come 972, 965, 958 not yet 951)

and he took his hand away, mindful of oversensitivity, and then she shivered in his arms and was still.

"Oh, God, Jason, that was so—you." She was looking up at him, wide-eyed. "You didn't . . . ?"

He stroked his thumb across her lower lip and she sucked at it, then kissed the tip as he pulled his hand away and reached down between her legs. "Now," he breathed against her mouth. "Again."

And started to move.

FORTY-TWO

Angela, being Angela, broke the afterglow with, "Don't think this was about today. I've been wanting this for a while."

"I didn't think it was a reflex," he said mildly. "Or the sexual equivalent of a sneeze."

They were back in the kitchen. She'd cleaned up a bit in the bathroom and gotten dressed; he'd cleaned up as well, and slipped into a pair of boxer-briefs. He'd poured her another glass of water and helped himself to a glass of milk.

"I was happy to spend the day with you. I was happy to bring you to my home. I was happy with the kissing and very, very, very happy with all that followed. I would have been happy if you'd spent the night. But we could have stopped at the napping and it would have been a day worth getting out of bed for."

She smiled, knowing that was no small thing to someone who wrestled with dysthymia. Then remembered what she was about to do and the smile dropped right off, poof, like it had never been there. "Happy. Right. The thing is, I *don't* bring happiness."

"My penis begs to differ." And, of course, that made her snort.

"Funny. Not in any large measure," she clarified. "That's what I meant. Or to put it another way: I'm no good for you, Chambers. I don't think we should see each other after this." She paused, adding so there would be no misunderstanding, "I won't see you again after tonight."

He had been setting the glass down on the counter and she heard the glass rattle when he started in surprise. He turned at once and replied, "Your uncle is a fool."

"It's not about him."

"No?"

"No." Probably. It was likely a Drake thing, but not necessarily a Dennis Drake thing. "No, it's about me. And the thing about me, Jason, is that I always screw it up and the innocents always pay for it. You can't get caught up in that, I won't let you drown in that whirlpool."

"Angela . . ."

"You know the worst of it? Even when I do *everything* right, call the cops, tell the truth, and do it over and over, make people hear me, fight for the ones in trouble, the innocent still get stuck with that bill. I haven't been able to fix it in four lifetimes."

He held up a hand before she could continue. "But that's what life is, Angela. It'll never be perfect. You'll never do everything right—that's not a condemnation, it just *is*. You act as though people don't have regrets, that they don't remember the heinous things they've done, that it doesn't tear them up. Of course it does. In that, you and I are no different from anyone else. But you can't hide from it, Angela. And you know it."

A lovely speech. And utter bullshit. Still, he was worth the effort. He was worth every effort. She couldn't be with him, but perhaps she could make him see. *Shouldn't have had sex with him. But I was weak. I wanted one small part of him, one lovely memory to carry into my next life. Whatever the fuck it'll be.*

"I was never an Insighter before," she began. "The difference— you wouldn't believe it. Suddenly I could see it all so clearly, like I was looking through sparkling clean glass: every wrong move, every lie, every selfish act of preservation. It was like watching an expert put a big, complicated puzzle together right in front of me: Everything fell into place while I watched. So. So I thought—"

"You thought this was the one you got right. That this time, you'd somehow be flawless while simultaneously exonerating all your past selves."

"Yes, but in my head it didn't sound quite so silly."

He smiled a little and a sad, horrid thought struck her: *This is the last time I'll see his dimple.* "It *is* silly, but not for the reason you think."

"Do tell." She could hear the chill in her voice and told herself to ease up. *You're banging him and dumping him; you can at least listen before you leave his delightfully appointed kitchen. The gal who dated via the real-estate section might have been onto something.*

"It was silly because it's the way a child thinks," he said, and somehow it didn't come out at all patronizing. "The way a child whose father was violently murdered thinks. 'I'll figure it all out and I'll fix everything and everyone will be happy.' You are intelligent and gorgeous and determined and funny and sweet, but a small part of you is still the fatherless fourth-grader who got the worst news in the world and wasn't allowed to mourn because she had to take over everything."

Well.

Your father's dead. Your uncle murdered your—

He wasn't wrong.

"You're wrong," she insisted, because fuck him. "I chose. I'm still choosing. It's why we won't be seeing each other again. If we get a case update, please don't follow up with me." That part was hardest. She almost choked on the words. The first thing she liked about Jason (after his socks) was that he immediately included her, kept her updated, always returned her calls, and she never had to chase him. She never had to follow him to a Walgreens and yell at him while he bought his second lunch (chocolate ice cream and Coke). All that was a dim nightmare by comparison.

And here she was a month later, spitting on all of it.

Klown, if you hadn't been so awful, I might not have fallen for Jason Chambers. This is mostly your fault.

No, not really.

"Do you know how my brother died?"

She shook her head. This, too, was shameful; she couldn't be bothered to get her head out of the files long enough to ask, though she knew it must have been bad.

"We were kids, and he caught me with drugs. Again. And when I refused to go back to rehab, he decided to show me how destructive it was, what it was doing to our family, so he smoked it right in front of me. Which was how we found out the cook was shit. His heart stopped while he was still holding the pipe."

It was like the muscles in her face and throat had locked; she couldn't say anything, couldn't swallow the sudden blockage in her throat. After a long moment, she managed, "I'm sorry."

"My parents did their best, but Pat's death was shattering. They both fell off the wagon—I hail from a long and distinguished line of substance abusers—and were killed when Dad mistook an oak tree for the turnoff. My grandmother took care of me while I finished high school. And then she . . ." He gestured to his beautiful home.

"I'm sorry." Stupid, worthless phrase. How was it that you could use the exact same phrase for when you spilled juice?

"I live with it every day. As you live with your burdens. But, Angela: This life is so, so hard. There's no guarantee the next one will be any easier, no matter what the Insighters or the priests or the therapists promise. Why not grab any bit of happiness you can? You're entitled to love. And on my good days, I think I might be, too."

"You *are*," she said thickly. "Jeez. Of course you are. Teenagers are dumb, right? Crack-addicted ones especially. They make stupid decisions and it's a miracle any of us lived through it. It wasn't your— I know if you could do it over again, you wouldn't buy the drugs."

"But you've got it wrong, Angela. Again." He said this to her in a gentle tone devoid of the smallest bit of pity for himself or condemnation for her. "I'd buy them and take them myself. With no hesitation. Because my brother was the one who deserved the fulfilling life with the beautiful home and the wonderful girlfriend and the challenging work. Not me. Never me." He gestured to his beautiful home. "I am living a stolen life, my brother's life. None of this should be mine. Most days, I know it, I believe it. Days like today? I wonder."

"No-no-no. I'm leaving for my own reasons, it's not a punishment I'm handing down to you because you were bad. My decision has nothing to do with your brother. We're both reading too much into this, because we're not breaking up. We weren't even dating, really."

"I suppose not," he said quietly. "Just hoping to. Or perhaps that was one-sided."

"No," she whispered. She cleared her throat and forced her voice to rise. "No, it wasn't, but it's just as well that our whatever-it-is ends now. Thank you for a lovely day, which got weird and unpleasant and then briefly lovely, and then I wrecked it again and where the hell are my shoes?"

He went to the living room and brought them to her without a word. Said nothing while she slipped them on, found her purse and slung it over one shoulder, made sure she had her phone. He just looked at her with that intense blue-eyed stare. Looked at her while he was standing there all brazenly gorgeous and lightly tanned and flat-stomached and big-dicked and a revelation in bed, that hour between the sheets had been the best sex of her life and if she kept thinking about it she'd go and do something *really* stupid like strip and spend the night and then possibly linger in the morning and maybe stay forever.

"I don't need a ride," she said before he could offer. If he was going to offer. "I'd like to— I'm going to take a cab."

He nodded.

"Okay." *It was nice meeting you? Thanks for all your hard work? Sorry about my fucked-up family life? Sorry about yours? You have a lovely home and no matter what anyone says, you deserve a nice life?*

Nope. None of it would work, and almost all of it would make things worse. "See ya." *Really? That's the platitude you went with?*

"One thing I don't understand."

She turned back, almost relieved. It wasn't over until she crossed the threshold.

"You indicated you've wanted me for a while."

"Yes." *The minute I saw the socks. And the dimple.*

"But not for a relationship."

"Right."

"And decided to have me regardless."

She cringed internally. "Yes."

"Despite knowing that you would make your feelings plain when we were finished."

"Yes."

"Cold."

"Warned you."

She left before he could see her tears. He didn't demand she stay. Or call after her to come back. Or rush dramatically after her.

It wasn't a movie. It was real life. Which was awful. And that was the point. Both their points.

FORTY-THREE

"Archer."

"Nnnnnn."

"Archer."

"Pigeon ate my burger."

"Archer!" This last was hissed right into his ear, which was a tactical error as Archer mistook her for a bug and swiped at her hard enough to make her ears throb.

"Friggin' mosquitos . . . nuh?" He rubbed his eyes hard enough to make her own water with sympathy. "Cuz, whassup?"

"I'm sorry," she whispered, already regretting the insane impulse that led her here. Fortunately, Leah was still deeply asleep. Loudly, deeply asleep. *My God. She sounds like a blender wrapped in a towel trying to blend a brick.*

"F'r what? Y'okay?" He was trying to prop himself up on his elbows, staring at her in the low light from the partially open bedroom doorway.

"I'm fine." Lie. "I'm just really sorry for all those times I was mean to you and said being mind-blind was like being developmentally disabled and that not remembering your past lives was like flunking a standard IQ test."

He gawped at her and rubbed his eyes again.

She rushed on. "I know we talked all that out before you brought Leah to visit, but I'm not just apologizing for that. I'm apologizing for waiting so long to apologize."

"If this isn't some bizarre dream I'm going to fart on your face."

By now she was kneeling beside the bed. "It's because of Leah that I was so mean. Wait, I said that wrong—it wasn't Leah's fault I was so horrible. I was horrible because I felt inadequate beside her and took it out on you."

"I will fart. On your face."

"Does that make sense? How it's about Leah but not really?"

"Hell *no* it doesn't make sense."

"Listen, this all goes back to our childhood and I know that's a cliché and maybe not worth waking you up for—"

"You might be onto something."

"But I have to explain why I was such a miserable, hateful bitch before— Wait a sec, was there a pastry swan on that plate?" She hadn't noticed the telltale empty dessert plate on the nightstand before, but now her eyes had adjusted well enough to see the crumbs.

"Yeah, there was, and it was delicious, and you can have the crumbs *after* you go away and let me go back to sleep." He fussed with the blankets and glared at her. Beside him, Leah murmured something, then went back to gargling gravel or whatever the hell she was doing, my God, how did he ever get a wink of sleep?

"Jack made that for her?" *How does she rate?* she thought but didn't say. Nothing against Leah, but the swans were special.

"I think your little brother is in love with my fiancée, which I assumed would be the most unsettling thought I'd have tonight."

"I'm almost done. Please be patient with me just a bit longer." She shook his shoulder a little for emphasis. "You know I'm a fan of hers. Lots of people are, the woman has groupies, for God's sake."

Archer nodded in the semidarkness. "You should see some of the stuff they send her. She has a fluoroscope at work."

"That's . . . sad, actually, but it doesn't surprise me. And when I found out I was an Insighter, I just knew I was going to be able to fix everything for everybody. That's what I told myself. So I pushed it and practiced my gift on everyone who would stand still and some people who wouldn't. But I could never see your lives. And I just couldn't face up to that. So I figured the problem had to be you."

"Angela." He fumbled for her hand and patted it, yawning. "There's no need for this. I don't know why you're doing this to yourself at . . ." He looked at the clock and his grip tightened. *"Two-thirty in the morning?"*

"Shhhhh!"

"You shhhh! And Leah doesn't sleep, she hibernates. Jesus Christ. Now? You need to do this now?"

"Need" was exactly the right word. Because this was about making amends, sure, but it was also about learning to live with the fallout from all her mistakes. *Even when I apologize, I'm selfish.* Was that funny? Sad? All of the above?

"No matter what I did, I was never more than a magician

doing card tricks. But Leah was already making a name for herself. She could make people appear *within other people*. She helped them see the dead. I could never do it so well, and—and I took that out on you.

"It drove me nuts that I couldn't see your other selves, it just reminded me of my own failings, made my amateur status *that* much more obvious. And it drove me nuts that you couldn't see them, either, couldn't learn like the rest of us, couldn't be *enlightened* like the rest of us, like I thought I was." She could hear herself practically snarling and couldn't stop. "I wouldn't admit you were special, and you paid for it. When I apologized last time, I didn't tell you the whole story. And I thought—I thought you deserved it. To know all of it."

Silence.

"Do you promise you're done?"

She thought it over, still kneeling beside the bed. "I . . . yes. That's all of it."

"Okay. My turn. Yeah, you were a jerkass, and not just when you were a kid. You were shitty to me when you were old enough to know better and that sucked, and you know it and I know it and everyone in the family knows it. But you made amends. We got right with each other. And then, mysteriously and to my intense aggravation, you were compelled to make amends again."

Compelled. Yes. Exactly right.

"But, cuz, even if you hadn't, your actions didn't define me and your apologies didn't, either. You were wrong about me. I was right about me, and that's what mattered more to me back then. But you're not the supervillain here. You're the stubborn baseball manager who tells the hero—*moi*—that I'll never make it in the big leagues. So I go out and work hard and make it to spite you and in the process end up rich and successful. You're not Lex Luthor, you're the B-villain who admits he was wrong at the end and respects the hell out of the hero. What you did, right or wrong, it helped make me a stronger person. Maybe even a better person."

"Okay . . ." She might have to mull that one over.

He sighed, picking up on her hesitance and confusion. "In other words, I was just as self-involved as you, my ego's just as fat as yours, we both got some things wrong about each other and some things right, I will fart on your face very soon now, the end."

That made a little more sense. Not the farting. The rest of it. "Okay. Thanks for indulging me, I got home from Jason's and couldn't go to bed until I amended my earlier apology."

Her eyes had adjusted quite well to the gloom by now; she saw him blinking at her. "So you got home from your weird date with Detective Chambers—"

"It wasn't weird!" she hissed, still mindful of waking Leah. Then she thought it over for a second. Tombstone cleaning, prison visit, uncle dropping the C bomb and promising at least one murder, a delicious fuck, a bitchy blow-off all culminating in a bedside confession. No wonder she was exhausted. "Well, okay. It was weird."

"And then you came up here to wake me up out of a sound sleep and remind me that you can be a self-absorbed jerkass but tonight, at least, you were an apologetic self-absorbed jerkass."

"No, I took a shower first."

He settled back and hauled the blankets up under his chin. "Good. Glad we got it all cleared up. But make a note, because in another ten years I want a middle-of-the-night apology for *this* middle-of-the-night-apology. Just make an appointment or mention it in the Christmas newsletter so I know when it's coming.

She giggled, something she hadn't imagined doing even once during this conversation. "Done."

"You promise?"

"Super done."

"Go away, you controlling, aggravating, bitchy idiot."

She wanted to hug him, but she'd disrupted his sleep cycle enough for one night. Instead she took the plate and quietly closed the door, and wasn't too proud to lick her finger to get every one of those delicious pastry swan crumbs.

FORTY-FOUR

His cell rang, which was unwelcome. Jason wasn't stupid enough to imagine it was Angela explaining she had waited until summer to pull an April Fool's prank.

He'd known trying to go to sleep was futile and it was too soon to wax the floors again. He wasn't hungry and he wasn't thirsty. He had no stomach for work and didn't feel like reading. So he was flipping through channels and rediscovering what most insomniacs knew: It didn't matter how many channels you had or where in the world you were, there was nothing on at 1:00 a.m.

The hell with it. He didn't recognize the number, but picked it up anyway. Woe betide the pollster in the wrong time zone who wanted his opinion on current events.

"Hello."

"I hear you been stirring shit with a stick over at ICC, Chambers."

"Mom?"

A gusty aggrieved sigh: "You know damned well I'm not your dead mom. This is Kline."

Perfect.

"Kline, why are you pestering me in the wee hours? Are you so bad at retiring they've kicked you out of retiring? And if you are, why the hell would you call *me* to complain?"

"Buddy of mine works Intake Processing gave me a call tonight. Name's Maller."

Hmm. "Yes, I met him this afternoon."

"He's not really a buddy," Kline explained, as if Jason had declared Kline had no buddies and demanded the exact truth of their relationship. "He's married to my niece. She's a nice kid, but he's a shithead. He's a gun owner and says he likes hunting, bullshit! He's a vegetarian! How the fuck does that happen?"

"This is fascinating, Kline. Please don't confuse that genuine sentiment with sarcasm. I'll be crushed."

"Anyway, turns out he was tryin' ta help you out and got fired for it. I coulda told him it was a waste of time."

Oh, hell. "Sorry to hear that." And he was. Maller had seemed like a good enough guy, and had appeared to genuinely appreciate Leah's offer of help.

"Well, he was short, outta there by the end of the month anyway, wasn't all bad. They're moving to the 'burbs and he hates the commute."

"It's kind of you to keep me up-to-date on the minutiae of your family's lives."

"You think I'm callin' you at . . ." He heard hissing and immediately knew what Kline was doing. He was fond of belching, but felt it was ungentlemanly to make a lot of noise indulging his frequent, Coke-inspired gas attacks. So he hissed the belch into his fist, which took longer, was more startling, and called more attention to him than just letting it rip would have. Of all the noises Kline's body made, the hissing was the one Jason missed least. ". . . one-fuckin'-thirty in the morning to give you updates on my niece's move?"

"Yes, Kline. That's what I think. Feel free to set me straight, unless you want me to commit to helping them move, in which case, I will cordially invite you to get lost."

"Lighten the fuck up. I swear you're the most uptight guy. Know what your problem is?"

"That would be problems, plural. And yes."

"You need ta get laid."

Jason laughed and for a few seconds, worried he might not be able to stop. He had to wipe his eyes before he could continue. "You were saying why you called."

"Yeah, I was. So whatever you and those Insighters did, ya freaked Dennis out."

"Astute and to the point, Kline, as ever."

"Shaddup. I got the whole thing from Maller when we hit the bar. So ICC hadda do a whole TD* and bundle his howling ass to seg, right? Well, while they were bringing Drake to his new digs, he was yellin' 'bout how his wife was gonna kill him, how even after all this time she was still pissed and she wasn't gonna let go until the kids let go."

---

*Take down

Jason, who had been slumped on his couch half watching a rerun of *The Tudors*

(pilgrimage of Grace and Jane Seymour, not bad but season two's more interesting. more and Fisher and the court of two queens)

dropped the remote. On his foot, but he hardly noticed. "Dennis Drake isn't married."

"Picked up on that, didja?"

"He's never been married."

"Yup."

"Jesus Christ."

"Thought you'd like that. Toldja something was weird about this case."

"You have said that about every single case that ever came your way." It was automatic. Jason hardly knew what he was saying. He couldn't hear Kline anymore. He was too busy remembering how he felt after Pat Chambers overdosed in front of him.

I am living a stolen life.

"Kline. I have to go. Thank you. For calling. My best to your niece and nephew-in-law." He fumbled for the button to end the call and dropped the thing; it fell beside the remote.

Holy shit.

FORTY-FIVE

"He did *what?*"

Angela wasn't too proud to bask in the group outrage, which was deafening and chaotic and made her feel better. A little better.

Paul had jumped to his feet. "I'll strangle him with my tape measure! Normally I only use it to measure, but for this? I'll make an exception."

Jordan stabbed a bite of French toast from Paul's unguarded plate. "I'll buy you another tape measure and we can choke him out together."

"Are you kidding me? Are you *kidding* me?" Jack slammed his spatula down for emphasis, which was why there were now drops of syrup in her eyebrows. "The minute this white chocolate bread pudding is out of the oven, we're all gonna pick out our favorite blunt object and pay him a visit." Jack checked the oven timer. "In seventeen minutes!"

The best part of all of this, Angela thought, was how menacing-yet-adorable Jack looked in his WHAT PART OF "IT'S NOT READY YET" DON'T YOU UNDERSTAND? apron.

Archer and Leah, motivated by hunger or curious about the source of the ruckus, came in. "Told 'em, huh?"

"Well, yeah." Angela quit trying to rub the syrup out of her eyebrows with a paper napkin. "I would have had to eventually."

"Good morning." From Leah. "You have napkin shreds in your eyebrows."

"Because of course I do. I'll go wash my— No!" Her hands shot out to keep Archer at arm's length since he'd crumpled up a napkin and licked it. "Don't you dare, don't you *dare* do that disgusting thing when a mom spits on a napkin or Kleenex and then scrubs your face with a spit-soaked napkin. *God.* Revolting."*

"At last we agree on something."

"Agh! Jeez, Mom. You scared me."

"In my defense, I was standing on the other side of the open fridge door."

Sure. That was it. Not the fact that you're fully dressed at 10:30 a.m. and having breakfast with the family.

"Say what you will about my parenting skills—"

"Nobody's got that kind of time." From Paul, who continued the vicious cycle of stealing food from other plates by taking Jack's bacon.

"I never did the spit-on-a-napkin thing."

"Y'know, I have to concede that point, Mom." *Hey, when*

---

*It is. I would literally rather be slapped.

*she's right she's right. And is it my imagination or are we having a
normal family-type breakfast the way millions do all over the world?*

"Ow!" From Paul, who jerked back and clutched his knuckles, but never stopped chewing.

"Keep your fingers off my plate and away from my bacon or
the next one goes between your eyes," Jack warned. He twirled
the spatula between his fingers like a rock drummer and Paul
pretended he didn't flinch.

"Auntie Em, did you hear? Did Angela tell you? About what
Dennis said?"

"I heard." She tsk'd and condensed a vague lecture into a
short phrase: "I warned you."

"You warned me that if I persisted, Uncle Dennis would
promise to randomly murder someone and call me a bitch and
then I'd throw up? I *thought* I was having some déjà vu yesterday. It was like you foresaw it all."

"Yes, yes, you love sarcasm, you've all made that clear over
the years. But if that admittedly unpleasant confrontation is
what it took to come to your senses, fine. Jack, is there any bacon left?"

"Sure, Mom." He went to the microwave, grabbed his tongs,
put a rasher* on a small plate and handed it over. "It's not as
crisp as you like, though. I didn't know you were— I mean, I
can cook it a little longer if you like."

Their mother shook her head. "It's fine, Jacky."

Paul finished Jack's bacon, then leaned in. "Can we get back
to the incarcerated shitstain who has invited all our wrath?"

---

*Three slices of bacon. I had to look it up, so I saved you the trouble. You're welcome!

"Must we?" Emma muttered.

"What are we gonna do to him? Shouting epithets at Angela while horrified onlookers pretend they can't hear or see anything is a privilege, not a right. He's gotta pay."

"He's serving a life sentence," Angela reminded them. "He'll never see his family again. He'll be in a cage until he dies. I think we can safely say that ICC has this."

"Speaking of ICC." Leah helped herself to a glass of orange juice and sipped while she looked at her phone, then up at Archer. "I spoke with CO Maller and it looks like we're going forward."

Leah hadn't been talking to her, but Angela jumped in anyway. "The guy with the gambling addiction?"

"Gambling problem. Yes."

"He got canned yesterday," Archer added, "so Leah's gonna see about getting him a new job."

"He did? She is?" *I slept for four hours and missed all sorts of updates!*

"Angela got someone fired again?" Jordan shook his head. "You're a general menace, you know that, right?"

"It wasn't me this time, it was Leah. And Uncle Dennis, who had something of a breakdown that after today we're not going to discuss anymore."

"Why'd you do that?" Jack asked Leah.

"*When* did you do that?"

"I set up an interview for him an hour ago, and I'll meet with him next week," Leah replied, seeming surprised at the sudden interest. "What? We always need good security people. A client tries to smack one of us around every month or so."

"Can we talk again about how much I hate that aspect of

your job?" Archer said. "Because I fucking hate that aspect of your job."

"Leah can take care of herself," Jack said stoutly.

"Of course she can, I knew that within ten seconds of meeting her."

"Hey, that's right!" Paul poked Archer in the shoulder. "She stabbed you!"

"Twice. So, yeah, Leah can take care of herself. I just hate that she has to."

"Regardless. We're always in need of good security, so." Leah shrugged. "I made some arrangements."

"Except." Angela cleared her throat. "Technically, he's not a good security guy. He totally ignored the rules because you butted into his personal life."

"That's another way to look at it," Leah admitted. "But we all know it was more complicated than that. He did us an enormous favor and suffered for it. Why wouldn't I try to help him? Chances are he won't make the same mistake twice."

"You hope."

"I hope," she conceded.

"But how did Maller even know to reach you?" she asked Leah. "Oh, wait—he must have gotten your personal info off one of the intake sheets."

"Actually." Now Leah was the one clearing her throat. "Detective Chambers called and told me a couple of hours ago."

"He called *you*?" *What are you freaking out for? You made it clear he sure as shit wasn't supposed to call you anymore.* Still, she couldn't help saying it again. "You?" First the pastry swan, now this? Usurper!

"Yes." Leah was doing a wonderful job pretending this was an ordinary morning. "And I think he'll be stopping by today."

Angela could feel herself getting pale, which was clinically interesting. *So that's why people faint. All the blood leaves your head and it becomes too hard to stand up.* "No. Oh no, he won't."

And because this wasn't an ordinary morning, because the Drake family could never have an ordinary morning, that was when someone knocked on the kitchen door.

"In fact," Leah continued, "I've got a very strong hunch that he'll be here any moment."

More knocking.

"Son of a *bitch*."

"You gonna finish that?"

Angela shoved her plate at Mitchell and stood in the same movement. "I'll take care of this."

"Why are you getting upset?" Jack asked. "Don't you like Detective Chambers anymore?"

"He's not working Dad's case. Which I made clear. He's not supposed to be here. Which he knows. So I will *handle* this."

"That's the problem," Leah said quietly. "You're not handling anything, Angela. You've been handled. For years."

"I don't know what that means," she replied flatly.

For whatever reason, that made Leah sad; she broke their gaze and stared down at her plate. "I know."

FORTY-SIX

"Nope."

    "I need to talk to you."

"Uh-uh."

"Right now."

"We're not doing this."

"It's important."

"Don't care."

"In private."

"It's never going to happen."

"Three minutes."

"No minutes."

"Two minutes."

"God, you're bad at this. No minutes!"

"Jeez, Angela." Her brothers were staring at her in amazement, and Paul added, "Give him a hundred twenty seconds. It's two minutes out of your life."

"Two minutes out of my life, then one day, then one year, and then you turn around and it's been a decade. No." And was she just supposed to pretend Jason didn't make himself extra-hot on purpose before coming over? Was she supposed to act like she didn't see how great he looked in dark jeans and an aqua polo shirt? And ignore the fact that he didn't shave *on purpose* just to fuck with her and flaunt his stubble?

Bastard.

"One minute," Archer said, "and that's our final offer."

"Done."

"Wait!" *Argh! What a stupid time for a lapse in concentration. It's the stubble's fault!* "This isn't an auction, it's not their decisi—"

"You've got sixty seconds, Detective." Mitchell looked at his watch. "Go."

Jason sucked in a deep breath and got started. "Our first visit to ICC. Dennis would only talk to us for five minutes, claimed he didn't want to go over his allotted visits for the month."

Angela frowned. "Yeah, but we knew that was a lie. You checked and he had plenty of hours left."

"But that's all I could do . . . see what he had left. I made a small assumption—he had plenty of hours because no one had been to see him. That assumption led to a mistake: I didn't bother asking for the log. If I had, I would have found out someone came to see him last month. Someone who hasn't seen him in quite some time."

"His lawyer?"

"Which one?

"He's fired two of 'em by my count—"

"Your count sucks. He's fired three."

"He's his own lawyer, remember? How can he visit himself?"

"Your mother," Jason said, raising his voice. "Emma Drake."

Abrupt silence, like a switch had been thrown. Angela felt like she was witnessing a miracle. Or witchcraft. Something about Jason made people want to stop and listen. Maybe it wasn't "people" (a general term), maybe it was just the Horde.

Jason started a little. "Oh. Sorry. I was waiting for another chorus of interruptions. You wanted me to continue?"

Silent nods. *Definitely witchcraft.*

"Last month, he wrote your mother and asked for a visit. A week after that, she came."

Dumbfounded silence. "Why—why did we not know that? She's always maintained zero contact, hasn't spoken to him since he took the plea and went to prison." Archer was shaking his head. "Why didn't we notice he wrote to her?"

Angela felt dull pain in her palm and realized she'd clenched her fist so hard her knuckles had whitened. "Because Mom checks the mail. It's the one thing she's consistently done for the last ten years. And we let her because, hey, at least she was engaged in *some* part of family life, right? That's what we told ourselves." She turned toward the fridge, where her mother had been standing a minute ago. "Isn't that right, M— Dammit!"

Emma Drake had left the building.

FORTY-SEVEN

"It's settled: Mom should be helping with the grocery shopping from now on."

"How did we not notice any of this?" Jordan cried. "She left and drove off right under our noses. Multiple times! She somehow got out of here without drawing attention to herself or asking anyone for a ride or for their keys?"

"Because of that." Angela pointed to the keyboard beside the fridge. Almost every hook had keys; the only one that didn't held the flyswatter. "There are so many of us and we've all got different schedules and we all need vehicles at different times. You remember—it's why we put the board up in the first place. If any of us get blocked in, we can come in here, grab keys, and move cars. Easy."

"Even so . . ."

"Are you new? This place is locked onto a 24/7 chaos cycle. Half the time we've got no idea what the other half is up to."

Archer was rubbing his forehead. "So she leaves now and again and nobody noticed. And my dad could have been writing your mom every month and we'd never have known. It's not like Dennis would mention it during one of the few visits he didn't refuse. Or in one of his rare letters. 'Dear son, how's it hanging? Also I write to your aunt every few weeks, which totally isn't a secret.'"

"Exactly."

"I don't get it." They all looked at Jack. "So she went to see him. So what? I mean, it's shocking in terms of nobody knew what she was up to, but it doesn't really mean anything."

"That," Jason said, "would depend on her motive for visiting."

"Maybe . . . to warn him off?"

"Nooooo. Auntie Em didn't warn him off. That would have involved caring. And dressing before noon. And driving." But even as he said it, Archer looked puzzled. Because if it wasn't to warn Dennis off, what possible reason would she have to go see him? Especially after spending years of energy making it clear that no one should see Dennis Drake under any circumstance?

"I think I get it." Jack was nodding, eyes bright as he reasoned it out. "I think she played the Widow Drake card and drove out there to tell Uncle Dennis to be a bastard to Angela and make her go away and never want to see him again so we could get on with our lives."

Archer and Angela traded glances. When Jack put it like that, it wasn't quite as mysterious and sneaky and terrible. Under those circumstances, Angela could almost understand. It was misguided and controlling, but in a weird way, it was also an act of love.

"That's not why she visited him," Jason said. He looked at Angela. "It's been sixty-three seconds. May I continue?"

Most of the group: "*Yes!*"

"I'm gonna vote no," Mitchell put in. "Just so there's one voice of dissent, but honestly, I think you should keep going."

"Very well. Once I realized Emma and Dennis had been in communication, I started to see things through a different lens. Things you told me, Angela. 'She's been after me to let Dad lie.' And his explanation for avoiding the trial, do you remember? 'I told the cops what I did because I essentially killed my brother and hurt your mother.' That was odd phrasing. 'I didn't take a plea to leave wiggle room if I got buyer's remorse.' How in the world could he get buyer's remorse? What did he buy? And 'this was always my mess. I bought it; it's mine.'"

"And aside from all of that—what has your mother been hiding all this time?"

"Guilty knowledge." There. It was out. She'd finally put it into words.

"Yes."

She was shaking her head numbly. She could almost see what he was getting at. But it was insane. Literal insanity: It was madness, an act of extreme foolishness or irrationality.

"The wrong one's in jail. You always maintained that; you built your lives around the concept. And you were always right."

Jacky was shaking his head so hard, he reached out to steady himself on the back of the chair. "No. You're wrong. Angela, tell him he's—" He clenched a small fist and looked up into Jason's face. "Are you saying our mother murdered our daddy? Which is why he's been protecting her and keeping away from us?"

"No." Angela couldn't remember feeling so calm in her life. Once again, it was like watching someone else put the puzzle together in front of you, the one you couldn't solve on your own. "He's saying our dad's still alive. Donald Drake is alive, *Dennis* is dead. And somehow, Mom got Dad to take his place."

FORTY-EIGHT

Pandemonium. (Understandable.) Most of the boys were yelling and Leah had gone to Jacky, who was crying, and put an arm around him, and walked him around the turtle table and made him sit down before he fell down.

But Angela wasn't touched by any of it. Instead she stood like a statue—like *Eternal Silence*, who showed you your death if you matched its gaze—and did what Jason had done: looked at "reality" through a different lens.

"This was always my mess. I bought it; it's mine."

You can't save him.

"He's dead. Let him stay dead."

And, particularly damning: "It should have been him." She thought about sitting across from "Uncle Dennis" and vowing to avenge the wrong brother's murder. How could he have just—just *sat* there and let her ramble on and on about all the time she was wasting?

He tried to make you stop. He and Mom both tried to make you stop.

Yeah? You know what a great way to make me stop would have been? Mentioning that HE WAS MY FATHER AND CLEARLY NOT DEAD. Christ, this was her life as Augusta Harrison all over again!

"He did tell us," she said. Her mouth felt like she'd gotten a shot of Novocain; it was hard to make her lips move. "He told us over and over. And he was right. I heard, but didn't listen."

She and Archer stared at each other and then said, almost in unison, "The wrong brother's in jail."

Paul, meanwhile, was holding his head in his hands. "This. Is. So. Fucked."

"Archer, you were right," Leah marveled. "You said it yourself on the way back from ICC: It was right in front of our faces."

"And I didn't recognize him." Archer was wearing the dazed expression of someone who was still standing despite taking a beating from a larger, more skillful opponent. "Why would I? It's been ten years. And they have the same build, the same coloring, sometimes people thought they were twins. If you look at the old pictures, you can see it." In his shock, his eyes showed the whites all around. "My dad's the one in the ground. Donald Drake—the 'good' brother—he's the one who's been locked up all this time."

"That's why he wouldn't see us," Mitchell said. He looked as punch-drunk as Archer did. "He couldn't stand to look at any of us, knowing what he'd done. We were kids, but he must have been scared we'd recognize him and blab."

"We've been in a soap opera for *ten years!*"

"Not even a good one, like *Days of our Lives*," Paul added, almost tearful. "A dumb, shitty one, like *Judge Judy.*"

"Wait. Wait. You've got it wrong." Jack was rubbing his face, smearing tears. "All of you. Think about it—Daddy just turned himself over to the police and said, 'Hi, I'm Dennis and I want to go to prison now'? And nobody questioned it? How is that possible?"

When was the last time he used the word "Daddy"? It's been years. Ten, in fact. "Who would he have to fool? Fellow inmates? The COs?"

"Who's gonna say 'What's this, you're reading Shakespeare? How out of character, that seems more like something Donald would do, you must be an imposter, someone get this man a new lawyer!'"

"That . . . seems farfetched," Archer admitted.

"But that's crazy!" Jack said. "It wouldn't have even gotten that far before he would have been busted. If nothing else, Mom would have—"

He cut himself off so abruptly, Angela heard his teeth click together. Her heart cracked for him in that moment. Because in order to believe in the Drake brothers switcharoo, you had to first acknowledge that . . .

"She was in on it."

"Worse," Leah said gently. "It would have been her idea. There's no other way this would have worked. And for whatever reason, your father went along with it."

"But why?"

The memory bubbled up to the surface again: her father, holding a bulging suitcase.

I never would have left him. And he never would have left me.

"That's the question, isn't it?" Angela was already slinging her purse over one shoulder. "I'm going to go ask her."

Jason, who appeared to have been waiting for her to reach that conclusion, got up and held the door for her. "You know where she went."

"I know where she went." Angela took a breath. "Will you take me there?"

"Of course."

"I don't want to go," Jack said at once. "I can't." The oven timer went off and she'd never seen him look so relieved. "Because of the pudding."

"It's fine."

"I'm not going, either. I might actually kill her. Kill her for real, not 'kill her but not really and then sit in jail for a decade' kill her," Archer said.

"You guys stay here and keep Jack company, okay?" She was amazed when uncharacteristicly quiet nods were the only response. A hundred years ago, she would have loved the deference. Now it looked wrong. Felt wrong.

"Felt wrong." Oh, boy, that was putting it mildly.

She pulled a Kleenex from her purse, handed it to Jack, watched him wipe his eyes. "I'll go take care of this."

He sniffed and looked up at her. "How?"

"I don't know."

I might kill her, too, Archer. For putting that look on Jack's face, if nothing else.

"Let's go," she said, and Jason was right behind her.

FORTY-NINE

It was a looooooooong drive. Angela sat with her arms crossed and her teeth clenched and her feet braced against the floor mat, mind whirling, peeking at Jason out of the corner of her eye.

A few miles in, she realized he was giving her the side-eye, too. *This is insane. And this car ride might be the strangest part. No, my dad being alive is the strangest part.* A snort escaped before she could lock it back. She crammed both hands over her mouth in a frantic attempt to block the noise, then made the mistake of glancing at Jason, whose eyes were watering with the effort of not laughing.

They lost it at the same time, each indulging in one of those full-body belly laughs that leave you gasping for breath. Jason had to pull over on a side street and park, and they both abandoned themselves. When they'd calmed down some, and Jason was wiping his eyes, she turned toward him, thinking she'd start with "Can you believe this shit?" or "Bet you're glad I broke it off last night" or "Will you hold my Mom down while I punch her in the throat?"

Instead, she started to cry. And somehow she was in his arms *(how long have I been able to teleport?)* and she was sniveling into his neck and rubbing her face against his stubble just a bit, just a little tiny bit so she wouldn't get tears on his shirt because dammit, she was considerate that way.

"I'm so sorry," he was murmuring into her hair. "I can't imagine. Can't imagine."

"It's a nightmare." She sniffed. "An ongoing nightmare where, in between the horror reveals, I get laid, which I have to admit is a new one." She pulled back to look at him. "How'd you know? How'd you figure it all out?"

So he told her about Kline and, in a way, it was the most infuriating thing of all: A random phone call had brought answers she'd been seeking for a decade. What were the odds of Klown retiring and Archer falling for Leah Nazir, setting in motion a cascade reaction that ended up with Dennis—with *Donald* shrieking the truth at Intake Processing?

Wait. *Think that over again.*

"Jeez. Maybe the universe really did want this to happen. I thought Leah would solve it, or point us in a new direction, and in a way . . . But now I don't know what to think." She rested her forehead on his warm shoulder for a few seconds, then pulled back into her bucket seat. "Thank you for coming to the house. It couldn't have been easy."

"Devastating," he said simply. "But in the interest of full

disclosure, I was thrilled to finally have answers. I ran two red lights getting over there."

"I can't condone your rampant disregard for the law, but it's an understandable reaction." A line from *The Silence of the Lambs*—the book, not the movie—had always stuck with her: "'Problem-solving is hunting; it is savage pleasure and we are born to it.'" She knew exactly why he'd been compelled to race over.

He fished out some napkins and handed them over. She blew her nose and tidied up as best she could. Flipped down the visor, observed her reddened, weepy eyes. Groaned.

In the low tone of a man confessing his greatest, most humiliating sin, Jason leaned over and murmured: "I streamed *Poltergeist*. It was horrifying. They just left the bodies! They only moved the headstones!"

That nearly set her off again. "That movie ruined chicken legs and closet ghosts for me. I already hated clown dolls, so that was all fine. You watched it?"

"I said, didn't I?"

"Ah. So I should always trust you will be a man of your word. Is that the message?"

"The message is, when a small round woman with a child-like voice declares the house is clean, it isn't."

"Point," she conceded.

He had been smiling, but sobered and caught her gaze again. "Angela, I'll take you wherever you wish, whenever you wish, but in terms of you and me, these new revelations are meaningless. They were not added to an imaginary column of negatives."

He really *was* a witch! "How did you know I kept imaginary columns of— Never mind. Go on."

"I still want to be with you, I want to give us a chance. You don't have to say anything. I just wanted you to know that your father being alive and your mother being an almost cartoonishly evil mastermind changes nothing. I'll always want you."

She could think of no reason why he would say such a thing unless it was the truth. But now wasn't the time. "Thank you," was all she said, because *cripes*, what a week. "I heard everything you said. Can we please drive on?"

"Of course."

Twenty minutes later, they were pulling into the cemetery parking lot. "There's the truck," Angela said with what she thought was a credible lack of surprise. It was Paul's used Ford, the dark blue one Jack had learned the stick shift on. It was usually parked off to the side, and it blended so well into their suburban street that it was small wonder they didn't notice it was missing at first.

"Could you stay here?"

He was already nodding. "For thirty minutes. Then I'll come for you."

"Okay?"

"I don't trust her," he said simply. She couldn't fault him for that.

⟲

ANGELA MARCHED PAST the newer graves, past the tombs, past the statue of Inez Clarke, past *Eternal Silence*, and stopped. She took a few seconds to glare at the thing in its cold stone face.

"You want a piece? Let's go!" she snapped and, when she wasn't struck by lightning, marched on.

She found her mother at her uncle's grave, as she'd known she would the moment Jason told them about the letter(s) and visit(s).

"Ah-ha! Look who's returned to the scene of the crime." *Okay, I already need a do-over. "Ah-ha" sounded great until I said it out loud.*

Her mother sat cross-legged in front of the stone and now looked up, squinting, so walking with the sun at her back was definitely the way to go. "I *ruined* my blouse that day."

"Because of course you did. But don't blame yourself. These things happen when you talk your dead husband into serving a life sentence for his own murder and later decide to desecrate his grave."

"It wasn't a decision. It's not like the second thing was part of any big plan," she said with . . . was that . . . reproach? "It was a reaction to stress."

Angela came a few steps closer. "Are you seriously tossing me attitude right now?"

"Ask."

Did she just call me an—oh. "Ask," with a "k." Not the other thing. "What?"

Her mother sighed. She was still in the outfit Angela had last seen her in half an hour earlier (red slacks, short-sleeved black blouse, black flats . . . business casual wear as opposed to grave-desecrating wear), her graying brown hair needed a good brushing, and she had her keys in one hand and nothing else.

"Left in such a hurry you forgot your purse," she observed. "I ought to have Jason arrest your ass. He might anyway. Obstruction of justice, for starters. Fraud." *Breaking your children's hearts. Consuming selfishness. That last one should be a felony.*

"'Fraud'?" Her mother's head jerked up. "I never stole from anyone."

"You've been collecting a dead man's pension! *And* screwing up your family like you were getting paid."

"That. Was. *Him.*" Emma Drake was uncoiling as she rose to her feet. *Kind of like a cobra*, Angela thought, fascinated. *And me without my lidded basket. Or a snake-charming flute.* "You can lay this entire debacle at your father's feet."

"'The entire debacle,' huh? Not just part of the debacle? Most of the debacle?"

"Yes."

"How did I never notice you were a sociopath?"

"Oh, please. People toss that word around too much. You know better."

"So let's talk about what I know." Angela started to pace around the stone. "Donald Drake is alive and well, or as well as anyone serving a life sentence can be. And he went out of his way to arrange his own life imprisonment for his own murder. Which you condoned and possibly planned." When her mom started to say something, Angela added, "And don't say 'Anything sounds bad when you put it like that.' There is literally no way to put that where it sounds anything but deeply, *deeply* fucked up."

"I don't expect you to understand."

"*Make me understand.* Break it down."

Emma studied her for a few seconds and said the last thing

Angela expected: "I really did love him. And never more than when he went to prison. It's how I finally knew."

"Knew what?

"That he valued our lives more than Dennis's lifestyle."

"Uh. 'Lifestyle'?"

"It was like your father was caught in a spell. It was always like that. The family myth was that Dennis was a no-good pothead who couldn't keep out of trouble, while Donald was a good and responsible man who deplored his brother's lifestyle. But it was always bullshit."

Angela rolled her eyes so hard her temples throbbed. "You pretended to be a widow for ten years and you're gonna bitch about family myths?"

"Do you want the story or not?" her mother snapped. "Less editorializing, more listening."

"We never made that deal. But fine. Talk about myths."

"It was all the time. It was constant. Dennis would call or drop by or steal your father's car and without exception, your dad would be out the door. Even if we had plans. Even if I was pregnant. Once, when I was in labor. *In labor*, Angela!"

"I can see how that would be aggravating," she said carefully.

"He was always leaving to bail his little brother out—literally, on more than one occasion. But worse, just to be with him. Donald couldn't stay away. I always thought that Dennis had to hit rock bottom so Donald would. I assumed Dennis would demand our attention one time too many and that would be it. Donald would realize that his brother would never change and would focus on the rest of his family.

"But it never happened. It was so pathetic, Angela. He didn't have the balls to out-and-out rebel, so he put himself on Dennis's fringe where he could see all the fun and face none of the consequences. Which made sense, because Dennis never had to face them, either."

"The dead guy," Angela said bluntly. "That's who you mean, right? The guy who's in the grave? No consequences for the corpse?"

Her mother waved that away: *Shoo, fly! Enough with your nitpicking.* "I couldn't break Dennis's hold, so I figured I'd start a family with Donald, make something new and beautiful and ours for him to hold. And we had you."

"You trapped him," she corrected. "You told me yourself and even then, I thought you told me more out of spite than a desire for me to know the truth."

Emma sighed the sigh of the greatly put-upon. "I can't win with you, Angela. If I tell the truth I'm a cold bitch, but if I try to pretty it up a little, I'm perpetuating a family myth."

"You know you're not the victim here, yes?"

Her mother ignored the interruption. "I made him a father, gave him a home—Dennis lived in a trailer, for God's sake—"

"Oh, and you're a snob on top of everything else. Nice."

"—and it *still* wasn't enough for him."

"Which should have told you something, Mom! Don't you think? Didn't you ever hear that saying? About when you love something let it go, and if it doesn't come back—"

"Bullshit trite nonsense. If you love something, you hold on with everything and you don't let anyone stop you."

"Uh. No. That's the sociopath's version."

"I warned him and warned him."

"At the top of your voice," Angela remembered. "A lot."

"I told him Dennis would get him killed. That it was inevitable. And then where would we be? Because by then I was pregnant again. And again. But—"

"But the more you tied him down, the more he wanted to get free. And wasn't that around the time that Grandpa died?" Angela had no memory of her paternal grandmother, who died of a brain aneurysm the summer Angela turned three. Her paternal grandfather died of lung cancer a few years later. "Okay, I see it now. He wouldn't risk disappointing his parents. But then his father died and Dad could be the guy he wanted to be. And you must have lost your shit."

"Everything I worked for, everything I gave him—"

"It's not a gift if it's got strings all over it, Mom."

"—was in jeopardy. Because by then, they were actually impersonating each other! You know how alike they looked. Your father still didn't have the guts to rebel, and he wasn't cheating on me—yet—but he'd go out with women and introduce himself as Dennis."

The memory bubble. Finally, Angela had context. "Is it that you don't remember, or that you think I was too young to remember? He might not have been cheating on you, but he was leaving you. I remember the suitcase, Mom. He'd crammed it so full, the thing barely closed. He was gonna be out the door and you were going to be stuck with the kids who were designed to trap him."

Nope. Emma wasn't listening. Clearly, some myths were cherished. "He'd introduce himself to strangers as Dennis, can you believe it? Meanwhile, the *real* Dennis was tooling around town—"

"In Dad's car. Without permission." For some reason, that seemed to irritate her mother the most.

"—ignoring his little bastards—"

"Nice, Mom."

"—living a life of zero responsibility and taking my husband along for the ride."

"Literally."

Her mother, who had been standing in one spot while Angela paced, abruptly sat again. "Then he started buying drugs as Dennis."

"Ah."

"A lot of them."

"Yep. Makes sense." *Dad, you sneaky shithead, you were doing everything to run away except actually running away.*

"He wasn't a pothead—yet. And by then I had an iron grip on our checkbook—"

"Oh, please. Mom, I know you. Well, sometimes. You had an iron grip from day one."

She nodded, acknowledging the point. "He didn't have ready access to money, is my point."

"Argh." She rubbed the bridge of her nose, having seen enough crime reports to guess the next step. "So he started selling them. He wouldn't smoke them all or pop them all, and he'd sell the leftovers."

"Yes."

"Without telling Dennis, who would have warned him what an unfathomably stupid idea that was."

"Correct."

"And the wrong people came looking for the wrong brother."

"Yes."

"So the dealers killed Dennis for poaching. And Dad must have come in—"

"As he told me, he got there in the nick of too late and realized what happened. He'd missed the killers by maybe two minutes."

Angela remembered her mother's harsh words from a few days ago. At the time, she'd put it down to resentment of her brother-in-law. She'd been dead wrong: The resentment had been aimed at Donald Drake.

It should have been your uncle bleeding out on that filthy floor in that shitty little drug warren. Not your father.

"So you decided it *was* my uncle bleeding out. For all intents and purposes."

"I told him," Emma replied, and she couldn't (or wouldn't) keep the triumph out of her tone. "I said to him, 'You wanted his life, now you have it.'"

"Oh, God. Mom." Angela shook her head, but nope: The words kept coming.

"'You wanted to be him?' That's what I asked him. 'So be him.' And he just sat there and stared at me. And went along with it."

"That's what you meant when you told me my father already got justice."

Even though it was (finally) laid out for her, Angela still had trouble grasping it. She knew Chicago had its share of crime and plenty of overworked cops, but it was still hard to believe that no one had questioned any of it. The cops? "This guy says he's Dennis Drake and that he killed *that* guy, who he says is Donald Drake. The wife/sister-in-law backed it all up."

His lawyer? "He fired me. He wants to take a plea."

The DA? "He wants a plea? Story checks out? I can keep a trial off the overcrowded docket? Rubber stamp that bitch. Next!"

It was a set of circumstances the likes of winning the lottery: unlikely to happen twice. No matter how often you tried.

"So not only was Dad trapped in Dennis's life, he had to take all the grief Dennis never did. 'You've always been the fuckup, of course you ended up in prison, why couldn't you have been like your wonderful good brother, etc.' That would have rubbed extra salt in the wounds."

"He took his own life for granted, *our* life for granted. That was brought home to him every time he had to answer to the name Dennis."

All the questions of my childhood are being answered, and I think I want to die now.

"That's why you never took us to see him. The first time any of us saw him was after we turned eighteen, when you couldn't prevent it anymore."

"I had to protect—"

"Your secret. That was your primary motivation. I was stupid enough to think grief was making you selfish. I closed my eyes to *everything.* Jason was right, one assumption led to a huge mistake, which led to years of reinforcing that mistake."

"You were too young, it would have damaged you, the—"

"Stop it. You were afraid we'd recognize him. Maybe not Jack and Mitchell, they were pretty young when Dennis was murdered. But some of us were old enough. We would have known Inmate #26166 wasn't Dennis Drake. That's why you kept us away. Anything else is one of those family myths you pretend to have no use for."

Angela had stopped pacing and simply stood and looked at her mother. She'd always understood Emma was selfish and vindictive, but this was pathological. And it sure as shit wasn't grief. Angela wasn't sure if it was *ever* grief. "You know you've broken any number of laws, right?"

Shrug.

"And I'll be having a chat with Dad?"

"You can't," Emma replied in that smug, triumphant tone Angela wanted to throttle out of her body. *Fooled you*, the tone said. *Still fooling you.* "He won't see you anymore."

"Mom. Look at me. Look at my face. Do you think anyone can keep me out, now that I know what I know? Do you think I won't talk to the DA?"

"It won't be as easy as—"

"The hardest part is seeing the big lie, since you and Dad hid it right in front of everyone all this time. But once you understand the lie, the rest of your lame-ass story falls apart. And I promise you this: Once the system gets clued in, everything you worked for will be undone."

It was gratifying to see the smug replaced with a scowl. "You wasted so much of your life."

"Back atcha, Mom. *Right back at you.* Look at yourself. You're so invested in the myth, even now, that rather than being glad for a chance to set the record straight, you still want to keep your head down and keeping playing the Widow Drake."

"I knew you wouldn't understand."

"It's hilarious that you're saying 'I should have known you wouldn't understand my psychotic need for revenge and my inability to take responsibility for this mess' like it's a bad thing. Like it's a character flaw I should feel bad about and try to overcome."

"It's not my mess," she insisted. "It's his."

"Wrong. Again. It's ours, all of ours. You won't take your share of the weight, so we'll have to." She doubted Emma was looking ahead. That wasn't her mother's strong suit. But her children and nephews wouldn't live with her after this. How could they?

So even if Emma didn't go to jail, the life she had was over. They'd all move, or she would. The support system Emma had built around herself would shatter. Christmas was officially ruined, probably for the next ten years.

And for what?

Emma wasn't looking at her anymore. It could have been the sun. Or her conscience, pricking her at last.

No, definitely the sun.

For a moment she imagined seizing her mother by the throat and wrestling her down the bank by the footbridge and tripping her and holding her head under the water and kneeling on her face until the thrashing stopped. The vision was clearer than any dream and the scariest part was how doable it was. She could overpower her mother. Jason might not get there in time.

Sure. Another Drake in prison for manslaughter, whose selfish act left the family in even more dire straits. Great plan, dumbass.

So Angela pushed away the sunny daydream and focused on the present. "You told me—told yourself—that you always loved Dad, but never more than when he went to prison for you."

Emma managed a smile. "I'm glad you understand some of it."

"Don't be glad. You're the one who doesn't understand. He didn't go to prison for you. And he sure as shit didn't go out of love. He went because the person he loved best was dead. His escape hatch was gone. He never gave a shit about you—"

"You're wr—"

"Which he proved when he practically sprinted into a prison cell. And he hasn't changed his mind, Mom. Not in ten years. Think about it. Every hour of every day, he is showing you that life in prison is preferable to life with you."

She opened her mouth . . . then shrugged and looked away.

"Do you know what is honest to God the most aggravating thing?" Angela kicked at a tuft of grass. "Jason and I wasted all that time cleaning a tombstone that wasn't even my dad's! If I'd known he wasn't dead, we could have gotten straight to the picnic! And the napping!"

"What?"

"And yes, I'm aware that my priorities are screwed!" More kicks. More tufts of dirt. "But for some reason that's the part that really bugs me right now!"

"It doesn't matter."

They both looked around and saw Jason standing fifteen feet away.

"That wasn't half an hour," she called.

He spread his hands. "I was worried. And it wasn't a waste. I was glad to spend time here with you. There will be other picnics." He smiled, flashing that dimple as he walked closer. "And other naps."

Angela jabbed a thumb at her mother, who was glaring at him like a Scooby villain. "It's way more fucked up than you knew, Jason."

"Of course it is."

Angela went to him, put her arms around his waist. Was

more than a little relieved when he let her. "I'm gonna need so much therapy."

"I have an excellent therapist. We can share."

"I'll have to move out."

"You can't stay with her now," he agreed.

"And I have to think about Jack, he's the only minor, he'll have to come with me."

"I have three bedrooms."

She blinked. "Yeah?"

"Yes."

"Just like that?"

"Just like that."

"I think the woman who used the real-estate section to date might have been onto something."

He laughed.

She pointed at her mother again. "This. This is the kind of obsessive madness you're risking if you want to be with me. We're all various degrees of crazy. I could actually turn into this woman."

"There will be days I won't get out of bed because my brain chemistry went haywire. Times when I'll miss a birthday because I'm literally wading through blood at a crime scene. And I have nightmares."

There was a pointed throat-clearing behind them.

"Oh, me, too. Not the wading-through-blood part. The bad dreams part."

"Excuse me?"

"My father-in-law faked his own murder."

"*Excuse me.*"

"My mother talked him into it," Angela added, in case Jason wasn't fathoming the full horror.

"We are fucked," he decided, and she laughed.

"Angela! I'm not finished with my story."

"It's not your story anymore, Mom," Angela replied without looking around. "It's ours."

FIFTY

"You warned him that you could turn into your mom?"

Angela could see Leah was trying not to laugh. "You bet I did. He deserves to know the cauldron of madness he's gonna be swimming in."

Archer snorted. "I'm sure he already knew."

"Yeah?"

"What, you thought it was a big mystery? Some huge reveal that you kept from him? I can't imagine he didn't figure that out half an hour into the Drake file."

"Isn't that something?" Angela knew she sounded pleased. "From day one he was in it up to his elbows and he never backed off, he never ga—" She cut herself off. *She* was the one who had given up. Except it was worse than that. She never had the courage to try in the first place, and shut it down the min-

ute she realized the depth of his interest. Not so much out of
concern for him, as terror for herself.

Tried to shut it down, anyway. He made it clear(er) on the
way home that he wasn't having it. What could she say? "You
don't really know me." Sure he did. "I have a complex family
history." Yeah, he was all caught up on that, too. "Your dysthymia and my controlling streak will clash." Again: They both
knew this. "What if we're not compatible in bed?" They could
check that box off, too.

She didn't think a decision to open herself up to love could
be so . . . logical. She'd been surprised to find that agreeing to
explore a relationship with the dimpled detective was as joyful
as the news of her mother's betrayal and her father's cowardice
was devastating.

"Yes, you might turn into your mom," Leah allowed. They
were back in the kitchen. Jason had driven Angela home, and
she would see him tomorrow. Their mother wasn't back. No one
knew where she was. No one wanted to go looking. "But no
more or less than any of us. Or your mom could turn into you."

"That's—what? I'm not following."

The smaller woman shook her head. "Sorry. I don't mean to
be cryptic. I want to—" She cut herself off and looked at Archer. "Do you mind if I tell her?"

"Jeez, sure. You can tell anyone you want, hon. I haven't
said anything because I figured on this one, I'd take my cues
from you."

"Such restraint!" Leah cried with faux wonder. Archer laughed
at her.

"What's—what is it? Is the baby okay?"

"Absolutely. In fact, we're having a daughter."

Angela smiled at Archer. "Congratulations, Dad. The good news is, the Drake men have set the bar incredibly low for you."

Archer groaned. "You've never said anything more true or more horrible."

"Sorry, I—"

"In fact," Leah said, raising her voice, "we're having my mother."

Annnnd Angela's smile was stuck. "I'm sorry?"

"The baby I'm carrying is Nellie Nazir reincarnated."

"Wow."

"Yes."

"I— Wow." This was obviously the month for incredible world-shaking news that Angela couldn't immediately wrap her head around and might not ever wrap her head around. "I. I got nothin'. I've never heard of such a thing. Is there— I don't think there's anything in the literature." She looked at the expert hopefully. "Is there?"

Leah shook her head. "Uncharted territory. But does it mean my daughter is doomed to be the stage mother from hell? That I'll hate and fear her? That she'll be psychotically vain? And will value her career—whatever it will be—over everything else in her life? Will I be a bad mother to a bad mother? How much can we change each time?"

"I don't know." Her brain was still trying to digest the idea of giving birth to a parent. Because pregnancy wasn't gross enough? "What does it mean?" Because if the entire purpose of reincarnation was to fix past mistakes, what does it mean when your imperfect parent comes from you? There were radicals who insisted that reincarnation was because there were a finite number of souls in the world, and they kept getting recycled. Their mantra was brutal in its simplicity: "Everyone's a rerun."

Angela had never subscribed to that notion, mostly because it didn't bear thinking about. "Leah? Do you know what it means?"

"No idea. But we're going to muddle through. We'll parent my mother and somehow we'll . . . um . . . No idea." She shrugged and Archer grabbed her hand and planted a noisy kiss in the middle of her palm. Angela suspected he did so because Leah had a downright delightful giggle. She was so

(dour? no, not quite that, but . . .)

solemn most of the time, to hear her laugh was to be charmed.

"Thank you for telling me about the baby. Who, regardless of who she was, *is* going to be your daughter. I think if you can hang on to that, the rest might be . . . not easier, exactly, but . . ." She realized she had no business giving anyone parenting advice, never mind a woman pregnant with her mom. Speaking of parenting . . . "I'll keep it to myself until you say otherwise. But right now I need to talk to Jack."

"He's in the backyard experimenting with the grill. Except he didn't take matches. Or food. And we all had supper. And the grill is closed. And he's been sitting on the back steps for half an hour."

"Ah." They all had their code words for wanting to be left alone. Sometimes the code was ignored. More often, it was honored. Unfortunately, Angela couldn't oblige this time. "Back in a bit. If Mom gets back, tell her I cordially hope she drops dead. Oh, and that we're out of milk. I see no reason why she can't help around the house more." *At least, while we're all still here. Which won't be for long, I think.*

~

ANGELA SAT DOWN beside Jack on the steps. Their small backyard had a wooden ten-by-ten platform that Jordan and Mitchell had cobbled together one weekend, and the rest was lawn. They all feared and hated gardening, though occasionally Jack would get ambitious and plant herbs in pots. Then they'd spend the summer drowning in mint and thyme and he'd swear off gardening of any kind. Until winter hit. Then he'd start thinking about thyme scones and mint macarons.

She cleared her throat. "So this is my cue to say something inane—can you believe how warm it's getting?—and then say something to acknowledge the fact that our world view has gone tits up in twelve hours, while also reminding you that life goes on and telling you to cheer up, l'il buckaroo."

He didn't laugh, but she got a smile. And though she'd been careful to leave some room between them, he shuffled a little closer to her and stared down at his knees.

"How could she?"

"Oh, Jacky. I don't know. She explained the whole thing and I still don't get it."

"How could *he*?"

She shook her head.

"I can't stay here," he said in a low voice. "I don't want to see her. I don't want to cook for her or take care of her anymore."

"Understandable. You probably don't need me to tell you this—"

"But you're gonna anyway."

"You're entitled to be upset. You're entitled to be *furious*. Christ knows I am." Angela studied her hands, flexed her fingers. "I thought about drowning her in Lake Willowmere. Then myself. And then being reincarnated and tracking her down and drowning her again. And Paul's so upset he hasn't asked anyone to measure him since this morning."

"That's how you recognize the depth of his trauma," Jack agreed.

"Mitchell's plotting something that involves chicken feathers, Mom's bed, and several neighborhood dogs."

"Yeah, I know, he left the schematic in the bathroom."

She cleared her throat. "You knew he was sad."

"What?"

"Jason Chambers. You'd only seen him twice. And you didn't touch him either time . . . Did you?"

He said nothing.

"But you knew about his dysthymia, the same way Leah did. It made a big enough impression on you to comment on it. And I notice you and Leah have gotten tight in a short time."

"We talk sometimes," he said cautiously.

"I'm glad you've had someone to talk to. But given that you live in a house full of people and have fifty friends, I have to assume you wanted to talk to her about a specific issue you had in common. So unless you're pregnant, I assume you were worried about being an Insighter."

"I'm not pregnant."

"Whew! Don't get me wrong, you'd be a great dad, but you're too young."

"Very funny," he said, smiling a little. Then he looked away. "I like talking to her. She's interesting. And nice."

"You don't have to sell me on Leah Nazir. I was practically the president of her fan club. I'm glad you went to her."

"I didn't. She came to me. Remember when we were all in the kitchen having hot chocolate?"

"Yes, that was one of the times I asked you if everything was all right and if there was anything you wanted to talk about and you said everything was fine." She managed (just) to keep the tartness from her tone.

Jack raced ahead, trying to outrun the argument he thought was coming. "So she hasn't been sleeping well and she knew I wasn't, either, and we got to talking and later she figured it out and came and asked me about it." He looked at her, distressed and pale. "Don't be mad."

"I'm not mad. Why would I be?"

"Because I didn't come to you."

I'm not mad. I'm a little jealous, but not mad. Well. A lot jealous. "I don't own your confidences, you goof. You can confide in anyone you like. If Leah helped you, how can I be anything but glad about it?" There was another mystery solved: why Leah couldn't sleep. Constantly fretting about giving birth to your mother would wreak havoc on anyone's REM cycle.

"And—and you're so busy with Dad's—with Uncle Dennis's murder."

"That's not it and you know it," she said kindly. "You were afraid to come to me because you were afraid you'd *become* me. You thought being an Insighter meant being an insecure, spiteful bitch. You didn't know that only applied to Insighters who are Angela Drake."

"That's what Leah said. Not about you being spiteful! Jeez, your eyes went to slits in half a second."

"Sorry. Reflex."

"She likes you, so don't worry."

"I wasn't," she lied.

"Leah said it didn't have to define me. That it was like being born able to throw a fastball . . . being able to do it didn't mean I had to devote my life to try and go pro."

Angela nodded. "That's a good way to put it. I don't make money from Insighting, I've never seen a client, I just studied the hell out of it because—well, you know. But it was never my job. And it doesn't have to be yours."

"Yeah." Jack gazed at the grill for a few seconds, then looked at Angela. "What happens now?"

"Oh. Um. I have no idea."

"Will Mom move out?"

"I doubt it." Why would she? The house was hers, free and clear. That was assuming she didn't go to jail, but Angela wasn't going to bring that up. The poor kid had enough to mull over. "I think we'll all have to leave. Paul and Jordan are talking about renting a house in Evanston, and Mitchell—"

"Philadelphia."

"Yep." Mitchell Drake had one great love in life: the show *It's Always Sunny in Philadelphia*.* He'd wanted to live in Philly and open a bar in homage to Paddy's Pub since he was eleven. He had been designing the drinks menu ("The Dee," which was mostly orange juice for a bird-yellow hue; "The Mac," which was three Cosmos served in a beer mug; "The Frank," which

---

*One of the darkest and most delightful comedies in the history of TV. And Philadelphia.

was skunk beer dregs; and "The Greenman," which is anything even vaguely alcoholic dyed green) since he was twelve.

"It's nice that the collapse of our family means he can pursue his dream," Jack said with touching loyalty.

"Nothing's collapsed," Angela corrected sharply. *Whoa. Modulate that tone.* "You and I still love each other, we love our brothers and cousins, there will be a new baby Drake in a few months, life goes on."

He just looked at her. "You don't think you're simplifying a bit?"

"What our parents did doesn't mean our generation—the cousins and brothers and future spouses and their kids—aren't a family. Emma and Douglas Drake do not have that kind of power over us. The backstory changed, but not how we feel about each other." She took his wrist, held it firmly. "Don't do that, Jacky. Don't give our parents that kind of power."

He let out a short, shuddering breath and nodded. "Will I have to switch schools?"

"I'm gonna try very hard to make that *not* happen. We'll get you through your senior year and then figure out the college thing." *The college thing.* Ah, yes, she certainly sounded in control and like she knew what she was doing. Perfect. But one thing at a time. "In fact, I was talking to Jason about that earlier. He has a beautiful home and he's invited us to stay with him."

"I *knew* you liked him!" A real smile this time, wide and gorgeous, the kind that crinkled up his nose. He used to grin like that in his crib. "You were always trying to be *sooooo coooooooool* around him, but I could tell. It was the socks, right?"

"You noticed?" She couldn't recall being more delighted with him. "Aren't they great? Not that it's just his socks. It only started with his wonderful, sexy socks."

"Barf."

"But listen: We have options, okay? However it works out. I've got savings, we can go and get an apartment somewhere. Or we'll stay with Jason. Or we'll come up with Option C, which might be a combination of A and B. My point is, you're not trapped here with her. None of us are. Okay?"

He nodded. "Yeah."

"And you'll be what you'll be. Whether it's chef to the stars or the next Leah Nazir or something in between. There's not one thing holding you back, Jack. Got it?"

"Got it."

"And I'm glad she helped you and I'm happy she's in our family and that's all fine. And I love you, but you made her a swan? Really?"

The grin became a smirk. "Don't be jelly."

"I really hate that slang."

"That's what a jelly person would say."

"You know I can still kick your ass, right? Even though you're almost as big as I am?"

"With your skinny arms and spindly legs? You'd use up all your breath being shrill and then I'd stomp you."

"You wanna go, pal?" She was already shrugging out of her jacket. "We can go right now. Next I'll roll up my shirt sleeves so you'll know I'm taking this seriously."

"Yeah, and then you'll notice I'm *not* rolling up mine," he scoffed. "I know you haven't been in your room yet. Or you would have noticed the plate."

"I haven't!" she cried, delighted, instantly putting her jacket back on—it was getting chilly out. "I ran into Archer and Leah in the kitchen and then I came to find you, I haven't been near my room!" She couldn't sit still, so she clapped her hands like a goof applauding herself. "I haven't had one of your swans in over a year. I can't wait to devour it!"

"You earned it."

"And all I had to do was devote a decade of my life to solving a murder that never happened."

He leaned in and said in a low voice, "That's why I made you *two* swans. Because for ten years, you've basically been our mom *and* our dad."

Don't cry. Don't cry. She did the fake-cough thing instead. "I can get behind your two-swan reward system." Jack got to his feet and held out a hand, then pulled her up. "You know the best part?"

"Archer's gonna be pissed."

"Archer's gonna be pissed," she agreed, and practically skipped into the house.

MaryJanice Davidson is the *New York Times* bestselling author of several books, most recently *Deja Who, Undead and Done, Undead and Unforgiven,* and *Undead and Unwary.* With her husband, Anthony Alongi, she also writes a series featuring a teen weredragon named Jennifer Scales. MaryJanice lives in Minneapolis with her husband and two children and is currently working on her next book.

Ready to find
your next great read?

Let us help.

Visit prh.com/nextread

Penguin
Random
House